TIME REMEMBERED

Recent Titles by Louise Brindley from Severn House

AUTUMN COMES TO MRS HAZELL
TANTALUS
VIEW FROM A BALCONY

TIME REMEMBERED

Louise Brindley

This first world edition published in Great Britain 2001 by
SEVERN HOUSE PUBLISHERS LTD of
9–15 High Street, Sutton, Surrey SM1 1DF.
This first world edition published in the USA 2001 by
SEVERN HOUSE PUBLISHERS INC of
595 Madison Avenue, New York, NY 10022.

British Library Cataloguing in Publication Data

Brindley, Louise
Time Remembered
I. Title
823.9′14 [F]

ISBN 0–7278–5668–5

Typeset by Palimpsest Book Production Limited,
Polmont, Stirlingshire, Scotland.
Printed and bound in Great Britain by
MPG Books Ltd, Bodmin, Cornwall.

Especially for Ollie.
You steer, I'll steady!

High massing clouds at day's end,
Pure alchemy of light where shines the river,
A day's dying breath where trees bend,
Could all I know and love but live forever.

Pale winter skies at life's end,
Inclemency of age from youth dismembered;
Once well-loved days their grace lend.
Eternity exists in time remembered.

One

This was what Thea thought of as a 'water-colour' morning, painted in understated colours of blue, white and gold, the paint still wet, so that the blueness of the sea and sky, the feathery white clouds on the horizon seemed blurred, slightly out of focus, as if seen through tears.

She was standing on the lower promenade of South Bay's seafront, looking out to sea, knowing her mother had been right in suggesting a change of scenery, a space of time away from London, to get her life back into perspective and decide what to do about the future.

'You really can't go on like this,' Fliss Bellamy had said decisively at breakfast one morning, watching her daughter dipping a spoon aimlessly into a bowl of cornflakes. 'Picking and poking at your food, not eating enough to keep a sparrow alive; acting like a character in a Victorian melodrama. All right, so you've been "dumped", to put it plainly, and it hurts like hell. But it isn't the end of the world, and I should know! After all, your father dumped me, remember?'

'I know, Mum, and I'm sorry. It's just I thought that Carlo really cared for me.'

'If so, he had a funny way of showing it,' Fliss said, 'beetling back to Italy the way he did, not even bothering to say goodbye, simply clearing the flat of his belongings and leaving a note on the kitchen table. The wonder is that he even bothered to put pen to paper!'

'No need to rub it in!'

'That's the last thing I want to do, believe me. All I'm

saying is, why not get away from London for a while? Go to South Bay for the summer. Stay with Bess and Hal Hardacre. I'm sure they'd be pleased to have you.'

'Oh, Mum, I couldn't bear to stay with the Hardacres for any length of time. They'd drive me nuts! Well, you know what Aunt Bess is like. The life and soul of the party, refusing to grow old gracefully. Not like you. If only she would calm down and act her age. I've never understood why you've been friends all this time. You haven't a thing in common.'

'We were girls together, that's what we have in common. But you're sidestepping the issue. You loved South Bay as a little girl, and I'd feel happier knowing you had someone to turn to if you needed help. Besides, you could find a little place of your own if you wanted: possibly even a summer job, to take your mind off things.' Fliss could be very persuasive. 'At least think about it, darling.'

Thea *had* thought about it, and had decided to take her mother's advice, staying with the Hardacres until she found herself a flat or bedsit. And so she had packed a suitcase, caught a train at King's Cross, and set off on her journey to Yorkshire.

Bess and Hal Hardacre had named their spacious dormer bungalow overlooking the South Bay Golf Course the Hacienda, which figured.

They spent the winter months in Spain, in a kind of English enclave on the Costa del Sol, doing all the things they would normally do at home: playing bridge, eating English food, playing golf, attending endless cocktail and dinner parties and drinking far more than was good for them, which probably accounted for Bess's leathery complexion and Hal's enormous paunch.

Crossing the threshold, Thea recoiled slightly at the décor: brightly coloured walls hung with framed posters of matadors, Flamenco dancers, Carmen, sangria adverts, and various other reminders of the Hardacres' Spanish holidays. Not to mention Bess's collection of Spanish dolls in the glass-fronted hall cabinet.

'Now, darling,' Aunt Bess said, 'Hal and I want you to feel totally at home here.' Her tanned leather skin contrasted oddly with her mop of bleached, tightly permed hair. 'Unfortunately, we have a long-standing dinner engagement tonight, but we shouldn't be late home.' She added archly, 'After all, old girls like me need all the beauty sleep they can get.'

'Not to worry, Aunt Bess, I'll be perfectly fine on my own,' Thea replied, stretching her mouth into a semblance of a smile, more of a grimace. 'OK if I take a bath, wash my hair, and watch television; maybe ring Mother to tell her I've arrived safely?'

'Whatever, darling, and help yourself to anything in the fridge. There's eggs, bacon, cold chicken and ham, salad, ice cream, plenty of bread and so on. There may even be a smidgin of paella left over from lunch. But no, perhaps not! You see, Hal and I are rather greedy pigs when it comes to paella!'

Ringing her mother after bathing, washing her hair, and wolfing a chicken sandwich, the only food she'd touched since her morning bowl of cornflakes, Thea blurted, 'I'm sorry, Fliss, but I can't stay in this ghastly house a moment longer than necessary. They've even got a mounted bull's head over the sitting-room mantelpiece!'

'Have you told them your plans? Finding a place of your own and a job?' Fliss asked.

'I mentioned it briefly, but they weren't really listening. They had more important things in mind – a dinner engagement, wouldn't you know? Bess went upstairs an hour and a half beforehand, to get ready: appeared at a quarter past seven looking like the fairy godmother in *Cinderella*. Honestly, Fliss, white satin and diamante shoulder straps. I ask you!'

'I take it they're not within earshot?'

'No, they haven't come in yet. Anyway, I'm off to bed now. Thanks for listening. Tomorrow, first thing, I'll set about finding myself a bolt-hole. Frankly, I think they'll be glad to see the back of me!'

The last thing Thea envisaged was a midnight visit from Bess, who came to her room, bubbling over with news of a job that might suit her down to the ground.

'What kind of a job?' Thea asked bemusedly, sitting up in bed.

'Well, I just happened to be sitting next to a quite charming man, Philip Gregory, at dinner – he's the owner of a dress shop in town, and a dear little summertime boutique on the lower promenade – and he confided in me – people *do* confide in me, you know, I can't think why – that he is in urgent need of someone to manage the boutique.

'Well, naturally, darling, I thought of *you*. The upshot being that, due to my recommendation, and if you are really interested, he's prepared to give you priority: to meet you first thing in the morning, on the promenade, discuss terms and so on. So you see, I had to tell you tonight, since you'll need to be up bright and early tomorrow morning. If you really want the job, that is?'

'Oh yes, and thank you, Aunt Bess!' Impulsively, Thea kissed her courtesy aunt's leathery cheek. So *had* she been listening, after all?

Driving along the promenade early next day, Philip Gregory wondered if he'd been wise in granting a priority interview to a friend of Bess Hardacre. He had never been introduced to Mrs Hardacre until last night, but South Bay was a comparatively small community and one knew most people by sight.

In the case of Mrs Hardacre, he had recognised her immediately as a woman who often came to his town centre shop to buy clothes. A rather silly woman, he suspected, usually accompanied by friends of her own generation whose presence in the showrooms and fitting cubicles caused endless problems for the assistants. According to the manageress, Miss Mould, an elegant woman of impeccable dress sense, who obviously regarded Mrs Hardacre and her friends as time-wasters, the women would emerge from the trying-on cubicles 'looking like mutton dressed as lamb, and giggling like a bunch of geriatric schoolgirls', issuing so many conflicting opinions regarding the suitability of this garment or that the assistants ended up never quite knowing who wanted to buy what, if anything at all.

Philip began to wish desperately that he'd held his tongue about needing a manageress for his boutique, that he had not mentioned the fact to Mrs Hardacre, of all people. Terrified of finding himself lumbered with some full-bosomed 'geriatric schoolgirl' friend of hers, he stopped the car near the boutique, noticing a tall, slim girl with light brown hair, wearing slacks and a thigh-length sweater, looking out to sea.

Turning at the sound of the car, Thea smiled and hurried towards him, moving as gracefully as a ballet dancer. A very attractive girl, nineteen or twenty, at a rough guess.

'Are you Mr Gregory?' she said eagerly. 'If so, I believe we have an appointment! I'm here about the job. My name is Thea Bellamy, by the way, and I am in urgent need of work right now.'

Not quite believing his luck, at the same time striving hard to maintain his dignity as a prospective employer, Philip said coolly, getting out of the car and unlocking the shop door, 'The job is not all that easy, believe me. South Bay is quiet at the moment, but it won't be when the summer visitors begin to arrive in full force.

'As you can see for yourself, there isn't much space as it is, so try to imagine the shop packed with holidaymakers waiting to be served; turning awkward at times if they are kept waiting too long.'

He continued, 'Meanwhile, you'd be hemmed in behind the counter, stuffing goods into bags; taking money, giving change; keeping your eyes skinned for shoplifters. Then, suddenly, you'd find you'd run out of change, at the same time spotting a shoplifter making off with a pair of earrings or whatever. Tell me, Miss Bellamy, how would you react to such a situation?'

Thea said thoughtfully, 'Being hemmed in behind the counter, I imagine I'd continue to stuff goods into bags. If I ran out of change, I'd probably request a larger float in future. One thing's for sure, I wouldn't waste my time or energy in running after a sneak-thief in possession of an item of costume jewellery, leaving the shop unattended.'

Deeply impressed, but wanting her to understand the full extent of what she'd be letting herself in for, Philip went on, 'Your duties would include checking stock with the invoices, re-ordering as and when necessary, arranging the window displays, polishing the mirrors; sweeping up at closing time and balancing the books and leaving the day's takings in the security box under the counter, ready for me to pick up and bank later.

'Your hours would be from nine till five thirty, an hour off for lunch. Any questions?'

'Well, yes. What happens if I need to spend a penny between times?'

'In that case, you would hang a notice, "Back in Five Minutes", in the window, and go along the promenade to the ladies' cloakroom in the concert-hall complex.'

'I see, but suppose I couldn't get there and back in five minutes?'

Philip laughed. 'Not to worry. No one would know what time you'd hung up the sign in the first place.'

'No, I guess not, but I have a terrible guilt complex,' Thea admitted, warming to Mr Gregory despite her earlier misgivings that the 'charming' man Aunt Bess had mentioned as her dinner companion last night might prove to be a stuffy old bore, totally lacking a sense of humour. How wrong she had been! Of course he was knocking on a bit, old enough to be her father, but he was still quite handsome in an elderly kind of way, and immaculately dressed in a lightweight tweed jacket, slacks, and a paisley scarf tucked into an open-necked brown silk shirt.

From his own viewpoint, Philip had already decided that here was a girl who could probably manage his boutique with one hand tied behind her back. Even so, he wanted to know something of her background: her connection with the Hardacres, for instance, and why she stood in such urgent need of a job. They had touched on everything, so far, except her wages, and the fact that she would be working six days a week, including Sundays.

He said, 'Well, Miss Bellamy, you've seen the shop for yourself, I've explained your duties as fully as possible, but I must warn you again of the hard work and the long hours involved, if you decide to accept my offer of employment.'

'You mean that' – Thea drew in a deep breath of relief – 'the job is mine? Oh, glory hallelujah! Now I can start looking for a place of my own to live. Thank you so much, Mr Gregory. Just wait till I tell my mother! And, if it's not too much trouble, would you mind very much calling me Thea, not Miss Bellamy, from now on?'

'Thea?' Philip queried, caught up in the girl's obvious excitement and delight. 'Is that short for Theodora?'

'No. I was christened Thea. Mother hates diminutives, a hangover from having her own name – Felicity – shortened to Fliss, I imagine. She figured that Theodora would be shortened to Thea anyway, so she cut out the "odor".'

Philip chuckled briefly. Pondering the subject of nicknames, he thought that never, during thirty-odd years of marriage, had has wife, Ruth, called him Phil. A serious-minded woman, albeit a splendid housekeeper and mother, she believed in calling a spade a spade, a Philip a Philip.

He'd tried calling her 'Ruthie', their two daughters Joan and Eva 'Joanie' and 'Evie', but that hadn't gone down too well. Serious-minded like their mother – a former school teacher – his daughters had invariably called him 'Dad' or 'Father', never 'Pop' or 'Daddy'. So where had he gone wrong?

In any event, did it really matter now that Joan and Eva were grown up and married to husbands named, respectively, John Barratt and Daniel Smith, destined never to be called affectionately, 'Johnny' or 'Danny'? Ah well! Philip sighed deeply, turning his attention to Thea Bellamy.

'So tell me, Thea,' he asked, 'why are you here in South Bay? Staying with the Hardacres?'

'Oh, that. Bess and Fliss were at school together. Not that they see much of each other, but they keep in touch: odd letters, Christmas and birthday cards, long-distance phone calls and so on. You know the kind of thing I mean? And, well, Fliss thought it would do me good to get away from London for a while to make up my mind what to do about the future – my future, that is. I have two options open to me, you see – art or stage design, and I'm not sure which to choose.

'Above all, I need a place of my own to live till September. Please don't get me wrong, but I don't feel quite at home with the Hardacres. I have the feeling I'm cramping their style. The generation gap, I suppose. I thought that if I found myself a job, I'd be able to afford a flat or a bedsit somewhere; cling on to my independence, pay my own way. Not that I'm on my beam-ends exactly! Fliss would pay my way, if I'd let her send me weekly handouts, but that's not what I want. I need to stand on my own feet from now till September, to have reached a decision between art and design as a career when the summer season is over.'

She continued mistily, 'I can't thank you enough, Mr Gregory, for your offer of a job, and I shan't let you down, believe me.'

Philip *did* believe her implicitly. There was something about this girl that inspired both trust and confidence in her ability to run his boutique – one of a line of small, lock-up shops beneath a sea-facing arcade – with a sense of pride in her work and a total commitment towards earning her own living, allied to her sense of purpose in finding herself a place of her own.

He said, 'Do take care when it comes to choosing accommodation. There are some greedy landlords about at this time of year, charging the earth for rooms the size of rabbit hutches.'

'It's the same in London,' Thea reflected wistfully. 'My ex-boyfriend and I shared a basement flat in Southwark Street, described in the advert as a "bijou residence". Bijou being the operative word. There was scarcely room to swing a cat! Not that I've ever felt inclined to swing a cat. Scarcely surprising that he got fed up with England and went back to Italy to live.

'Can't say I blame him, really. We were beginning to get on each other's nerves, I suppose. Poor Carlo. He was never free of colds, one after another. He seldom stopped sneezing. I spent a small fortune on man-size tissues. Of course I was devastated when he left me. I thought ours was the love affair of the century, but I never could cook spaghetti bolognese the way he liked it – and he liked it the way his "Mamma Mia" made it, with sun-dried tomatoes and lots of grated parmesan cheese. I didn't even have a cheese grater, let alone any parmesan. I used Cheddar, pared with a blunt kitchen knife!'

She laughed suddenly, 'Know what? I think I'm beginning to get over him! Fliss, in her wisdom, sent me to South Bay to do just that. I was just moping about when I went back home; driving her bonkers because I wouldn't eat properly. Now, I could eat a horse. Must be the sea air!'

'There's a snack bar at the end of the promenade,' Philip said. 'May I buy you a bacon sandwich and a cup of coffee?'

The snack bar opened early to accommodate council workmen engaged in painting railings, planting flowerbeds and cutting grass, in need of refreshment before starting work. There was a long counter with a tea urn and a coffee machine, stacks of cups, saucers and plates, piles of sandwiches and meat pies under plastic covers, a microwave oven behind the counter, and the nose-twitching smell of frying bacon from the kitchen.

'Well, what'll it be?' Philip asked his new manageress. 'A bacon butty or a full English breakfast – bacon, eggs, sausages, mushrooms and baked beans? In other words, the full mazuma!'

'Oh, the "full mazuma", if you don't mind,' Thea said ecstatically, finding a window seat while Philip did the ordering, thinking how lucky she had been to find herself a job at such short notice, with so nice a boss as Philip Gregory.

Bringing the coffee over to the table, plus the necessary cutlery and a couple of paper serviettes, he said, 'Harking back to the accommodation discussion, a business acquaintance of mine, Bill Cumberland, owns a block of flats on the upper promenade, bought as a source of income when he retired from the rag trade several years ago. Trouble is, I can't for the life of me remember what it's called. The Villa – something or other. A former hotel, gone to rack and ruin until he bought it for a song and set about turning it into flats and bedsits.'

Frowning slightly, Thea said, 'Years ago, when I was just a kid, before Fliss and my father split up and went their separate ways, we spent our summer holidays in South Bay. At the Villa Marina Hotel.'

'Yes, of course, that's it. The Villa Marina,' Philip confirmed happily, as a young waitress brought the food he had ordered to their table. Two platefuls of sizzling hot bacon and eggs, sausages, mushrooms and baked beans, plus fried bread and tomatoes.

He said light-heartedly, 'Bon appetit, Thea.'

Thea replied unthinkingly, 'Bon appetit, Philip.'

Seldom had he felt happier or more relaxed than he had done then, watching Thea tucking into bacon and eggs. Here was a lovely young girl with her life before her, treating him not as some old fuddy-duddy, but as a contemporary. Realisation that her use of his Christian name had been unintentional, that, in all probability it would never happen again, made no difference to his quiet feeling of pleasure that she regarded him not as a 'has-been', but as a friend.

Two

The Villa Marina stood at the end of a terrace of tall Victorian houses, once privately owned, now mainly hotels. Houses whose front gardens had been paved to accommodate wrought-iron tables and chairs, sun-loungers and notice boards announcing 'En suite rooms, colour TV, bar snacks available' and so on.

Strange, Thea thought, that the Villa Marina, built as a hotel, had now been carved up into private residences, the houses vice versa.

Walking up the front steps and ringing the doorbell, she recalled mounting those steps before, as a child, clinging tightly to her father's hand, tired out with sunshine and fresh air after blissful days on the beach riding donkeys and making sand pies. Wading into the sea under the watchful eye of her mother – who must have known, even then, of the 'other woman' in her husband's life – she had screamed with delight as the waves lapped at her ankles.

When the door opened, Thea was faced with a man wearing jeans and a polo-neck sweater. 'Oh,' she said brightly, pushing aside memories of the past, 'are you Mr Cumberland?'

'That I am, young lady. But if you're selling double glazing, you're wasting your time.'

'No, not at all,' she assured him. 'I'm in search of somewhere to live. My employer, Mr Gregory, mentioned your name to me, and I just wondered—'

'Philip Gregory?' Mr Cumberland interrupted heartily. 'I

haven't seen much of him since my retirement from the rag trade. Frankly, I'm working much harder now than I ever did then, but I'm a damn sight happier.' He paused. 'You'd best come in, then, Miss . . . ?'

'Bellamy. Thea Bellamy,' she said, crossing the threshold – a threshold she had crossed many times before in the carefree days of childhood. Not that she immediately recognised her surroundings. There was no sign of the old reception lounge with its potted palms, chintz-covered sofas and armchairs, broad, carpeted staircase leading to the upper landing or mahogany reception desk with its leather-bound visitors' book, 'sit-up-and-beg' telephone, and notices reminding guests of meal times – and not to forget to hand in their keys on the day of departure.

Now, it seemed that the building had been carved up as precisely as the segments of an orange, with the peel, pith and pips removed, and much of the flavour. But nothing in earth or heaven comes as it came before, and she did desperately need a place of her own to call home.

Mr Cumberland said, 'As a matter of fact, I do have a bed-sitting room to let at the moment. The previous tenant moved out a few days ago. You can take a look at it, if you like.'

'Yes, please,' Thea said gratefully, following her prospective landlord through a glass door marked 'Strictly Private' to a broad staircase leading to the upper landings. The old staircase she remembered so well.

Unlocking a door on the first landing, Mr Cumberland preceded her into a room as familiar to her as breathing. This was the room that she, Fliss and her father had occupied many moons ago, with a bay window overlooking the promenade; but it was far different now than it had been then, apart from the window and the view of the sea beyond.

Not that Thea disliked what she saw, though it was very different from what she remembered. There was now a kitchenette in a corner of the room, separated from the living space by a kind of bar-counter. The living quarters comprised a single divan bed with a fitted cover, a drawer beneath for the bedding, a small settee and armchairs, a coffee table fronting a TV set, a wardrobe and dressing table cheek-by-jowl with the divan, and a bedside cabinet crowned with a pink-shaded lamp.

'Well, Miss Bellamy, what do you think of it?' Mr Cumberland asked, struck by the girl's expression of joy and sadness combined, her smiling lips contrasting oddly with the hint of tears in her eyes.

Thea said mistily, 'I think it is just too good to be true! I'll take it, Mr Cumberland, if that's all right with you.'

'Sure; glad you like it! Of course you'll have to share a bathroom. You'll need to work out a rota with the other tenants. Fortunately they are working girls about your own age.

'There's a bathroom on every landing,' he explained, 'four tenants to a landing in this, the main part of the building. The flats in the west wing are all self-contained, let mainly to elderly couples, on a permanent basis.'

Mr Cumberland, obviously proud of his achievements, continued, 'There's a laundry on the ground floor, where the kitchen, larders and store-rooms used to be in the old days, when this was a hotel.

'You should have seen the state of it when I bought it! Every damn thing had gone to rack and ruin! It cost me an arm and a leg to modernise the place, as you can imagine. I had to strip out the antiquated kitchen equipment for starters. I shudder to think what kind of food was served up to the hotel residents in those days.'

Thea harboured fond memories of the meals she had once enjoyed with her parents in the now non-existent dining room, swallowed up, apparently, in the modernisation process. 'The food was great, as I recall,' she said longingly. 'You see, I've been here before.' She added, not wanting to make a mountain out of a molehill, 'The reason why I want this bed-sitting room so much is it's the room I shared with my parents a long time ago.'

Against her Hacienda background of Spanish dolls, framed posters, and the mounted bull's head over the sitting-room mantelpiece, Bess Hardacre said petulantly, 'You certainly don't believe in letting the grass grow under your feet, do you?' She added huffily, 'Well, all I can say is, "act in haste, repent at leisure!" Your mother won't be best pleased, I dare say, when she finds out about this bed-sitting room you've rented out of the blue, when you were perfectly welcome to stay here with Hal and me until September. Akin to a slap in the eye, in my opinion!'

'I'm sorry you feel that way, Aunt Bess,' Thea said contritely, 'but one thing led to another. Thanks to you, Mr Gregory offered me a job which I was happy to accept. But let's be honest. You and Uncle Hal have your own lives to live. Can you cross your heart and tell me that you wouldn't have grown tired of having me under your feet until September?'

'I guess not,' Bess sighed. 'Frankly, Hal and I are at a bit of a loss when it comes to coping with the younger generation. So when are you thinking of moving into your bedsit?'

'This morning! As soon as I've packed my suitcase, tidied my room, and ordered a taxi.'

'But today is Sunday,' Bess protested, 'and I'm cooking something special. You must stay for lunch!'

Not wanting to disappoint her hostess, Thea compromised. 'Fair enough; I'll change my plans, book a taxi after lunch. A couple of hours won't make much difference, just as long as I have time to settle in before starting work at nine tomorrow morning. You see, I'll need to buy bread, milk, coffee, tea-bags and so on, beforehand; something for breakfast. Fliss would kill me if I set out to work on an empty stomach!'

'If there's anything we can do to help,' Bess suggested, determined to poke her nose in. 'After lunch, Hal will drive you to Tesco to do your shopping, lend a hand with your luggage, and I'll help you to unpack. Besides, I'd better take a look at this bedsit of yours.'

Accepting the inevitable, the well-meant interference of Bess and her husband, which she could have well done without, and realising that to refuse the offer would be unkind, Thea said brightly, 'What a lovely idea.'

Later, in the supermarket, wheeling a trolley when a shopping basket would have done, Thea wished that Bess would stop dumping into it things she didn't need and couldn't afford anyway – tins of asparagus, salmon, anchovies; soup and pasta; a lettuce the size of a cabbage! Several bunches of spring onions, pounds of tomatoes, exotic cheeses, a whole roast chicken, plus bottles of red wine, mayonnaise, bleach, washing-up liquid and scented candles. Cheeks pink with excitement and the several glasses of sangria she'd drunk at lunch, to complement the paella, Bess chucked everything that caught her eye into the trolley with gay abandon.

Eventually, Thea said, 'Please, Aunt Bess, I'm not sure there's room in my kitchenette for all this food.'

'Then we must *make* room,' Bess declared forcefully. 'Leave it to me. I'll have a word with the landlord, if necessary; tell him you need more fitted cupboards. Not to worry, darling, I'll foot the bill for whatever you need to make you feel at home in your new surroundings, just as I insist on paying for all this lovely food I've chosen for you as a "Welcome Home" pressie.'

Normally a man of few words, overshadowed by his wife's far stronger personality and long inured to her extravagance allied to her determination to have her own way, Hal said quietly, 'Steady on, old girl. Pay for the food if you want to, but leave Thea alone to get on with her life in her own way without the interference of a couple of silly old buffers like us!'

Despite her husband's advice, Bess insisted on accompanying Thea upstairs to her room – leaving Hal to hump her suitcase and the box of groceries – to peer into every nook and cranny, finding fault with this and that: the poor quality of the carpet (of the rubber-backed variety), for instance.

So what had Bess expected, for forty pounds a week rent? A scattering of antique Persian rugs?

The divan bed, also, had not met with Bess's approval. 'What you need here,' she announced forthrightly, 'is a new mattress, otherwise you'll never get a decent night's sleep.'

She continued, 'As for the kitchenette, words fail me! Just that postage-stamp cooker, one electric kettle, a pop-up toaster, a sink and draining-board of dolls'-house dimensions, and that inadequate refrigerator! Well, all I can totally say is you've exchanged your fiddle for a gewgaw, in my opinion, choosing to live here instead of with me and Hal at the Hacienda. But *why*? That's what I'd like to know!'

Remembering that mounted bull's head over the sitting-room mantelpiece, the glass-fronted cabinet of Spanish dolls in the hall and the ghastly paella she'd choked down at lunchtime, Thea knew exactly why she had exchanged her 'fiddle for a gewgaw'. She had come to South Bay in search of independence, a new beginning, to forget about the past and reach certain conclusions about the future.

She said, 'Because I'm young and headstrong, wanting everything my own way. You understand, don't you, that I really need to stand on my own feet?' She added, 'And I'd hate the other tenants to think I'd been given preferential treatment in any shape or form.'

'Thea's right.' Hal nodded. 'In any case, I can't see anything wrong with the room. I mean, how many kettles and pop-up toasters does one person need? It isn't as if she'll come home from work wanting to cook herself a three-course meal. Happen she'll settle for egg on toast, or a salad: something nice and easy, the way young girls do nowadays.'

'Oh? And what do *you* know about the eating habits of young girls, I should like to know?' Bess flung back at him.

'Not a lot,' Hal admitted, 'but it stands to reason. They have their waistlines to consider.'

Sensing a heated argument between husband and wife, Thea broke in, 'It isn't as if I'll be living on another planet, Aunt Bess. I'll visit you and Uncle Hal quite often, if I may?'

Sidetracked, Bess said warmly, 'But of course, darling; feel free to visit us as often as possible! I am, after all, a very good cook, though I say so myself. Paella being my *spécialité de la maison*. Isn't that so, Hal?'

'Yes, dear.' Having spoken his piece and reaped the whirlwind, he decided that retreat from battle was the safer option. Thinking to pour oil on troubled water, he said, 'Paella is the only Spanish food we care for. Most of our time abroad, we settle for British grub: steak, chops, ham and eggs, that kind of thing. Bess can't stand sardines, garlic or too much olive oil; her tummy gets upset.' He sighed deeply. 'I often wonder why we bother to go abroad at all.'

If looks could have killed . . . Bess said scathingly, 'I happen to be allergic to garlic, and I prefer sardines in tins, quite small and manageable, not staring up at me from my plate. Oh, do come along, Hal! Remember we're dining out this evening, and you'll need your afternoon nap beforehand!'

Poor Aunt Bess, Thea thought, when they had gone: so well-meaning yet so foolish, ever in pursuit of eternal youth – quite unlike Fliss, who, faced with her husband's defection, had acquired a kind of inner beauty and strength of character in her determination to bring up her daughter alone. After her mother's divorce from Charles Bellamy, the father she had adored, Thea had been distraught: she still missed him acutely from her life. Just as much, she suspected, as Fliss missed him from hers.

Thea had not understood, as a child – how could she? – that her beloved Daddy had gone away to live with someone else. Even when Fliss had explained to her that such things often happened when one person fell out of love with another, she had not understood why her father had gone away so suddenly after that seemingly happy last summer holiday at the Villa Marina.

Growing up, Thea had begun to realise the debt of gratitude she owed to her mother for never uttering a harsh word against her father. Instead, the delightful, commonsensical Felicity Bellamy, a tall, proud, slender woman with thick brown hair drawn back from her lean, intelligent face into a heavy chignon at the nape of her neck, had chosen to work hard to give her daughter a good education. She had encouraged her to stand on her own feet, to make her own way in the world, holding fast to her strong belief that letting go of the people one loved, allowing them the freedom to make their own choices, would some day bring about a long-awaited and longed-for reunion. A continuance of interrupted love. A kind of homecoming of the wayward heart to its place of rest.

Thea began unpacking and stashing away the contents of Aunt Bess's Welcome Home hamper, thinking, What a waste – a whole bird when a couple of drumsticks would have done. Moreover, the vast amount of salad stuff Bess had bought wouldn't fit into the vegetable drawer. No matter how hard she tried, the drawer wouldn't close properly, and neither would the refrigerator.

How she would eat her way through all this food, Thea had no more idea than the man in the moon. Oh well, might as well have a bath first and decide what to do about the grub later.

Sallying forth to the bathroom across the landing in her

dressing gown and slippers, she twisted the doorknob this way and that, but to no avail. The door remained firmly closed. Someone was already in there, by the sound of running water and the faint but unmistakable smell of Badedas bath essence permeating the air.

'Hang on just a sec,' a voice called out to her, 'I won't be more than a few minutes. Just cleaning the bath!'

Thea hung on. Suddenly the door opened and a redhead, draped in a bath sheet, feet bare, appeared in the aperture. 'Hello,' the girl said, raising her eyebrows in surprise, 'who the hell are you?'

'My name's Thea Bellamy. I've just moved in to Flat Four.'

'Oh, great. Old "Fanny Adams", the previous tenant, was a pain in the whatsit! Pleased to meet you, I'm sure. I'm Bunty Macintosh, Number Two. Stella Johnson's in Number One, and June Blake's in Number Three. Anyway, Thea, enjoy your bath, and if you need any help, just holler!'

'Thanks, I will.' Thea liked Bunty enormously at first sight: a clear-cut kind of girl, she imagined, fun-loving and uncomplicated. A very pretty girl to boot, with her mane of red hair, hazel eyes and generously smiling mouth displaying splendidly large white teeth. Above all, there was an air of innocent naughtiness about her which Thea warmed to at once.

She asked, 'What are the other girls like? Stella and June?'

Bunty wrinkled her nose, 'Hmm, well, it really isn't up to me to say, is it? Stella's a bit moody at the moment; up to her eyes in an affair with a married man, which is going nowhere fast, only she hasn't the sense to see it, whilst June, bless her, can't find herself a boyfriend, married or otherwise, which troubles her a good deal, I'm afraid, though I can't for the life of me understand why not, with her looks!' Bunty sighed deeply. 'I guess it has to do with her lack of self-confidence due to the midwife who hadn't the sense to cut the umbilical cord joining June to that ghastly mother of hers.'

Making up her mind in a split second, thinking of the chicken, the iceberg lettuce and the rest of the greenery stuffed into her refrigerator, deciding on a plan of action to get rid of most of it in one fell swoop, Thea suggested a housewarming buffet party in her flat later that evening, to include Bunty, Stella and June. Nothing special, just cold roast chicken, washed down with a couple of bottles of Beaujolais.

'Hey, that sounds great to me,' Bunty enthused. 'I'll round up June and Stella then, shall I? Tell them to bring their own glasses and cutlery! I know for certain that Stella's at a loose end tonight, and June's always at a loose end, poor lass. As *pour moi*, I'll be there with bells on!'

She added, with a twinkle in her eyes and a smile as wide as a sunburst, 'My financial status being what it is at the moment, and with nary a rich boyfriend in sight, no way could I resist the offer of a free meal, much less a few glasses of Beaujolais into the bargain!'

After her bath, Thea set about carving up the chicken, chopping lettuce, peeling spring onions, slicing tomatoes, and hard-boiling eggs to add to the salad, which she arranged on the counter separating the kitchen from the rest of the room. The room she now thought of as home was filled to overflowing with never-to-be-forgotten memories of her childhood days: the translucent beauty of the sky beyond the bay window as darkness fell and the lights of South Bay shimmering down into the mysterious depths of the waves lapping the shore.

Checking to make sure she had not forgotten anything, feeling suddenly nervous at this, her first ever shot at entertaining, she had just run a comb through her hair and applied a soupçon of lipstick when a knock came at the door and Bunty called out, 'We're here!' The party had begun.

Three

Bunty had plaited her Titian hair into a thick rope secured with rubber bands of the kind often discarded by postmen delivering letters, and exchanged her bath towel for a multi-coloured kaftan worn with lots of dangling jewellery.

Darkness had fallen. The lights of South Bay glimmered like fireflies along the promenade. Before the girls arrived, Thea had switched on her bedside lamp, another near the TV, and lighted the candles Bess had given her, which she placed at strategic points around the room to create a romantic atmosphere.

'Gosh, this looks great,' Bunty enthused, glancing about her, taking in the lamplights, candle-shine and the array of food on the counter. 'If old "Fanny Adams" could see it now, her eyes would pop out of her head! A right misery she was, forever complaining, a bit like the old girls next door. Ah well, it takes all kinds to make a world! Oh, by the way, meet the neighbours, Stella and June. Girls, this is Thea Bellamy.'

June, a blue-eyed blonde, wearing a pleated grey skirt and a white embroidered blouse, said softly, 'Pleased to meet you, I'm sure. My room's next to yours. I hope I shan't disturb you.' She added nervously, 'Miss Adams didn't like music, you see. Whenever I switched on my stereo, she would bang on the wall as a signal to turn it down. In the end, I stopped listening to it at all. What I mean is, Pavarotti singing "Nessun Dorma" isn't everyone's cup of tea.'

Thea laughed. 'Know what, June? In your shoes, I'd have given Miss Adams Tchaikovsky's 1812 Overture full blast: cannons, bells and all!'

'Really? You mean you *like* music?' June's eyes glowed in her beautifully modelled face.

'Like it? I love it!' Thea assured her, turning her attention to Stella Johnson, an unsmiling brunette wearing black velvet trousers and a trendy black, thigh-length sweater. The girl who, according to Bunty, was deeply involved in an affair with a married man.

Little wonder that she looked so po-faced and miserable, Thea thought, an attractive young woman intent on luring away another woman's husband. Just as the woman called Carol Lindsay had lured away Charles Bellamy from Fliss.

Stella said briefly, dismissively, 'Can't stay long, I'm afraid. I'm expecting an important phone call. Anyway, I'm not in the least bit hungry.'

Bunty burst forth, 'Well, if you're not, *I* am! Thea has gone to a lot of trouble to lay on this party for us! So at least make the lass feel at home. As for that phone call you're expecting, you know damn well that bloke you're stuck on won't risk ringing you until his wife is in the shower.'

Stepping into the breach, Thea said equably, 'At least have a glass of Beaujolais, Stella. Bunty, June, help yourselves to the food. I'll open a bottle.'

Handing Stella a well-filled glass, Thea noticed that the girl's colour had mounted unbecomingly, a result of Bunty's plain speaking. Obviously her *liaison dangereuse* with a married man was not working out well, hence her lacklustre eyes, the down-curve of her mouth and her prickly, defensive attitude allied to her air of aloofness, as if her affair had set her apart from her friends – which it probably had, Thea realised.

Breaking up a marriage merited no kudos. Becoming a man's mistress – the 'other woman' in his life – must, of necessity, carry with it soul-destroying burdens of guilt, bitterness and jealousy, uncertainty and fear of the future. Suffering would be on the cards for all those involved in the love triangle if the affair came to light. Particularly the man's wife.

Thea longed to tell Stella not to squander her youth in pursuance of an affair which might well end in heartbreak. But how could she? She scarcely knew Stella Johnson. All she knew for certain was that the girl was deeply unhappy.

Having spoken her piece, Bunty had apparently forgotten the incident. Not the type to harbour grudges, she had helped herself and June lavishly to roast chicken and salad and carried their plates to the table where Thea poured out wine for the pair of them and a less generous amount for herself.

Bunty and June were together on the settee; Stella had perched on the edge of an armchair, as if poised for flight. Thea sat down in the chair opposite.

'You're not eating,' Bunty said in surprise. 'Shall I fetch you something?'

'Not right now. I'll have something later.'

'Aren't you feeling well?' Bunty frowned anxiously.

'I'm fine,' Thea said, 'just a bit over-excited, I guess. It has been quite a day, and I'm starting a new job tomorrow morning.'

'Oh, where?' Bunty asked, a forkful of chicken halfway to her mouth.

'At Mr Gregory's boutique on the lower promenade.' Thea added, 'I said a *new* job. The fact is, I've never had a job before and well, to be honest, I'm feeling a bit nervous about it.'

'Good God!' Bunty exclaimed. 'What a coincidence! Old "Fanny Adams" was all set to manage that when suddenly she packed her duds and did a runner, leaving the owner in the lurch.'

'Did she say why?' Thea asked.

'I'll say she did,' Bunty supplied avidly. 'Said she couldn't stand the thought of being cooped up in a confined space six days a week. Went on and on about the state of her nerves and suchlike. I hadn't a clue what she was on about half the time. Anyway, we were glad to see the back of her with her highfalutin ways and constant nagging and complaining about this and that.'

She added mischievously, 'I say, Thea, you're not subject to panic attacks, are you?'

Thea wasn't too sure about anything, at that moment.

Bunty worked in the cosmetics department of a Debenhams store in the main street and, she confided after a second visit to the buffet to replenish her plate, the rate she was going, soon she wouldn't fit into her overall. 'In which case I shall visit Stella's salon for a session on the toning tables,' she announced gaily in her lilting Scottish accent.

'It isn't *my* salon,' Stella said scathingly. 'I just happen to work there.'

'All right, no need to snap my head off,' Bunty said mildly, embarking on her second glass of Beaujolais, 'just a manner of speaking.'

'The trouble with you is, you speak without thinking,' Stella said tartly, 'let your tongue run away with you.'

'I know,' Bunty admitted cheerfully, 'but it comes in handy at times, especially when selling anti-ageing cream to women with wrinkles like tramlines.'

'And that doesn't worry you?' Stella demanded, determined to carry on the vendetta.

'Not really; why should it? It's what I'm paid for, and most women only see what they want to see anyway, in their bathroom mirrors. They *feel* better, having spent fifty quid on a pot of face cream, therefore they *look* better. Ask Sigmund Freud if you don't believe me.'

Thea expressed a deep feeling of relief when Stella, glancing at her wristwatch and rising to her feet, announced her departure, presumably to take her important phone call in the privacy of her own room.

When she had dramatically taken her leave, like the Wicked Witch in a Christmas pantomime, Thea asked June what she did for a living.

'Nothing very interesting, I'm afraid, I'm just a clerk at the Town Hall, dealing with housing claims and suchlike.' She added wistfully, 'I'm not very keen on the job, but at least it pays my way, enables me to stay on here at the Villa Marina, well away from my mother's apron strings!'

She added quickly, nervously, 'Not that I have anything against her. It's just that, having left home, I wouldn't want to go back to Batley to help with the housework and take care of my brothers and sisters. I *hate* Batley! But South Bay is different. I love living near the sea; being independent for once in my life. Even so, I can't help feeling guilty, at times, leaving Mum in the lurch the way I did.'

Thea said, sympathetically, 'Not to worry, June, we all have choices to make and if happiness comes high on the agenda, what's wrong with that?'

June said, thoughtfully, 'You may be right. Even so, I can't help feeling guilty.'

Bunty and June insisted on helping with the clearing up. Thea gave them a portion of chicken each to take with them for tomorrow's supper. 'But you haven't had any yourself yet,' Bunty reminded her, 'and there isn't much of it left.'

'That was the general idea,' Thea laughed. 'It was beginning to haunt me, and I couldn't close the fridge door.'

Drying plates and polishing the glasses and cutlery Bunty had washed at the kitchen sink, June asked innocently, 'What made you buy so much food in the first place?'

'I didn't. It was a Welcome Home present from my courtesy aunt, Bess Hardacre, along with enough tinned stuff to last me a lifetime. If I die young, that is!'

'Bess Hardacre?' Bunty gasped. 'Golly, she's one of my best customers! Honestly, you wouldn't believe the amount of money she spends in Debenhams' beauty department; Stella's Salon de Beauté too, having non-surgical face-lifts, clay wraps and so on. Well, good luck to her; she's certainly well preserved for her age. I admire women who make the most of themselves.' She sighed wistfully. 'I'm only twenty-three, and look at me, as fat as butter and getting fatter by the minute! Perhaps I should follow Stella's example; find myself a rich married man with money to burn. Trouble is, rich blokes never give me a second glance. I usually end up with students as poor as church mice who borrow money off me, then scarper off into the wild blue yonder, leaving me, if not broke, then sadly bent.'

'Tell me about it,' Thea said ruefully. 'My student ex-boyfriend went back to Italy when the going got tough. That's the reason why I came here to South Bay: to get him out of my system.'

'And have you?' June asked.

'I'm not quite sure. I really did love him, you see. And I thought he loved me. Apparently I was wrong, but I can't help thinking about him, wishing he hadn't left so abruptly, without a word of explanation, just a note saying he'd decided to go back to Italy. That really hurt!'

'At least you've had a boyfriend, a love affair in your life, which is more than I've ever had,' June said regretfully. 'I'd like to meet someone really nice, no matter how poor, just as long as he cared for me. But men never seem to notice me at all, as if I were invisible, downright ugly, or whatever, and I don't know what to do about it!'

Bunty said forthrightly, 'The trouble with you, June, is that you don't make the most of yourself! Tell me, who chose that embroidered blouse and pleated grey skirt you're wearing? No, don't tell me, let me guess: your mother! From some fuddy-duddy catalogue, I shouldn't wonder. Am I right?'

'Well, yes, but Mother has always helped me choose my clothes. What's wrong with that?'

'Just about everything,' Bunty said bluntly. 'What you need is a whole new wardrobe of really smart clothes: trouser suits and sweaters, plain and simple skirts and well-tailored, unfussy blouses to show off that Audrey Hepburn figure of yours to its best advantage. Not to mention a drastic haircut, a low-cut cocktail dress, plus a nightly regime and first-hand advice on make-up to enhance your natural beauty. Take it from one who knows. So what do you think, June?'

At that moment, June didn't know what to think. Turning to Thea for advice, she asked uncertainly, 'What do *you* think?'

'For what it's worth, I agree with Bunty. But far more important than new clothes and beauty treatments, you'll need to get rid of your guilt complex.'

June smiled lopsidedly. 'I know what you mean. But you don't know my mother. She hates me being here; keeps on bullying me to go home. I'm afraid she'll wear me down in the end, and I never know exactly when she'll turn up to make sure I'm all right. What she'd say if she came to find me wearing trousers and make-up, I shudder to think.'

'Don't Batley women wear trousers and make-up?' Bunty asked.

'Not in our house, they don't,' June said.

When they had gone, Thea made ready for bed. Switching off her lamp, she saw the lights of the promenade reflected on the ceiling, and heard the distant sound of the sea washing in on the shore, as she had done a long time ago. She could almost see the room as it used to be, with a double bed facing the window and her own single bed near the far wall, in the space now occupied by the kitchenette.

The room had been furnished with solidly built Victorian wardrobes, chests of drawers and a marble-topped wash stand, in those days, and her parents had moved about quietly and spoken in whispers so as not to disturb her when they came up to bed.

Not that she had always been asleep, though she had pretended to be, awaiting the moment when Fliss would bend over to smooth her coverlet and kiss her forehead. Thea had loved the womanly fragrance of her mother, that immutable blend of eau de cologne, oatmeal soap, and sandalwood bath cubes.

Drifting to sleep on a tide of memories, Thea experienced no sense of loneliness, rather a feeling of homecoming in this room of hers. Despite the changes wrought by time and modernisation, it was still the same space once occupied by herself and her parents in time long gone. Time remembered with joy.

Up early next morning, Thea slipped across to the bathroom long before her fellow flatmates had opened their eyes to the insistent clamour of their alarm clocks.

Relaxing in the bath, taking care not to use too much hot water, she mulled over the events of the party the night before; the disparate personalities of the extrovert Bunty, the nervous, self-effacing June, and the emotionally mixed-up Stella, so obviously at loggerheads with Bunty, who believed in speaking her mind, let the barbs fall where they might.

Curiously, it was Stella who came uppermost in Thea's mind. Getting out of the bath to wash her face and clean her teeth before going back to her room to dress, comb her hair and apply her make-up, she wondered what would happen to Stella if the man she loved let her down in the long run. Perhaps he had already done so, and she wasn't prepared to admit it. Not even to herself.

Was she, Thea pondered, becoming morbidly obsessed with Stella's relationship with a married man because of her father's adulterous relationship with Carol Lindsay?

She was desperate to know more about the role played by the mistress in an illicit love affair. Had Carol Lindsay, for instance, suffered in much the same way that Stella Johnson was suffering now?

Philip had opened the shop when Thea arrived, having

unloaded several cartons of stock from his car, which he stacked on a long fitment, with shelves and drawers, on the wall opposite the window.

Not an inch of space had been wasted. Thea loved the neatness of it all, down to the tiny fitting cubicle with full-length mirror in the far corner, its candy-striped curtain reminiscent of a Punch and Judy cabinet.

Philip said cheerfully, 'When we've unpacked the cartons, we can begin stashing things away in drawers and on the dress rail. The smaller items – stockings, silk scarves, rain hoods, and so on – go on the counter. You'll soon get the hang of it.

'Most of the customers will be holidaymakers on the lookout for things they've forgotten to bring with them, or finding they're in desperate need for a particular item all of a sudden, depending on the weather. Hence the sun-tops, sun-tan lotion and babies' sun-bonnets for if the weather turns hot; the plastic macs, rain hoods and cagoules for if it turns wet.'

This was like Christmas, Thea thought, awaiting the opening of the cartons, anxious to see the contents, the goods she'd be selling when the season got fully under way. Apart from sun-tops, there were Italian silk over-blouses, cardigans, swimsuits and bikinis; rings, brooches and bracelets of the costume variety, of no intrinsic value, but tastefully designed; plus brightly coloured cotton squares alongside the more expensively priced Italian silk scarves.

Philip smiled, aware of her excitement. He said, 'In case you're wondering, a window cleaner comes once a week to wash the windows and the exterior paintwork. I'm afraid you'll have to clean the inside of the window yourself, hence the bottle of Windolene and dusters in this cupboard.' He opened the door to reveal the aforementioned equipment, plus a Bissel carpet sweeper, a bucket, and an electric kettle.

'There's a standpipe further along the prom,' he explained,

'where you can fill the kettle, and I've brought you these.' Lifting the lid of a cardboard box, he produced mugs, spoons, jars of Nescafe and Coffee Mate, a packet of tea-bags and a tin box labelled 'sugar'.

Thea laughed delightedly. 'My cup runneth over,' she said, tongue in cheek. 'So what's next on the agenda?'

'A coffee break at the snack bar,' Philip said decisively. 'Have you had breakfast, by the way? Or are you in need of another full mazuma?'

'Not this time,' Thea assured him, on their way to the café. 'I'll have you know that, on your advice, I am now safely ensconced in a bedsit in the Villa Marina, complete with a kitchen and all mod cons, doing my own catering. I had a bowl of cornflakes for breakfast, plus two slices of toast and marmalade, thanks to you – and Mr Cumberland, who just happened to have a room to let.'

'Really? Well, that is good news,' Philip said, ordering the coffee and sitting opposite her to drink it. 'And is the room all right?'

'More than that, it's perfect! Believe it or not, it's the room I shared with my parents many moons ago when we spent our summer holidays in South Bay, and I was knee high to a grasshopper.' She paused, misty-eyed with happiness. 'I could scarcely believe my luck when Mr Cumberland unlocked the door and said, "Well, this is it! What do you think of it?"'

She continued excitedly, 'What's more, I threw a flat-warming party, last night, for my fellow flatmates. You see, Aunt Bess had been with me on a shopping spree to Tesco, beforehand, lumbering me with more food than I could possibly cope with on my own: salad, tinned food, a cooked chicken the size of a – bustard; you name it!

'They ate up most of the chicken, but there's enough left over for my supper tonight. After I've rung my mother to tell her the news! I haven't had a phone installed yet, but there's a payphone in what used to be the reception area.

Not that I recognised it as such any more, without the old sofas, armchairs and potted palms, and with everything partitioned off. It seemed much smaller, somehow; the mahogany reception desk's a thing of the past, along with the glass doors leading to the dining room. But that's the way of the world, isn't it? Everything changed except in memory.'

When they had finished their coffee, they went back to the boutique to continue unpacking the cartons, Thea determined to gain more information about what her job entailed apart from the 'fun' aspect to it. The necessity of knowing the stock from A to Z, for example, so as not to waste time, when the crunch came, in attempting to sell a size 42 cardigan to a size 36 customer, or vice versa; or of never allowing a client to take into the fitting room more than two garments at a time, lest she paid for just one of them, and walked out of the shop wearing the others secreted beneath the one she had paid for.

'When it comes to window dressing,' Philip said, 'include as many items of stock as possible. Those wicker "busts" on the top shelf will come in useful to display the sun-tops and cardigans, suitably embellished with scarves, beads or whatever.'

Thea knew what he meant. The dummies, suitably robed, would add the dimension of height to the display. Smaller items such as jewellery, boxed hankies, stockings, rain hoods, sun-tan lotion and brightly coloured scarves, placed to the front of the window, would catch the eyes of passers-by, luring them into the shop to browse, hopefully to invest in goods they hadn't meant to buy until, doing her sales spiel, she talked them into it.

'You're looking decidedly pleased with yourself,' Philip remarked. 'What's on your mind?'

Thea glanced about her. 'This shop, this place, South Bay, the sea on my doorstep. My room at the Villa Marina. I've seldom felt as happy before as I do right now. Thanks to you. Oh, so many thanks to you for giving me this job.'

Later, on her way home to ring Fliss and polish off the remains of the chicken, since she was now feeling decidedly peckish, Thea caught sight of an elderly woman, limping badly on account of a bandaged ankle, attempting to climb the front steps of the house next door – the only one which had not, so far, succumbed to modernisation as a hotel. Still a private dwelling judging by its somewhat seedy, run-down appearance, it had old-fashioned lace curtains and Venetian blinds at the windows, and a neglected front garden overgrown with weeds and spotted bushes – hence the name of the house, 'The Laurels', displayed on a tarnished brass plaque near the front door.

Feeling sorry for the old lady, Thea said quickly, 'Please let me help you up the steps,' offering an outstretched hand as a means of support.

The woman said icily, 'If and when I need help, I'll ask for it, not before. I do not accept help from strangers.'

Frowning slightly, trying hard to remember, concentrating on her childhood days, Thea said, 'But we are not quite strangers, Miss Ashcroft. I came here a long time ago on holiday; my ball landed in your back garden several times, and I asked your permission to look for it. Do you remember?'

'No, I don't! Now just go away, young woman, and leave me alone. I can manage perfectly well on my own!'

The front door opened suddenly to reveal a shorter, plumper woman, with wispy grey hair, who cried out, 'I did warn you, Abigail, not to walk on that bad ankle of yours, but would you listen? Now look at you, all hot and bothered, in pain, and being rude into the bargain.'

'I am not in the least hot and bothered,' Abigail Ashcroft retorted sharply. 'I just wish you'd stop fussing, Vi! I wish everyone would stop fussing; as if I were in my dotage, when all that's wrong with me is a slightly sprained ankle!'

'A *badly* sprained ankle,' Vi reminded her sister. 'And I daresay Dr Watts won't be best pleased to find out you've been walking on it when he told you to rest it as much as possible.'

Thea could tell that Miss Ashcroft was in pain. Beads of perspiration were gathering on her forehead, she was breathing heavily, and her face was grey with fatigue. Tucking a hand firmly beneath the old woman's elbow, she said quietly, 'I intend helping you whether you like it or not. The sooner you're indoors and resting that ankle of yours, the better. Then I'll go away, but not before. All right?'

Past caring one way or the other, Miss Ashcroft made no reply. She simply took the steps one at a time, leaning heavily against Thea until they reached the front door of the Laurels, where Thea delivered her burden safely into the outstretched arms of the woman called Vi.

Four

Ruth Gregory was in the kitchen preparing the evening meal when Philip came home. Theirs was a red brick-built detached house, set back from the main coast road. It was a house he hated, having set his heart on a stone-built cottage further inland – a charming beamed cottage, at the sight of which Ruth had, figuratively speaking, thrown up her hands in horror.

That was in the early days of their marriage, when Joan and Eva were mere toddlers. Ruth, a neatly packaged woman, still as slim and self-contained now as she had been then, had pointed out to him that, growing up, their daughters would need more space, separate rooms of their own. Far more space than a two-bedroom cottage, however charming, would allow. No, they'd be far better off investing in a modern, detached, four-bedroom house, closer to town.

Inevitably, Philip had bowed to his wife's better judgement, kissed the cottage goodbye and settled for a modern monstrosity, totally lacking in charm.

Entering the kitchen, planting a perfunctory kiss on his wife's forehead, he asked, 'What's for supper? I'm starving.'

'Chicken and mushroom pie, from yesterday's left-over chicken,' she said patiently, putting pans of potatoes and carrots to boil on the Aga cooker.

Why had he bothered to ask? Philip wondered, long inured to his wife's mile-wide economy streak, her intentness on never letting anything edible go to waste if she could help it.

Left-over beef from Sunday lunch, for instance, usually appeared on Monday in the form of rissoles; lamb in cottage pies crowned with well-browned mashed potatoes. Left-over chicken usually came shrouded in pastry.

Ruth said, 'Why not take a shower? Supper will be ready in half an hour. Oh, by the way, good news. The children are coming to stay with us in a couple of weeks to celebrate our wedding anniversary. Isn't that splendid?'

Guilt-stricken, Philip realised that he had forgotten all about the up-and-coming anniversary. Thank God that Ruth had reminded him in time to get his act together; to buy her a suitable present – a ruby and diamond ring, perhaps; to reserve a table at the Mirimar, complete with champagne and red roses. Possibly even to present her with a surprise weekend trip to Paris, in September, when the summer season was over, the boutique closed, and Thea had gone back to London to become either an artist or a set designer.

Thea!

'Oh, do come in and sit down,' Violet Hastings advised her strong-willed sister, leading her to a chair in the parlour and placing a stool beneath her poorly ankle, 'while I put the kettle on for a nice cup of tea.'

In the high-backed chair near the fireplace Abigail wondered how long she and Violet, two vulnerable, lonely old women caught up in memories of yesteryear, could continue to live together in a kind of time warp. At the same time, she realised she faced a bleak future ahead of her if, on the pretext of wanting to be close to her in her declining years, Violet's son Peter persuaded his mother to enter sheltered accommodation in Norfolk.

Sooner or later, Abigail imagined, gazing about her at the lace-curtained windows with their acorn-adorned Venetian blinds and the towering overmantel above the empty grate, would come social workers – do-gooders, alerted by Dr

Watts – to pry into her affairs, with a view to putting her into a home.

The doctor had asked searching questions, she recalled, about her fall downstairs, wanting to know if she had turned giddy, suffered a temporary blackout, or misjudged her distance. How recently she had had her eyesight and blood pressure checked? Did she and her sister employ a home help? He had hinted that they were, perhaps, not 'feeding' properly.

Feeding? Deeply angry and upset, Abigail had said scathingly, 'My sister and I are not pigs at a trough. We do not "feed", we *dine*!'

The doctor shrugged his shoulders, 'Just a figure of speech,' he said dismissively. 'Now, if you'll roll up your sleeve, I'll take your blood pressure.'

Abigail said coldly, 'You were called in by my sister – mistakenly, in my opinion – to attend to my ankle. I suggest that you get on with it, then leave here as quickly as possible. Do I make myself clear?'

'Abundantly so, Miss Ashcroft, but your ankle is badly sprained and needs strapping.'

'I scarcely need you to tell me that, young man! It's as plain as the nose on your face. I do have some medical knowledge, you know: my father was a physician, and the room we are in now was once his surgery!'

'No need then for me to tell you that you must rest your ankle as much as possible,' Watts said imperturbably, having strapped the ankle and scribbled a prescription for painkillers. 'I'll call in to see you again next week; apply a new strapping, if necessary.'

Later, Abigail and Violet had exchanged 'words' over the incident of the sprained ankle.

'I did what I thought was best,' Violet confessed, weepily, 'when I found you lying there, in the hall, with your poor ankle black and blue, not knowing what had happened to cause your fall. For all I knew, you might have suffered a heart attack or a stroke, and the thought of losing you was more than I could bear!'

Abigail said forbearingly, 'What really happened was that I tripped over that worn-out patch of carpet halfway down, but I couldn't very well have told Dr Watts as much, could I?'

The trouble was, every carpet in the house needed replacing. There just wasn't enough money. The Laurels had been left jointly to herself and Violet when their father had died twenty years ago, and since then they had survived on the meagre income from the investments he had made during his lifetime, plus their old-age pensions supplemented by Vi's widow's pension. But never at any time had they thought of selling their home, despite tempting offers from developers wanting to turn it into a hotel.

The irony of the situation struck Abigail forcibly. Their one asset, the home they loved, was virtually worthless so long as they refused to part with it.

Another worrying thought occurred. If Vi decided to move to Norfolk to be near her son, his wife, and her grandchildren, the Laurels would have to be sold to realise her half-share in the property. Peter Hastings would insist on that, Abigail knew, having no great regard for her only nephew, a greedy, shiftless man, in her opinion.

And if Vi went away, where would that leave her? The answer came pat: financially better off, but rootless; a sad, lonely old woman robbed of her sister's presence in her life. She would end her days in a retirement home for the elderly, alone with her memories of happier times, when her parents and their brother George had been alive, and the Laurels had been filled with love and laughter – until the war had claimed the life of their brother, who had been killed at Monte Cassino, and whose remains now lay buried in Italy.

The laughter in life had died away suddenly so far as their mother, Caroline Ashcroft, was concerned, Abigail remembered. Receiving that telegram from the War Office, deeply regretting the death of her son, she had seemed to fade away before their eyes, no longer interested in her home, her husband, or her surviving children, until, a year later, she had died of leukaemia. More likely of a broken heart, Abigail thought bitterly.

She realised, of course, that the house was far too big for just two people. Not that they used all the rooms. The top-floor bedrooms and the attics had long been out of commission; seldom visited except when missing roof slates needed replacing, and workmen were called in to do the necessary repairs.

Now, she and Vi occupied bedrooms on the first landing, close to the bathroom and the Victorian lavatory, and the ground-floor rooms: the draughty, old-fashioned kitchen, the back parlour, and occasionally the drawing room overlooking the promenade. When the weather turned warmer they could sit at the bay window watching visitors coming up from the beach in readiness for hot baths, a change of clothing and dinner at whichever brightly lit hotel they had chosen to stay at, before embarking on evenings out at the theatre, a concert, cinema, or public house.

Apart from the top-floor bedrooms and the attics, another room in the Laurels remained unused – the ground-floor dining room. Once the epicentre of the house, breakfast, lunch and dinner had been served there by a parlour maid wearing a black dress, white cap and a starched pinafore, as befitted the household of a well-respected physician.

Her parents, Abigail remembered, had also employed a kitchen maid in those days, to help with the preparation of the food and attend to the washing-up afterwards. But it had been her mother who had planned the menus and done most of the cooking herself, believing in the old adage that food, cooked without love, has no taste.

In this day and age, Abigail thought tenderly, Caroline might well have published a wealth of cookery books, complete with glossy photographs of mouth-watering meals. On the other hand, she might have proved incapable of expressing, on paper, what exactly she did to food to make it taste so good. All that was a far cry from the kind of food that she and Violet ate nowadays, Abigail reflected wistfully: cornflakes and prunes for breakfast; boiled eggs and bread and butter for lunch; tinned spaghetti on toast or sausages and mash for supper. On Sundays, if they were lucky and had not overspent during the week, two roast chicken breast portions served with root vegetables, followed by either rice, sago, or tapioca pudding.

Once, just once more, Abigail thought, before she shuffled off this mortal coil, she would sell her soul to the devil to sink her teeth into roast sirloin of beef, crispy Yorkshire pudding, roast potatoes, leeks masked with a light cheese sauce, onion gravy, and profiteroles smothered in chocolate and filled with fresh Jersey cream.

In short, she was hungry. Desperately hungry! Hungry not only for food, but for peace of mind, a return to the carefree, taken-for-granted happiness of a past way of life now over and done with forever.

In her bedsit, Thea's thoughts centred not on herself but the two old women in the house next door, wishing she knew what, if anything, she could do to help them. They seemed so insular, somehow, so alone in the world.

She had glimpsed, through the open front door, the dingy hall paper and threadbare carpet. The poor old things must have fallen on hard times to be living in such poverty-stricken circumstances, and yet the message had emerged clear and strong that the taller and statelier of the two women would go to any lengths to maintain her stiff-necked independence.

Ringing Fliss from the payphone in the hall to impart the glad tidings of her own new-found independence, her job and her bedsit, she spoke quickly in the event of her money running out. Her mother said calmly, 'Give me your number, Thea, and I'll ring you back. You're not making much sense, and I want to know about everything in detail, without interruption of those blessed tones!'

When Fliss rang back, Thea waxed lyrical about the boutique, her boss and her bedsit: the self-same room they had occupied during their summer holidays in South Bay long ago, she told Fliss ecstatically.

Then came the saga of her shopping spree in Tesco with Aunt Bess and Uncle Hal, plus thumbnail sketches of her new neighbours and the flat-warming party she had thrown for them to get rid of the surplus food Bess had lumbered her with.

Fliss said happily, 'Well done, darling.' She added mischievously, 'Shall I send you a food parcel, by the way? Just in case you feel like another party?'

'Don't you dare!' Thea laughed, inured to her mother's dry sense of humour.

'A cheque, then?' Fliss suggested. 'To cover your first month's rent. I'll pop it in the post first thing tomorrow morning. That way you'll be able to spend your wages on having a good time, and getting out and about a bit with your friends. I really do want you to enjoy yourself.'

'I know, Mum, and thanks,' Thea said gratefully. 'I'll heed your good advice.' She paused, then added wistfully, 'I only wish there was something I could do to help the two old ladies in the house next door. Do you remember them at all?'

'Yes, but not very clearly. Let me think . . . oh yes, two sisters living together in genteel poverty. The older sister a bit of a dragon, very thin, tall and upright; the younger shorter and plumper. Don't tell me they are still living in – sorry, the name of the house escapes me – Laurel something or other.'

'The Laurels,' Thea supplied, jogging Fliss's memory. 'And yes, they are still living there – or existing, more like. I just feel so dreadfully sorry for them. Do you think they'd mind if I offered to clear their front garden of weeds? It's in such a mess, and obviously they can't do it themselves.'

A wise woman, Fliss replied warmly, 'Why not ask them? And if the answer is no, at least you'll feel better, knowing you tried.'

Hanging up the phone and passing the glass inner door of the Villa Marina, Thea noticed a red Mercedes parked near the front steps, the driver of which appeared to be engaged in a heated argument with the dark-haired girl in the passenger seat – Stella Johnson.

Suddenly, flinging open the car door, Stella stormed up the steps to the vestibule. Caught unawares, feeling guilty, Thea ducked back into the phone box. Stella was obviously angry and upset, in no mood for an exchange of pleasantries with a neighbour. In her present state of mind, were she to discover Thea hanging about in the hall, she might well accuse the girl of spying on her.

Not that Thea had meant to pry. She had simply wanted to gain an impression of Stella's gentleman friend. This she had done, and she had not liked the look of him one little bit: a heavily built, middle-aged man, red-faced, with a receding hairline. She wondered what on earth had possessed Stella to become involved with such an unattractive man in the first place.

Deep down, she knew why. Money. It *had* to be money! Why else would a pretty girl like Stella Johnson waste her time on a middle-aged Lothario when there must be plenty of handsome men her own age more than willing to show her a good time?

None of her business, Thea knew. After all, hadn't she wasted her own time on an Italian with a passion for spaghetti bolognese, when she might have dated a thin English student, floppy-haired, with a passion for poetry, not pasta? Attraction in her case had had nothing whatever to do with money, however; all her boyfriends so far had been as poor as a pauper's Christmas.

When Stella had disappeared through the door marked Strictly Private, Thea left the phone box and went down the front steps towards the Laurels, not relishing the thought of a second rebuff from the redoubtable Miss Ashcroft, but determined to offer her help in clearing the front garden of weeds.

The red Mercedes was still parked outside. The man at the wheel, lighting a cheroot, looked hard at Thea as she walked down the steps. Close to, she disliked him even more than she had done at a distance. Success had obviously settled on him like an expensive camel-hair overcoat, but the results of good living had settled in the region of his waistline, hence his flabbiness, his heavily jowled features, and the network of broken thread-veins on his cheeks.

Aware that she, especially her legs, were being given the once-over, Thea realised that she was being sized up for her 'bedability', as Stella must have been initially, before this 'toad-in-the-hole' had made his play for her. Presumably he had turned her head with gifts of flowers, jewellery and perfume, and candlelit dinners in out-of-town hotels, telling her that his wife didn't understand him, in all probability.

Thea shuddered involuntarily at the thought of Stella's liaison with such a man. A poor excuse for a human being, in her opinion. Treating the owner of the Mercedes to a withering glance, head in air, she walked on down the steps and along the pavement towards the Laurels, bumping into Bunty as she went.

'Hey, where are you off to in such a hurry?' Bunty asked in surprise. Thea breathlessly explained her mission.

'Hmm, rather you than me,' Bunty said wryly. 'I once hung some washing out of my window. Next thing I knew I was being read the riot act by Mr Cumberland, who had received a letter of complaint from the old girl next door saying washing hanging out of windows let down the tone of the neighbourhood.'

Catching sight of the red car and its occupant, she frowned. 'Oh Lord! What's Dracula doing here at this time of day? I thought vampires only came out after dark! He must be waiting for Stella to show up. Honestly, I've a good mind to give him an earful!'

'I think he's already had one, from Stella,' Thea said. 'She's gone to her room to cool off. I imagine they'd had a pretty heated argument. Stella shot out of the car like a bullet from a gun, with a face like thunder. I happened to be in the hall at the time. I'm afraid I took the coward's way out and hid in the phone box till the coast was clear.'

Bunty pulled a face. 'In your shoes, I'd have done the same,' she admitted. 'I like Stella, but there's no getting through to her these days, not since Flash Harry came on the scene, filling her head with all kinds of nonsense. Frankly, I could strangle that man with my bare hands – especially since his wife is a client of mine, a really nice woman. My feeling is that she suspects something is going on behind her back, and that's the reason why she's forever buying rejuvenating creams, make-up and so on. The poor soul, making the best of herself for a bloke who couldn't care less about her!'

She added fiercely, 'Not that he'll leave her! Oh no! Men like him want the best of both worlds. A nice ordinary wife to clean and cook for him, and an attractive "bit on the side" to bolster his ego in bed!'

Food for thought. Parting company with Bunty, Thea mounted the steps of the Laurels and rang the bell.

Violet Hastings, a far less fearsome personality than her sister, came to the door. 'Oh, it's you again. What is it you want?'

When Thea explained, Mrs Hastings said pleasantly, 'Well, that's very kind of you. But I'm not sure that my sister would approve. She's resting at the moment, and I shouldn't care to disturb her. Shall I talk it over with her and let you know in due course?'

She added, sotto voce, 'You see, she is a very proud, independent person. On the other hand, this is my home too, and the state of the garden worries me a great deal. Abigail too. So will you leave it with me, my dear, to try to persuade her?'

'Yes, of course I will,' Thea assured her. Then, yielding to a sudden impulse, leaning forward, she kissed the old lady's wrinkled cheek.

Five

Returning to the Villa Marina, Thea went up to her room to tackle the remains of the chicken and the left-over salad, which she set in front of the television. The news was on, mainly depressing reports to do with famine in the Third World. Closer to home, a full-scale police search for a missing three-year-old child was taking place, and a damning report had been issued of the physical abuse of the residents of a geriatric nursing home by members of staff.

Deeply troubled by man's inhumanity to man, and in sympathy with the victims of the famine, Thea pushed aside her plate, knowing that to eat another mouthful would choke her. Switching off the TV, she consigned the remains of her supper to the pedal bin, and made herself a cup of strong black coffee.

At that moment, the sound of music filled the air. June had put on a recording of Pavarotti singing 'Nessun Dorma'. Nothing could have been more welcome. 'Music that gentler on the spirit lies, than tired eyelids on tired eyes', Thea mused. Not that she was tired, merely restless, in need of spiritual refreshment. The news had upset her; so had the incident with the man in the Mercedes, the calculating look he gave her which had made her flesh creep. *Ugh!*

Someone knocked on the door. 'Come in,' Thea called.

Bunty entered the room, wanting to know how she had got on at the Laurels, and if she had enjoyed her first day at work.

Glad of her company, Thea invited her to sit down for a

cup of coffee. Refusing the offer, Bunty said, 'The reason I came was, I just wondered if you feel like a night out? There's a place in town called the Mirimar. The restaurant's a bit on the posh side, but there's a smashing cocktail bar, soft lights and sweet music, and plenty of talent.' She meant men.

'Not that I'm on the lookout exactly,' she added quickly. 'It's just that I have a dress I'd like to wear while I can still get into it, and the odd admiring glance wouldn't come amiss right now.'

'Any particular reason why?' Thea asked.

'Not really!' Bunty sighed deeply. 'Oh, who am I kidding? I had a letter from home this morning. Apparently an old flame of mine got married last week. Mum sent me a newspaper cutting with a photograph of the happy couple leaving the church, and I couldn't help thinking the bride might have been me, if I hadn't been so – pig-headed!'

'I'm sorry,' Thea said sympathetically. 'Were you very much in love with him?'

'No. But I might have been if I'd tried a bit harder.' Bunty laughed suddenly. 'Oh, take no notice of me. I'm just feeling sorry for myself, that's all. Ready to drown my sorrows in a couple of dry Martinis. How about you?'

'I'll be ready in half an hour,' Thea promised.

Over supper, Ruth Gregory asked her husband how he'd got on at work that day, making no secret of the fact she thought he'd acted hastily in appointing an inexperienced girl to manage the boutique. 'You can't put an old head on young shoulders,' she reminded him in a schoolmarmish voice.

'Miss Bellamy may be young, but she is highly intelligent, enthusiastic, and she came well recommended,' Philip said, wishing the topic had not arisen. 'I had a quick decision to make when Miss Adams left me in the lurch. So far as I'm concerned, I made the right decision in offering the job to Miss Bellamy.'

'You should have discussed it with me first,' Ruth said primly. 'After all, I *am* a major shareholder in the business.'

'There wasn't time for discussion.' He lay down his cutlery amid a sizeable portion of pie crust and uneaten vegetables, having lost his appetite all of a sudden.

'You were starving when you came in,' Ruth commented, 'now you've hardly eaten a thing. What's the matter with you? You might as well tell me. I shall find out sooner or later.'

'Very well, since you ask. I wish you would leave the running of the business to my better judgement from now on. A shareholder you may be. So what do you want, a shareholders' meeting every time there's a snap decision to be made?'

Ruth raised her eyebrows in surprise. 'There's no need to adopt that tone of voice with me. After all, I *am* your wife as well as your business partner.'

Sick and tired of this, a far older argument, Philip said impatiently, 'For the umpteenth time, you are not my business partner. You are one of four shareholders, none of whom have so far complained at the annual rake-in of dividends. So I must be doing something right!'

'All right, Philip. No need to get hot under the collar. At a rough guess, I'd say you are not certain yourself that Miss Bellamy is up to managing the boutique. You are just too stubborn to admit your mistake. I'm right, aren't I?'

Philip gave up the struggle, as he had done so many times before. The trouble with Ruth was that she was always right, in her opinion. If only, once in a while, she would admit to being wrong.

'The trouble with you, Abby,' Vi Hastings told her sister, 'is you're too proud and stubborn to accept that we need help. No, don't interrupt. It isn't often I speak my mind, but this time I intend having my say!

'Before you fly off the handle again, just remember, this is my house as much as yours. Oh, I don't care about the state of it indoors, that it needs money spending on it to make it habitable. Money we haven't got. I don't care about being poor. What I *do* care about is the state of the front garden; displaying our poverty for all the neighbourhood to see.

'Now, a decent young woman has come forward with an offer to tidy up the garden for us, and all you can do is witter on about not accepting help from anyone! Well, I think differently! That garden is nothing short of a disgrace. Just think how Father would feel if he were alive to see it, choked with weeds and overgrown bushes!

'You call yourself a proud, independent woman. So ask yourself if you are proud of that garden out there. Are you independent enough to tackle it yourself? No, and neither am I! The truth is, we are just a couple of worn-out old women near the end of our tether, in need of all the help we can get. And that is the reason why, whether you like it or not, I intend writing a note to Miss Bellamy, accepting her offer. So there!'

Abigail said tartly, 'In that case, you had better include the key to the shed in your letter. I daresay the girl will need tools – a fork, a spade and secateurs – to do the job properly.'

Violet said warily, 'You mean that you really don't mind?'

'*Mind*? Of course I *mind*! I mind growing old and useless. I mind being poor and looking ugly. I mind never having quite enough to eat. I mind having a sprained ankle, poor eyesight and high blood pressure, and worn-out carpets and curtains! How about you?'

Violet said wistfully, 'I don't mind anything at all, as long as we're together.'

Flinging herself face downward on the bed, Stella beat the pillows violently with her clenched fists.

It had happened again: the last-minute cancellation of a dinner date she'd been looking forward to all day; the third such cancellation in the past two weeks. This time she'd gone off the deep end, had told Brian Felpersham exactly what she thought of his broken promises.

Losing her temper completely, she'd shrieked, 'Have you any idea what this uncertainty is doing to me? No, and you couldn't care less, could you? Well, I'm sick and tired of playing second fiddle to your wife and family. If it's them you want, why not have the guts to say so, and leave me alone?'

'You're talking nonsense, Stella, and you know it. Have you any idea how hard it is for me to drum up excuses to get away from Audrey and the kids even once in a while, let alone as often as I've been doing lately?'

'Then why not tell her the truth for a change? Stop making excuses and tell her straight that you're in love with someone else?'

Brian said heatedly, 'How many more times must I tell you it isn't as simple as all that? The last thing I need right now is to give Audrey grounds for divorce. She'd take me to the cleaners! For God's sake! Is that what you want? Think about it, Stella.'

'*Think* about it? I'm sick and tired of thinking about it! Fed up to the back teeth of being stood up whenever your wife crooks her little finger at you, and you come running! Have you any idea how cheap that makes me feel? Being your "bit on the side", the other woman in your life? Well, that's all over now! Stay with your wife and kids! See if I care!' At which point, Stella had flung open the door of the Mercedes and rushed upstairs to her room to beat hell out of her pillows.

Later, when the phone rang, picking up the receiver, she asked, 'Yes? Who is it? What do you want?' She knew full well who it was, and what he wanted.

Brian's voice came on the line. He said, 'Listen, Stella.

I'm really sorry about tonight, that silly misunderstanding between us. Please tell me you didn't mean what you said about ending our relationship. All I'm asking for is a little more time to sort out my domestic problems, and I promise faithfully not to let you down again. So how about Friday night? Dinner at the Chase Hotel? Pick you up around seven. All right?' He added persuasively, 'I really do love you, you know.'

'Very well then, if you say so,' Stella replied, hanging up the receiver, wishing, deep down, she'd possessed enough courage to say no, wondering, not for the first time, how she had become so deeply involved with a married man.

It boiled down to flattery, she imagined; that and the excitement of having an illicit love affair with a man rich enough to shower her with expensive gifts, who made no secret of the fact that he wanted to make love to her in the privacy of some hotel bedroom after a candlelit dinner for two.

It was too late now to withdraw from her *liaison dangereuse*, Stella realised. Having become inured to rich living, champagne, caviar and candlelight, how could she possibly return to a life devoid of excitement, of sexual fulfilment in the arms of a charismatic lover?

She could not, and that was that.

Relaxing in a chair, eyes closed, wearing slippers and an old dressing gown, June let the music she loved wash over her like warm, scented bathwater, thinking how lucky she was to be able to listen to music to her heart's content in this spacious room of hers. It was a far cry from the cramped confines of the house in Batley, occupied by her prim, over-protective mother Agnes, her two riotous brothers, Alfie and Billy, and her mischievous ten-year-old sister Angela, in which she had never known a moment's peace of mind.

It hadn't been easy telling her mother she was leaving

home. She had studied hard for her A-level exams, with a view to finding herself a decent job when she left school. Frequent visits to the Job Centre in Batley had proved futile, however, despite the many job application forms she'd filled in. Not once had she been shortlisted or interviewed for a job of any kind – not even as a supermarket check-out girl, a hospital cleaner or a snack-bar assistant.

Her mother, relieved, told her she'd be far better off at home, helping with the housework, cooking and shopping, just as long as her weekly Giro cheques continued to cover the cost of her board and lodging and the monthly payments due to the catalogue firm from which the family's clothing derived. Boots and shoes, shirts, trousers and anoraks for her brothers; petticoats, knickers and dresses for Angela; blouses and skirts for herself; brushed nylon nightgowns, towel bales and bedding for Agnes.

What had prompted her to reply to an advert for a job as a clerical assistant in South Bay, June would never know. Desperation, perhaps? A last throw of the dice before she was swallowed up completely by the noise and confusion of her home in Batley: the coming and going of her siblings; the slamming of doors; the quarrels at mealtimes; her mother's frequent headaches; and the seemingly endless piles of dirty plates, pots and pans in the kitchen sink, awaiting her attention when her siblings went missing after supper and Agnes had retired to her room to nurse her migraines.

Never would June forget that sublime moment when, after a long bus journey to South Bay and a nerve-racking interview at the Town Hall, she was requested to report for duty the following Monday morning, to start work there in the Benefits Department, subject to her acceptance of the terms listed in an official contract of employment.

All she'd had to do then to escape from her over-bearing mother and the house in Batley was to sign on the dotted line, which she had done with a sweet feeling of relief that she was free at last to live her own life. But was anything ever quite that simple or straightforward?

Returning home to pack her belongings, she had become involved in an argument with her mother, who called her selfish and thoughtless for even thinking of leaving her to manage on her own. And just where did June propose to live?

'I'll find somewhere,' June said, 'a hostel or a bed-sitting room.'

'Huh. Throwing good money away, if you ask me,' Agnes said scornfully. 'But that's typical of kids nowadays, never stopping to think of the practicalities, the cost of food, heating and so on. Well, don't say I didn't warn you, when you're living on toast and sandwiches.'

'I'm not a kid, Mum. I'm eighteen,' June replied. 'I'll be earning good money, and I shan't be living on sandwiches. There's a canteen where I can get a proper midday meal during the week. At weekends, I'll have boiled eggs, soup, bananas, stuff like that. I shan't starve. Besides, it will do me good to fend for myself for a change.'

The argument dragged on, but June stood her ground and, two days later, had returned to South Bay to begin her new life.

The Mirimar restaurant and cocktail bar occupied the ground floor of a Regency building which, despite alteration and modernisation, still retained an aura of bygone elegance. Indeed, discreet floodlighting had enhanced rather than diminished its charming, balconied façade, and there was nothing in the least brash or jarring about the heavy plate-glass doors opening on to a luxuriously carpeted reception area dotted about with velvet-covered sofas and armchairs, exquisite items of antique furniture and breathtakingly beautiful flower arrangements.

'Well, I told you it was posh, didn't I?' Bunty said, sotto voce, as they made their way to the cocktail bar separated from the restaurant by curved glass partitions fronted with stone troughs of trailing pink geraniums and variegated ivy.

Overhead lighting had been kept to a minimum to ensure a warm, romantic atmosphere. The restaurant tables were adorned with pink-shaded lamps. The discreetly lit cocktail bar exuded the glamour of a Hollywood film set of the 1940s. Not that Thea remembered that era, but she had seen it portrayed often enough in late night films on television. *Cover Girl*, for instance, starring the lovely Rita Hayworth – Fliss's favourite film, with music by Jerome Kern.

No matter what the future held for her, Thea would never forget that night: the soft lights and sweet music, the spotlit grand piano in the far corner of the room, the man seated at that piano, and the tune he was playing, Jerome Kern's 'All the Things You Are'.

Thea had never believed in love at first sight before. She did then.

He was the most incredibly handsome man she had ever set eyes on, dark-haired, with strong, symmetrical features. Looks which might have made little or no impact on Thea had the man been younger, fully aware of his physical assets, and ogling the unattached members of the opposite sex that were perched on high stools near the bar.

The man at the piano was doing no such thing. He hadn't even looked up from the keyboard, as if the music he played was for himself alone and no one else in the world except, perhaps, one very special person.

It was the air of sadness about him that Thea found so appealing, the intensity of his playing, the haunting tunes of the past: 'Smoke Gets in Your Eyes', 'Stardust', 'These Foolish Things'.

'God, isn't he marvellous?' Bunty breathed in Thea's ear. 'I'd say yes to a date with him any night of the week, wouldn't you?' She sighed deeply. 'Chance would be a fine thing. Any road, I'd hate playing second fiddle to a piano!'

As if he had caught wind of Bunty's remark, the pianist looked up from the keyboard, frowning slightly. His eyes were dark, etched about with faint lines of sadness and fatigue, as if he had undergone some recent illness or bereavement. Bypassing Bunty in her tightly fitting black dress, his eyes momentarily focused on Thea. Then, returning his gaze to the keyboard, he began playing softly 'Long Ago and Far Away'.

Six

Thea looked forward intensely to her day off. She had worked hard that week, washing the fixtures and fittings, polishing mirrors, unpacking and putting away stock, attempting her first window display, concentrating on the job in hand. At the same time she had felt strangely disorientated, unable to rid her mind of the Mirimar's soft lights and sweet music, the impact the pianist had made on her. Beguiled by his looks, that air of sadness about him, she had begun to think she might have fallen in love with him. How utterly ridiculous. Even so, he lingered on in her subconscious mind as a man in desperate need of love and understanding.

Not that she expected to see him again. No way would pride allow her return to the Mirimar to make a fool of herself once more, perching on a bar stool, imagining that he had noticed her. How gullible could one be?

Apart from her work at the shop, she had spent her evenings clearing the front garden of the Laurels. Delighted that her offer of help had been accepted by her eccentric next-door neighbours, she had entered the shed to the rear of the premises by means of the key enclosed in the letter Mrs Hastings had sent her. There she had found an assortment of rusty tools, spades, forks, trowels and shears, an ancient wooden wheelbarrow; and a grass mower of pre-war vintage, the latter apparently meant for use in the wilderness of a garden to the rear of the house.

Not that any sign of a lawn remained. The entire area

was choked with weeds, nettles, overgrown borders and flowerbeds in which a few lupins, delphiniums and rose bushes struggled for survival.

Ye gods, Thea thought, staring about her in dismay, what had she let herself in for? Tackling the front garden would be child's play compared with restoring order to this – shambles! But could she, in all conscience, leave it in this state? Of course not. In for a penny, in for a pound. Besides, the exercise and fresh air would be good for her. More to the point, the restoration of the property would hopefully please the charming, slightly scatty Violet and her far less charming sister Abigail.

One thing for certain, the tools at her disposal would need oiling and cleaning before she could begin to tackle the 'shambles'. No use approaching Miss Abby, she reckoned; far better to utter a quiet word or two in Vi's ear. Sometime next week, perhaps? This Friday evening, Thea was too full of her Saturday off to bother about the state of the women's rear premises.

Tomorrow, she had planned a bit of a lie-in followed by a trip into town to do her weekend shopping, a visit to the local art gallery in the afternoon, and an evening's outing to the theatre, depending on what was on. In need of solitude to come to terms with the many and varied facets of her new life in her own way, she would spend the day alone.

Coming home on Friday evening, she saw Stella, carrying an overnight case, getting into the red Merc, the driver of which glanced round furtively before nosing the car away from the pavement and heading inland. So the affair was on again, Thea conjectured, despite the blazing row she had witnessed earlier that week. No wonder Lover Boy looked so guilty. 'Conscience doth make cowards of us all', she thought wryly, going upstairs to her room.

On Saturday morning, up bright and early, thoughts of a lie-in forgotten, Thea borrowed the communal vacuum and cleaning materials from the store cupboard on the landing and set about housework. Rejoicing in the sunshine of a perfect May morning, she stripped the bed and turned the mattress, remaking it with a pile of fresh linen prior to taking the cast-off bedding down to the basement laundry to be washed and ironed and returned to her the following week. 'All part of the Villa Marina service,' Mr Cumberland had assured her, when she had agreed to rent the room, adding, 'Of course, personal garments you'll have to iron yourself. Understood?'

'Yes, of course, Mr Cumberland,' she'd replied, not about to reveal to him that she had never ironed a garment in her life before, not even Carlo Gambetti's shirts, worn to Mass on Sunday mornings. No wonder he had left her, she thought ironically. Unironed shirts linked to her inability to cook spaghetti bolognese!

Thea knew now that a stable relationship between a devout Catholic and a part-time Protestant was doomed to failure sooner or later. Not that their disparate religious beliefs had seemed important when they'd made love, only on Sunday morning, and when her spaghetti bolognese had ended up resembling a Welsh rarebit smothered in tomato sauce with a crusty topping of roughly cut-up Cheddar.

Even so, Carlo had been her first lover, whose sudden departure from her life had caused her a great deal of pain, anguish and mental suffering, linked to those passionate nights they had spent together in that weird basement flat of theirs until he had opted out of his final year at the Lambeth College of Art to return to the bosom of his family in Milan.

All of this he'd explained briefly in the note he had left for her on the kitchen table.

> Dear Thea, I see now that our relationship is leading nowhere, the reason why I have decided to return to Italy. I regret opting out of my final year at college,

> as I regret leaving you. A choice had to be made, and I have chosen to accept my father's offer of a junior partnership in his firm. Yours, Carlo.

Ah well, Thea thought resignedly, vacuuming the carpet, all that was over and done with. Thanks to Fliss, she had a new future ahead of her, albeit a future devoid of love – apart from the inexplicable tugging at her heartstrings that night at the Mirimar, when the sad, handsome pianist had played 'Long Ago and Far Away'.

Driving to work, Philip hoped that Thea would enjoy her day off. She had already made an appreciable difference to the boutique. He had not asked her to wash the paintwork or clean an accumulation of sand from the tough fibre floor covering; that she had done so of her own volition further convinced him that he had chosen the right person for the job.

Moreover, she had added an unexpected dimension of happiness to his days – a bonus, at his age – as if her youth and vitality had infected him with feelings of joie de vivre and optimism. He felt a renewed interest in his business affairs, and turned aside thoughts of retirement, of selling up – to do what, exactly? Potter in his garden? Improve his golf handicap? Take up a hobby of some kind? Photography, or writing his memoirs – *My Life in the Rag Trade*? The mind boggled.

He loathed the uninteresting half-acre of land surrounding his red brick villa, a garden devoid of hidden corners, just lawns and flowerbeds, almost as much as he hated playing golf – his wife's favourite pastime. As to photography, clicking a camera was not the seamark of his utmost sail. He remembered the sheer boredom of social evenings spent perusing other folks' albums – or, worse still, watching jolly holidays captured for posterity by means of some intrusive camcorder enthusiast determined to catch his victims at a disadvantage, usually with their mouths stuffed full of food. As for writing his memoirs, he would not, in all probability, get beyond the first chapter.

Right now he must give some thought to buying his wife a ruby wedding anniversary present: some item of jewellery that she would really like and appreciate, perhaps, not that Ruth wore rings, apart from the plain gold band he had slipped on to her finger on their wedding day.

Ruth was not, and never had been other than a practically minded person, and as a young man he had needed a woman of her calibre to bolster his ego. Faced with the dilemma of whether or not to set up in business for himself, he had lacked the self-confidence to terminate his employment as the manager of a clothing factory: it had been Ruth who had advised him to find out more about the town centre shop he was interested in buying.

Apart from her common-sense outlook on life, he had deeply admired her looks: her trim figure, her clear hazel eyes beneath well-shaped brows, her abundant dark brown hair cut in a no-nonsense bob. True to form, on their wedding day she had worn a well-tailored skirt and jacket and a halo hat, and carried a spray of roses, forgoing the traditional white bridal gown, veil, headdress and the kind of mammoth shower bouquet chosen by most women for their walk down the aisle. And she had been right to do so, Philip realised. Ruth was not a 'floaty' kind of person. Besides which, she had no intention of wasting money on an outfit of no earthly use to her after the wedding ceremony, when they would need to save every penny to invest in the future.

With her usual propensity for clear thinking, she had everything worked out beforehand. She would keep on teaching full-time until she became pregnant. Thereafter, when the baby was born, she would work part-time in order to spend as much time as possible with the child until she had finished breastfeeding. Meanwhile she would take on tutoring, in a private capacity, to ensure the continuance of her income following the birth of their child, or children, as the case might be.

Today, faced with the difficult decision of what to give his wife on their fortieth wedding anniversary, Philip recalled that never once during their married lives had he told Ruth he loved her, and never once had she voiced her feelings for him. It was as if some unbreachable barrier existed between them, which neither of them had ever really noticed or regretted, immersed as they were in pursuit of financial stability and providing a solid home background for their offspring.

Now, Philip regretted the passionless nature of his relationship with his wife these past forty years, the perfunctoriness of their love-making, more of a ritual than a pleasure. An act of duty on the part of the husband. A kind of meaningless assurance of his continuing fidelity to her, hers to him. Now, remembering her wedding vows, she still allowed him occasional access to her long since infertile body.

Parking his car, Philip thought that, with a modicum of luck, he would drum up an excuse to visit the boutique tomorrow morning, when Ruth would be busy in the kitchen preparing and cooking their roast beef, Yorkshire puddings and vegetables for Sunday lunch.

She would complain, of course, about his absence. Having invited golfing friends for lunch, she would ask why he felt it necessary to visit the boutique on his day off, when he would be better employed mowing the lawn and setting the dining-room table. He would cross that bridge when he came to it.

Art had always fascinated Thea. As a lanky, pigtailed schoolgirl, she had often been taken during school holidays to the Tate Gallery, and sometimes to theatre matinées, so that she had grown up with an awareness of the cultural aspects of life and a deep appreciation of various means of self-expression.

Not that Fliss had rammed culture down her daughter's throat. Far from it. In her role as a single parent, she had simply wished to foster in a highly intelligent young girl an appreciation of the richness of creativity: art, music, ballet, books, the theatre. Of course there had been lots of other fun too: visits to the Regent's Park Zoo, Madame Tussauds, the Planetarium, hamburger restaurants, Covent Garden, Billingsgate and Petticoat Lane. At the end of long, happy days spent together, they would enjoy a warm homecoming supper before bath and bedtime, a tucking in of Thea's coverlet, an affectionate goodnight kiss and the leaving on of the landing light outside her room as a reminder that she was not alone in the dark.

South Bay Art Gallery had once been a privately owned house in a quiet, tree-lined avenue near the town centre. Today, its façade of honey-coloured stone glowed in the sunlight. Crossing the threshold, Thea found herself in a spacious octagonal hall with a curving staircase leading to the upstairs rooms. To the right of the entrance there was a reception desk displaying literature announcing forthcoming exhibitions and selling picture postcards and a visitors' book, behind which stood a uniformed attendant who bade her a cheery good morning.

'On holiday, are you?' he asked pleasantly.

'Yes and no,' Thea said, smiling back at him. 'I'll be here till September. I've taken a job for the summer.'

The man, elderly, with receding grey hair, said, 'Well, you couldn't have chosen a nicer place. I've lived here all my life, an' I wouldn't live anywhere else for all the tea in China.' He paused. 'Fond of art, are you?'

'Yes, very. In fact, I'm thinking of taking up art as a career.'

'Well, I'll be blowed!' The attendant looked suitably impressed. 'To be honest, most of the folk who come here haven't a clue about art; they either come in out of the rain to make use of the toilet facilities, or they're in need of a cup of coffee and a scone in the basement café. Probably all three in the long run.' He chuckled drily.

'Anyway, miss, take your time looking round the exhibits, an' don't forget to sign the visitors' book when you leave, just in case you become a famous artist one of these days when, more than likely, I'll write you a begging letter! My name's Tom Fenby, by the way.'

'Mine's Thea Bellamy,' she said, enjoying the nonsense conversation, 'but I shouldn't hold my breath, if I were you. Re that "begging letter", chances are I'll be writing one of my own – addressed to *you*!'

Thea wandered round the gallery, in which she appeared to be entirely alone. This being a fine Saturday, it seemed scarcely likely that floods of visitors would turn up out of nowhere to break the silence of her concentration on the wealth of paintings on display, by artists of the calibre of Holman Hunt, Ford Madox Brown and Alfred, Lord Leighton. Above all, on loan by courtesy of a London gallery, John Atkinson Grimshaw's *Liverpool From Wapping* depicted lights from shop windows gleaming on wet pavements, hansom cabs adumbrated against gathering twilight, and the masts of sailing ships at anchor. Gazing at the sublime brushwork and stepping back to gain an overall view of the masterpiece, Thea inadvertently bumped into someone standing close by.

Turning abruptly, she said, 'Oh, I'm so sorry, please forgive me. I got so carried away, I hadn't realised that I wasn't alone.'

'No need to apologise,' the man standing behind her said quietly. 'I should have coughed or whistled, perhaps?'

Thea's heart skipped a beat. The man she was looking at was the pianist.

Frowning slightly, he asked, 'Haven't we met somewhere before? Your face seems familiar.'

'No, we've never met.' What else could she have said?

No way was she prepared to admit to having seen him at the Mirimar, from a bar stool.

He said, 'This is a marvellous painting, isn't it? But then, John Atkinson Grimshaw is one of the all-time great artists. Certainly no one else ever captured moonlight on canvas the way he has done.' He paused, then, 'A tricky thing, I imagine, painting something as elusive as moonlight.'

Glancing up at him, Thea noticed the finely etched lines about his eyes, that indeterminate air of weariness about him which she found so attractive, as if he were nursing some deep, inner sorrow which had coloured his life with regret. There was sorrow expressed in his piano playing, no matter how trite the music he played might be. Sad songs for sad people, perhaps?

She said, 'Painting anything at all isn't as easy as it looks. Even still life. There's so much technique involved.'

'You speak as one who knows,' he remarked.

'Up to a point,' she admitted. 'I've been at the Lambeth College of Art in London for the past year, studying design as well as painting, not knowing which to choose as a future career.'

'And have you a preference?' he asked.

'Oh, sure,' she smiled ruefully, 'to capture moonlight on canvas. The fact is, I've yet to capture, on canvas, a banana that remotely resembled a banana.'

The pianist chuckled. 'So what does the alternative entail?'

'Design? Well, that's a much broader spectrum, a course involving various aspects of stagecraft, for example: lighting, set design and so forth. I adore the theatre – which reminds me' – she glanced at her wristwatch – 'I must book a ticket for tonight's performance on my way to the shops.'

The man said quietly, 'Are you in a hurry? If not, would you care to have coffee with me?'

Thea hesitated briefly, and was lost. 'Well, yes,' she

replied, 'if you wouldn't mind leading the way. I've never been here before – have you?'

'Yes, quite often.' He smiled reflectively. 'You see, I think of this place as my spiritual home whenever I return to South Bay for a summer season.' He added, 'My name is Ross Drummond, by the way.'

'Mine is Thea – Thea Bellamy,' she responded warmly, liking everything about him. Quite apart from his looks, his appreciation of art was akin to her own, as if they had met somewhere before. Long Ago and Far Away?

The girl intrigued Drummond. Unlike most young women of his acquaintance, she had not tried to flirt with him to impress him, had not patted her hair, preened or giggled. Indeed, this girl appeared unaware of her fresh young beauty, her grace and charm, rendered more potent by her lack of artifice, of heavy make-up or provocative clothing.

Leaving the Mirimar when the place closed for the night, chances were there'd be groups of girls awaiting his appearance, wanting his autograph or to engage him in idle conversation, when all he wanted was to go home to the small furnished flat he rented for the summer months, to have a shower, slip into a bathrobe and try to relax before bedtime.

Bringing coffee and scones to the café table, he noticed that Thea was writing a shopping list, frowning slightly with concentration, jotting down ideas as they occurred. Looking up, she said, 'I should have done this before I left home, but it's such a lovely day I wanted to make the most of my time off.'

'So you're a working girl?' he queried, sitting down to pour the coffee.

'Yes. I was lucky enough to be offered a job right away, at a little shop on the lower promenade. Then I found myself a bedsit at the Villa Marina, with a marvellous sea view, so I'm on cloud nine at the moment.' She smiled. 'A case of "all this and heaven, too".' She wondered what he'd think of her if she told him that 'all this and heaven, too' included their unexpected meeting; being here with him now, feeling entirely at ease and relaxed in his company.

He said, 'You spoke of the theatre. What are you going to see?'

'I haven't a clue. I don't even know where it is.'

'Perhaps I could show you the way,' he suggested, 'when we've finished our coffee?' He felt reluctant to part company with her, knowing that he wanted to see her again some time in the not too distant future, despite the barrier imposed by his anti-social working hours, those long evenings spent playing sad songs for sad people very like himself. Apart from the 'bar-flies', of course, the nightly contingent of sexually aware self-conscious young women perched on bar stools, obviously far more interested in him than his music.

The theatre, scarcely a stone's throw away from the art gallery, had most probably been extant in the late Georgian era, Thea imagined. One of those bijou theatres that now mounted restoration comedies by Richard Brinsley Sheridan and plays by Oscar Wilde, George Bernard Shaw and so on.

To her delight, Thea saw that tonight's play was Noel Coward's *Private Lives*. Next week's offering was to be *What Every Woman Knows* by J.M. Barrie; thereafter, Emlyn Williams's *Night Must Fall*, Oscar Wilde's *Lady Windermere's Fan* and Sheridan's *School for Scandal* would be presented.

Smiling up at the pianist, she said, 'Thank you so much for showing me the way.' She hoped against hope that they would meet again one day, wanting desperately to know more about him, this man who had coloured her life with dreams of romance, with whom she had fallen in love at first sight. Not that she would ever venture to tell him so. Pride, after all, was a potent weapon in every woman's armoury.

On the point of his departure, he said suddenly, 'May we meet again, next Saturday? Same time, same place?'

'Yes,' she replied quietly, despite her rapidly beating heart. 'I'll look forward to it.'

Seven

The hotel Brian Felpersham had chosen for his assignation with Stella was so far off the beaten track that more than once he lost the way and had to consult a road map of the area.

'I thought we were going to the Chase,' Stella said huffily, thinking what a waste of time it was to be driving round in circles when they might have been safely ensconced in their usual suite by this time, enjoying champagne cocktails before dinner.

'For God's sake, Stell, stop nit-picking and leave the decision-making to me,' he replied sharply, stabbing the road map with a well-manicured forefinger. 'Oh yes, I've got it now! We should have turned right half a mile back.'

Clinging grimly to her seat belt as he swung the Merc into a two-point turn and headed back towards a hitherto unnoticed sign announcing 'The Inn Thing', Stella wondered what the hell he was playing at, bringing her to a dump like this. Approached by a series of steeply angled hairpin bends, the hotel lay at the heart of a valley, the slopes of which were clothed with vegetation – thickly crowded trees and towering rhododendrons – creating a claustrophic atmosphere.

'If you think I'm staying here, you're wrong,' Stella said stubbornly, refusing to get out of the car. She stared mutinously at the flight of steps leading to a rustic veranda swathed in masses of unpruned clematis. 'I wouldn't spend the night here if you paid me!'

Seriously out of temper, hot and hungry, unwilling to

admit that he had made a mistake in his choice of venue, Brian said hoarsely, 'The room is already booked, so stop bitching and start walking. I mean it!'

'I've already told you—'

'And I'm telling *you*! We're stopping here whether you like it or not. You stay in the car if you want to. Me, I'm going indoors for a good stiff drink, a slap-up dinner and a good night's sleep, with or without you!'

Stella knew when she was beaten. Brian held all the aces. Getting out of the car, she followed him up the steps to the reception lounge, bearing in mind the – albeit tenuous – security that their relationship afforded her. His gifts of jewellery, perfume, flowers and clothing. Above all the monthly cheques he paid into her bank account to cover her rent at the Villa Marina.

Seething inwardly, she thought that one day, perhaps, if she played her own cards right, she would come up trumps. And if playing her cards right entailed making certain that his wife found out about their affair, so be it.

Dressing for dinner seemed scarcely worth the bother, Stella thought bitterly, since she and Brian were apparently the only guests in this cock-eyed hotel. So why take the trouble to put on her black velvet skirt, sequinned top and diamond earrings? She might just as well wear the slacks and jumper she'd arrived in.

Brian said placatingly, 'I know you're upset, Stell, and I admit this place isn't quite what I'd expected. But look on the bright side. At least we have it to ourselves. Not likely to bump into anyone I know here, am I?'

Sliding his arms round her waist, nuzzling his cheek against her hair, he inhaled the scent of the Chanel No 5 perfume he'd given her on her birthday, which had cost him an arm and a leg, not to mention the diamond earrings and the black lace lingerie.

Even so, she was worth it, he persuaded himself, pushing aside thoughts of his wife and their two teenage sons, along with his ever-present feelings of guilt about the lies and evasions necessary to a man involved in a passionate affair with another woman.

If only Stella were as sweetly compliant as his wife Audrey. On the other hand, a compliant mistress would scarcely have satisfied the sexual needs of a middle-aged man bogged down in domesticity, married to a woman at the so-called 'change of life' and no longer interested in the sexual aspect of their marriage.

So what did any woman expect, at her menopause: that her husband would live like a monk? He, for one, had no intention of doing so. Nevertheless, his deep-seated guilt complex nagged at him like toothache, at the root of which lay the fear of divorce: the legal jiggery-pokery involved if Audrey found out about Stella; his loss of face; more importantly, the loss of his money, the division of his property, and the draining away of his cannily accumulated wealth in alimony, lawyer's fees, and so on. His blood ran cold at the thought.

Yet here he was, holding a desirable young woman in his arms, risking his entire future for the scent and softness of her, scarcely able to restrain his desire for her until nightfall, when, replete with food and wine, he would make passionate love to her in the four-poster bed occupying the central space of the room.

He had reckoned without Stella's reaction to his initial embrace, the abruptness of her question, 'Well, are we going down to dinner or not?'

She added huffily, 'Some fine place you've brought me to, I must say! The whole damn hotel is under repair, if you ask me.'

Catching her derisory remark on the stairs leading down to the reception area, a man stepped forward to apologise for any inconvenience the repair work to the hotel may have caused them.

'In which case,' Brian said pompously, 'someone should

have warned me, when I made the booking, that the hotel was in no fit state to accommodate visitors. My wife and I are not accustomed to second-rate service, believe me!'

Grant Edwards, the hotel owner, believed him implicitly. He could read the man like a book. The world was full of his kind, men who liked giving waiters a hard time, believing that the trappings of wealth made up for a lack of good manners. He said quietly, 'Of course, sir. Now, if you and madam would care to follow me, I'll show you to the dining room. Hopefully the service will be entirely to your satisfaction.'

'It better had be,' Brian said gruffly, 'or I shall want a word with the owner.'

Having bought the hotel for a song due to its sorry state of dilapidation and the near bankruptcy of its former owner, Grant Edwards had set about updating the property.

An astute businessman, he had ascertained beforehand that no legal problems would arise from remodelling the land involved in the sale: creating a landscaped garden, for instance, comprising rockeries, floodlit water features, a miniature waterfall and a swimming pool.

Common sense warned him that the access road to the hotel might cause problems in its present state of disrepair, and that it might take some time and a great deal of money to have its 'bumps' ironed out. But he was comparatively young and enthusiastic, and he had long dreamed of one day owning a place of his own, a really great hotel catering to the needs and comfort of its guests.

Most of the bedrooms, the bar and the dining room had already been upgraded. The worrying factor, so far, was that bookings remained thin on the ground, due, he imagined, to the poor reputation of its former owner, plus its appalling appellation 'The Inn Thing', unfortunately still extant in the local phone directory.

This weekend, for example, the hotel was empty apart

from Felpersham and his so-called 'wife'. Edwards had been long enough in the hotel business to suss out an illicit relationship when he saw one: in this case, an overbearing bully of a man escorting a girl half his age. A very pretty girl, come to think of it, apart from her down-turned mouth and lacklustre eyes, her general air of dissatisfaction with herself, her lover, and the world in general. An intelligent, well-bred girl, he imagined, worthy of someone far better than the lout she was lumbered with, presumably because of his well-filled wallet.

The poor kid, he thought compassionately as he ushered the pair of them to their table and handed them the menus.

Sitting down by courtesy of Edwards, who had held back a chair for her, Stella noticed that every table in the room held its full complement of starched napery, polished silverware, pink-shaded lamps and gleaming wine glasses.

'Thank you,' she murmured gratefully, glancing up at the man she imagined to be the head waiter. 'I am sorry I said what I did when I came downstairs.'

Meanwhile, greedily eyeing the menu, Brian butted in, 'I'll have smoked salmon for starters, followed by a thick juicy sirloin steak and chips. Have you got that?'

'Certainly, sir,' Edwards acknowledged urbanely, 'and how would you like it cooked? *Bien* or *pas-de-bien cuit*?'

Brian's mouth sagged open. 'What the hell are you on about?' he demanded angrily. 'I want it bloody well cooked.' Unaware of the solecism, he added, 'So tell your chef to get a move on! What's up with you, man? Are you hard of hearing? Why are you standing there like a tailor's dummy?'

Grant said urbanely, 'Because your order is incomplete. Madam has not yet decided upon her choice of food.'

Stella said wearily, 'I'm not very hungry. I'll just have a green salad with a vinaigrette dressing, a glass of iced mineral water, and an orange.'

'*Mineral water?*' Brian burst forth indignantly. 'Bloody

lettuce and an orange? You'll have the same as me, and like it! If you think I'm paying through the nose for a dinner for two with you nibbling a lettuce leaf and sucking an orange, you have another think coming, my girl! Which reminds me, where's the bloody wine waiter?'

Grant Edwards broke in respectfully, 'Excuse me, sir, but in case you hadn't noticed, there's a bottle of champagne in an ice bucket near your chair, by courtesy of the management. Would you prefer to pour it yourself, or shall I do it for you?'

Felphersham said rudely, dismissively, 'No, just you bugger off to the kitchen and tell the chef that I shall want lots of vegetables with the steak and chips – for my wife and myself, after our smoked salmon starters.'

Glancing across the table at her obese lover, Stella shuddered inwardly at the thought of the night ahead of her, sleeping with him, being touched by him.

'There's something about that Grant Edwards character that gets up my nose,' Brian said, towelling his hair as he emerged from the bathroom. 'Well, people won't pay good money for that kind of treatment. Word gets around. In his case, I'll make sure that it does.'

'Tell your friends you spent the night here, you mean?' Stella said disdainfully. 'Why not write a letter of complaint to the local paper? Perhaps they'll take it up, make a news item of it, send a reporter, take photographs.'

'All right, all right, no need for sarcasm. I'm beginning to wish we'd never set foot in the damn place.' Throwing aside the towel, he vented his anger on her. 'It's all your fault, bitching all the way here, acting like a spoilt kid, harping on about the Chase, upsetting me, making me feel guilty—'

'Oh, that's right, blame me,' she broke in fiercely. 'That Grant character, as you call him, had the decency to give us a bottle of champagne. Perhaps you got up his nose, too, when you didn't even bother to thank him!'

'Look, Stell, I didn't come here for a row,' Brian said. 'Is that bed comfortable, by the way?' He laughed unpleasantly. 'Must say you look very fetching propped up against the pillows.'

'The bed's fine.'

'Pleased to hear it.' Stretching out beside her, laying a bare arm about her and drawing her closer, he murmured, 'Come on, love, relax, let's not waste time arguing. We got off to a bad start. So what? I'm crazy about you. You know that, don't you?'

'I guess so. It's just that I . . . Oh, never mind, it doesn't matter.'

'Go on! Spit it out!'

'If only we had a little place of our own where we could meet more often, get to know each other better, where we could both relax properly, not having to worry about being seen together, being on edge all the time.'

'Oh, not *that* again. If I've told you once, I've told you a dozen times that it just wouldn't work! I'm well known in South Bay, in case you've forgotten. How long before tongues start wagging? No, Stella, it's out of the question, so just forget it. The trouble with you is, you're never satisfied. Always wanting more, trying to pin me down. Well, I can't be pinned down, and you know why. I'm a married man, for God's sake! But you've known that all along, so what's wrong with things the way they are?'

A great deal was wrong, in Stella's opinion. Apart from sex, presents and occasional nights in hotel rooms, she stood in desperate need of recognition as something more important than the other woman in his life.

But things were unlikely to change in the foreseeable future, so she had best make the most of what she had.

Next morning at breakfast, a waitress came to take their order. Brian wanted a full English: bacon, eggs, sausages, tomatoes and mushrooms, with plenty of hot buttered toast, tea and marmalade. Stella settled for orange juice, toast and coffee.

'At least the fellow' – he meant Grant Edwards – 'has a serving wench,' Brian remarked in a loud voice. 'I'd begun to think he was running the show on his own. Wouldn't surprise me if he were, with all going out and nowt coming in. I suppose you realise he's doing the cooking himself?' He laughed. 'Wouldn't mind betting he'll be chamber-maiding when we're out of the way. Which reminds me, I want to be back in South Bay by eleven thirty at the latest, so we'd best get a move on.'

Stella frowned. 'But this is Saturday. You don't usually work on Saturdays.'

'Oh, for God's sake, do I have to spell it out for you?' he muttered impatiently.

'No,' she said wearily, 'I suppose not.' She knew that he would have concocted a carefully fabricated cock-and-bull story to explain last night's absence from home, assuring his wife that he'd be back from wherever he was supposed to have been to before lunch. Meanwhile, she would be left alone the rest of today and all day tomorrow – doing what, exactly?

Brian had settled the bill and gone outdoors to check his tyre pressure, awaiting Stella's arrival with her overnight case. Why was it that women always found some last-minute excuse to cause a delay of departure? he wondered, glancing impatiently at his watch. He'd had the forethought to bring his luggage down with him before breakfast. Why couldn't she have done the same?

Coming downstairs, Stella came face to face with Grant Edwards on the half-landing. He said, 'I hope that you and your husband have enjoyed your stay here, despite certain – disadvantages.'

Throwing caution to the wind, Stella said dully, 'He isn't my husband. But you guessed that all along, didn't you? My name's Johnson, not Felpersham. Now, if you'll excuse me, he's in a hurry to get back to his wife.'

Brushing past him, she hurried on down the stairs until, turning halfway to look back at him, she said, 'Thank you for the champagne, by the way.'

Driving back to South Bay, she wondered what the hell had come over her to confide to Grant Edwards that she and Brian were not married.

Was it because she had wished to dissociate herself in some way from Brian's insensitivity and bad manners?

He had not uttered a word to her since they left the hotel, giving her the silent treatment to underline his displeasure at being kept waiting, driving recklessly, grim-faced, to make up for lost time, increasing the tension which soured their relationship nowadays.

No use pretending otherwise. Stella knew deep down that their affair, so sweetly begun, had run its course; that familiarity, in Brian's case, had bred contempt. Hence, perhaps, that warning light at the back of her mind she'd been aware of at dinner last night, watching him wolf his food and guzzling champagne. She had read in Grant Edwards' eyes his utter contempt for the man, as well as veiled pity for herself, supposedly Brian's wife.

The last thing on earth Stella wanted was pity. She'd had enough of that to last her a lifetime when her parents had died in a boating accident off the Scilly Isles, after which she had been handed on to relatives, none of whom had really wanted the responsibility of bringing up a nine-year-old orphan. The wonder was that she had not been on that boat when it capsized. She often wished that she had been.

'For God's sake slow down,' she cried hysterically as Brian swerved recklessly to avoid an oncoming car on the crown of a hill, 'before we end up in hospital.'

'Oh, telling me how to drive now, are you?' he snapped back at her, deeply shaken by the near collision but unwilling to admit to his mistake in overtaking a vehicle in front, too close to the summit of a hill, in his hurry to get home in time for lunch.

On the outskirts of South Bay he said, matter-of-factly, 'I'll drop you off at the Villa Marina. Ring you this evening.'

Drop her off? Dump her, more accurately, Stella thought bitterly, akin to a bag of washing dumped at a launderette. And she was right. Drawing up the Merc at the kerb fronting the villa, Brian fairly bundled her out of the car, engaged first gear, and drove away without so much as a farewell kiss or a backward glance in her direction.

Later that day, having bathed, washed her hair, and changed her bed linen, Stella went into town to do her shopping, more as a means of filling in time than filling her supermarket basket with food, none of which she actually needed or wanted, apart from fruit, milk and eggs.

Returning to the Villa Marina, she stripped off her outdoor clothes and underwear, shrugged into a terry-towelling bathrobe, and lay down on her bed to relive memories of The Inn Thing. She could see clearly, in her mind's eye, that rickety veranda swathed with riotous masses of unpruned vegetation; could remember Brian's belligerent attitude towards her when she had announced her intention to spend the night in the car rather than enter a hotel reminiscent of a gothic horror movie.

And yet, surprisingly, she'd had no fault to find with its interior: the en suite bedroom, the dining room with its pristine napery, lamplit tables and gleaming silverware and, above all, the deferential treatment they'd received from their host, Grant Edwards. A courteous man, in her opinion, middle-aged, with a 'lived-in' kind of face, a warm smile, and something more besides, less easily defined. Nothing whatever to do with his personal appearance, more to do with his persona, a kind of integrity, and self-containment, allied to a quirky sense of humour, an educated way of speaking, and his skill as a chef. Even Brian, in his most nit-picking mood, had not been able to fault his steak *bien cuit*, crisply fried chips, battered onion rings, asparagus and glazed carrots.

Brian! Her reluctant, guilt-ridden lover! Staring up at the ceiling as twilight shadows invaded the room and lights sprang up along the seafront beyond the window, Stella awaited his promised phone call in a state of acute nervous tension. What should she say to him? she wondered. 'Hello, darling?', pretending that nothing had changed between them? Selling her soul for diamonds, perfume, flowers, designer clothes, money?

Or should she tell him the truth: that she was sick and tired of all the lies and subterfuge, the very sight of his fat-larded body, his florid face and receding hairline, his temperamental outbursts and lack of good manners and the cavalier treatment of her which had brought her to her present state of mind.

When the phone began ringing at around nine o'clock, Stella, curled up on her bed in her terry-towelling robe, made no move to answer the call. She simply let the phone go on ringing until it stopped.

Half an hour later it rang again, then again and again.

Lying on her side, looking at the lights beyond her window, hearing the faint wash of the sea on the shore and listening to the clamour of the phone on her bedside table, Stella knew that the best, the most dignified way of ending a burnt-out affair was to say nothing. Nothing at all!

Eight

Thea awoke to the realisation that something wonderful had happened. Her chance meeting with Ross Drummond had bordered on the miraculous.

To add to her soaring feeling of happiness, she had gained enormous pleasure from her theatre visit last night. The warm, intimate atmosphere generated by its red plush seats, gleaming brass handrails and crimson velvet curtains had evoked reminiscences of the older London theatres she had visited with Fliss, allied to an awareness that the theatre – that magical world of make-believe closely associated with art and music – had long ago become an integral part of her life.

Thank heaven there had been nothing make-believe about her meeting with the pianist, nor had she been mistaken in her feelings towards him, which she had kept well under control. Perceptively, she had realised that here was a man in need not of starry-eyed adulation but of conversation – a means of self-expression far removed from his work playing sad music for lonely people.

Or was she being fanciful? The coterie of young women perched on bar stools, watching him intently as he played, saw themselves as neither sad nor lonely, she imagined. Smitten by his mature good looks and his air of detachment, they were more than likely planning to waylay him at the rear entrance of the Mirimar, when the bar closed, to ask for his autograph, each doing their best to attract his attention.

Regarding him as a kind of 'dream lover', those sexually

aware, giggling girls had probably laid bets, beforehand, on which of them he would choose to sleep with later that night.

Curiously, Thea had not considered the possibility of a physical relationship with the pianist. Her brief, abortive affair with Carlo Gambetti had taught her that sexual gratification was no guarantee of happiness. There had to be something far deeper than mere physical attraction to cement a lasting relationship, based on understanding, respect and – love.

In any case, she thought, on her way to work, how could she be sure that the pianist would want an affair? For all she knew, he might be married with children. Possibly his sadness stemmed from being parted from them during the summer season in South Bay. All Thea knew for certain was that she would never regret having met him, that she would count the days, the hours, the minutes, till their next meeting.

When Philip arrived at the shop at around ten thirty, ostensibly to bring glass shelves for the window display and a few swatches of brightly coloured silk, really to find out how she was coping, Thea said excitedly, 'Guess what? I've sold three sun-tops, two pairs of tights, a bracelet and a baby's sun bonnet!'

'You have? Well done! Any problems?'

'Not a one! They were day trippers from Leeds, dying to spend money. What's more, they'll be back later. One of the women fancied herself in a Bellino over-blouse, only she couldn't decide on the colour.' Thea grinned mischievously. 'She doesn't know it yet, but she's going to buy both the blue and the orange.'

Philip thought how well and happy the girl looked, bright-eyed and brimming with enthusiasm.

'Did you enjoy your day off?' he asked, buoyed up by her warm, outgoing personality, wishing he could whip up similar enthusiasm for a roast beef luncheon followed by an afternoon on the golf course.

'Oh yes, I had a wonderful time. I went to the art gallery in the afternoon, and to the theatre at night to see *Private Lives*.' She sighed happily. 'I'd never realised before what a charming place South Bay is. I was far too young to care about anything except the sea and the sand, donkey riding and building sandcastles, when I came here with my parents all those years ago.'

She added reflectively, 'One day, when I'm a famous designer, perhaps I'll buy myself a little pied-à-terre in South Bay, away from the London rat race. I'd really like that.' She smiled wistfully, 'Well, I can dream, can't I?'

'A designer?' Philip queried gently, 'Does that mean you've made up your mind about your career?'

'Oh yes, I think so. The theatre's in my blood. Not as an actress, far from it. I couldn't learn lines to save my life. It's what goes on backstage that fascinates me. Props, lighting, and so on; creating an authentic on-stage atmosphere complimentary to the actors.'

She continued, 'Fliss once took me to see *Gaslight* at the Adelphi. I'll never forget that set, a perfect facsimile of a Victorian drawing room, correct in every detail from the carpets to the curtains, the gilt-framed paintings on the walls, the green chenille tablecloth, silver epergne, cases of stuffed birds and domes of artificial flowers. When the curtain rose, the audience applauded spontaneously the skill of the designer responsible for the setting.'

She added, 'I know I have a long way to go, a great deal to learn, that I shall most probably end up neither rich nor famous. On the other hand, I'll have the satisfaction of taking a step in the right direction in choosing design, not art, as a career.'

'Then I wish you all the luck in the world, which you richly deserve,' Philip said wholeheartedly. He paused. 'I've brought you these shelves and swatches for your window display but, since you appear to have nothing better to do for the time being, how about some coffee? Will you make it, or shall I?'

Returning to the Villa Marina after locking up the shop, tired but happy, Thea thought that this had been a marvellous day. Not only had she persuaded the lady from Leeds to purchase both Bellino over-blouses, she had also sold numerous items of jewellery, sun-tops, tights and stockings, five Italian silk scarves, six cotton squares and a bottle of sun-tan lotion, amounting to the sum of one hundred and fifty pounds. She had left the cash in the security box under the counter for Philip to pick up later, hoping that he would be pleased with her first day's takings.

On the landing, she came across Bunty, looking distraught, saying she knew that Stella was in her room, but no way could she get her to open the door. 'Something must have gone wrong between her and that pudd'n-headed Romeo of hers,' Bunty said fiercely. 'The phone kept on ringing last night, three or four times, then shut off abruptly the way it does when there's no answer, but I know for a fact she was in 'cos I knocked, and she told me to go away.'

'Perhaps she's ill,' Thea suggested, uncertain how to help. 'Should we ask Mr Cumberland to have a word with her?'

'Darned if I know,' Bunty demurred. 'If she's having one of her sulks, like as not she'd tell him to go to hell; then the cat really would be among the pigeons.'

'I know, but we can't just leave her alone. What if she is unwell, in need of a doctor?'

They were on the landing outside Stella's room door, debating on the best course of action, when the door opened abruptly to reveal the girl in question standing there, hair awry, eyes blazing, wearing her bathrobe and no make-up, her face blotched and swollen with the tears she had shed.

'If you must discuss my private affairs,' she cried hoarsely, 'at least have the decency to do so somewhere else. To satisfy your bloody curiosity, I am *not* ill, and I don't need a doctor. All I want is to be left alone. Now go away, both of you!'

Thea said, 'I'm sorry. We were worried about you, that's all.'

'Oh, *really*?' Stella said bitterly. 'How very noble of you. The truth is, you couldn't care less about me. I'm just some kind of joke to you, an object of ridicule. Well, go on, admit it! Have a good laugh at my expense.'

'No one's laughing at you,' Thea said gently. 'And you're wrong about no one caring. Why else would we have thought of sending for a doctor?'

Stella's face crumpled suddenly, and her tears welled up once more. Thea held out her hands appealingly. 'Please, can we get you anything? A cup of tea? A sandwich?'

'No. I don't want tea, and I don't need patronising. I just want to be left alone!' Stepping back into the room, she slammed the door behind her.

'Well, that's us put in our places,' Bunty commented drily. She paused to let the message sink in, then suggested, 'Don't know about you, but I could do with a bit of light relief. What say we have a drink at the Mirimar?'

'Thanks, Bunty, but I'd rather not, if you don't mind. I've just come home from work, and I'd planned an early night.' A lame excuse, but the best Thea could think of at the moment.

Bunty said, 'Oh yes, I'd forgotten you work on Sundays. Well, another time, perhaps?' she added cheerfully. 'I'll have a word in June's shell-like. A night out on the town will do her the world of good – listening to piano music for a change, instead of that blessed "Nessun Dorma" she's so fond of.'

Later, alone in her room, Thea heard the closing of doors and footsteps on the landing as Bunty and June went out together for their night on the town.

Earlier, she had bathed, washed her hair, cooked a mushroom omelette, switched on her radio to listen to a concert of classical music broadcast live from the Wigmore Hall, and opened wide the windows to let in the freshness of a warm summer breeze drifting in from the sea and the whisper of the tide running in on the shore.

Relaxed and happy, wearing a dressing gown and slippers, a cup of coffee on the table beside her, she relived memories of her meeting with Ross Drummond. From the chair she had turned round to face the bay window she could see the daylight fade to the dusk of evening, the blossoming of street lamps along the promenade and the slim sickle of a new moon and a scattering of stars in a turquoise-coloured sky. Listening dreamily to a Chopin nocturne, the last thing she expected was a repeated knocking on her door.

Switching off the radio, she swiftly crossed the room and opened the door. 'Oh, it's you, Stella! Come in. I'm pleased to see you.'

'I can't think why,' Stella said ruefully, 'after all the rotten things I said to you and Bunty. Telling you to go away, to leave me alone, when what I really needed was someone to talk to.' She added, 'It's all my fault; I'm entirely to blame for ending a relationship with – someone who meant a great deal to me. Now I can't help wondering if I did the right thing.'

'That rather depends why you felt it necessary to end the affair in the first place,' Thea said quietly, leading Stella to a chair near the window. 'Sit down, and take your time. You must feel worn out. Could you do with a cup of tea or coffee?'

'Coffee, please. Milk, no sugar.'

'I'll put the kettle on.'

Obviously the girl needed to talk, but Thea wanted to give her time to relax, to gather her thoughts before blurting out details of her broken love affair, which she might later regret revealing to a comparative stranger.

The coffee made, she carried it to the table between the chairs. Stella said, gazing up at the moon and stars, 'It's so peaceful here, so quiet. This feels like a real home. That first night you came here to live, the night of your party, I couldn't help thinking how lovely the room looked, with the lighted lamps and the candles. Truth to tell, I felt jealous of the atmosphere you'd managed to create within the space of a few hours.

'I've been here almost two years now, but my room has no atmosphere at all. But then, I've never had a real place to call home. After my parents died, I lived in other people's houses, being passed from pillar to post like a parcel. An unwanted parcel. That's why, when I was old enough, I decided to make my own way in the world, to stand on my own feet. Huh.' She laughed mirthlessly. 'Now look at me! A fine mess I've made of things.

'I really thought, when I met Brian, that my luck had changed for the better. Oh, I knew he was married, much older than me, but that made no difference. For the first time I had met a man who really wanted me. Everything was going fine, until' – she drew in a deep breath – 'until it dawned on me that I – I didn't really want *him* any more.'

Her lips trembled. 'That's why I didn't answer his phone calls. I just lay there listening to the phone ringing and ringing, willing myself not to answer. It's the hardest thing I've ever done in my life. A bit like drowning, ignoring a lifeline; wondering if I'd live to regret not answering his calls.' Tears welled up again. 'Now I have nothing left to look forward to. No good times.'

'No bad times either,' Thea reminded her, 'if you meant what you said about your change of heart. There must have been a good reason why. Look, Stella, I'm in no position to give advice. I've just come out of a relationship myself. I was happy at the time, or thought I was, but I knew all along that something was missing.

'The differences between my boyfriend and I became

more apparent when we shacked up together. My mother told me that you don't really know a man until you live with him. How right she was.'

'Was he – married?' Stella asked. She was puzzled by Thea's laugh.

'Only to his faith. He was a Catholic. An Italian, a fellow student of mine at the Lambeth College of Art, tall, good-looking, very attractive. You get the picture? I fell head over heels in love with him, he with me. Except that it wasn't love, but lust. The cracks appeared when we moved in together, when nothing I did seemed right for him.'

'Go on,' Stella said, drawing a parallel with her own situation, wanting to know more about Thea's abortive love affair.

Thea continued, 'I couldn't cook spaghetti bolognese properly for starters, or starch and iron his shirts. I'd never starched and ironed a man's shirt in my life before, to his disgust. To *my* disgust, he would spend hours locked in the bathroom when I was dying to spend a penny. And when I finally got into the bathroom, he'd used up all the hot water! It was then that I begun to realise that the only person Carlo really loved was himself, not me.'

'Then what happened?'

'He dumped me!' Thea admitted ruefully. 'Left a note on the kitchen table saying he'd decided to go back to Italy.'

'How did you feel about that?' Stella asked intently.

'Terribly hurt and confused. Shattered, to put it mildly,' Thea confessed. 'The way you are feeling right now, I imagine – until that wise mother of mine advised me to stop moping and make a new life for myself. I'm here in South Bay to do just that.'

'Then you really think it's possible to forget about the past and make a new beginning?' Stella asked wistfully.

'Oh yes,' Thea said, looking up at the night sky beyond the window, thinking that everything seemed possible on a night like this. She said softly, 'Remember, Stella, that you are worth far more than a second-hand love affair. You're really attractive – why not take it from there? Forget about the past, just feast your eyes on the future.'

Rising to her feet, Stella said gratefully, 'Thanks, Thea. Thanks for the coffee, for being my friend. Thanks for – *everything*.' Turning at the door, she added, 'Goodnight, and – God bless.'

At the Mirimar, June Blake was perched on a bar stool, intently listening to the music of the man seated at the spotlit piano. Deeply conscious of her own lacklustre appearance compared with other girls her own age, she wished heartily that she had not accepted Bunty's invitation of a 'night on the town'. The atmosphere was totally inimical to a girl without a pair of high-heeled shoes, black stockings, a thigh-length skirt, or a low-cut blouse to her name.

'Well, whose fault is that?' Bunty reprimanded her bossily, during the interval. 'If I've told you once, I've told you a dozen times to stop wearing those catalogue outfits of yours, to get yourself a decent haircut; start wearing make-up, and splash out on a wardrobe of up-to-date gear for once. Still, if you prefer going through life looking like a frump, that's your business, not mine!'

June was deeply wounded. 'Do I really look a frump?' she asked, close to tears.

'No, of course not. I'm sorry. I shouldn't have said that. You're far prettier than any of the girls here. You could be a real stunner if you tried a bit harder.'

'I wouldn't want to look – common,' June demurred, looking worried.

'With your face? Impossible!' Bunty laughed.

'What's wrong with my face?'

'Not a damn thing. It's just that you don't take care of your skin properly. Washing it with soap and water twice daily is the road to ruin. What you need, my girl, is a good cleansing and toning routine, lots of moisturiser, a tinted foundation cream, a soupçon of lipstick, a gamine haircut to accentuate your bone structure, and some new duds to show off that catwalk figure of yours. You know it makes sense, so what do you say?'

'How much will it cost?' June asked nervously.

'You mean you'll put yourself in my hands?' Bunty said gleefully. 'Right then, you come to the store tomorrow in your lunch hour, and I'll have a little parcel ready and waiting for you. Not to worry about the cost, I'll give you the benefit of my ten per cent discount.'

She added mischievously, 'First things first. I'll sort out your wardrobe later. You have a cheque book, I take it?'

'Yes, but . . .'

'But *what?*'

'I'm saving up for a new stereo,' June reminded her.

'Huh,' Bunty chuckled. 'When I've finished with you, you won't even have time to listen to it!'

Nine

When Violet Hastings had read the letter from her son, she stuffed it, with trembling fingers, into her overall pocket. The thing she'd been dreading had happened at last. Peter had announced his intention of coming to South Bay within the next month to discuss plans for his mother's future.

Vi knew she should have shown the letter to Abby right away. She would have to read it sooner or later, had every right to do so. After all, discussion of her own future would involve her sister's also if Peter insisted on the sale of the Laurels.

Secreting the letter for the time being was scarcely the solution to the problem, Vi realised, but how could she possibly break the news to Abby that the years they had been together would, if she moved away from South Bay, soon be over?

On the other hand, how much longer could they continue living in poverty, growing older day by day, clinging together like shipwrecked mariners on a waterlogged raft? But if she acceded to her son's plans for her future, how could she contemplate Abby's, robbed of her independence, the home she loved?

That evening, Thea unlocked the door of the garden shed in search of tools to aid her attack on the rear garden. Turning around she saw Violet standing in the doorway. Realising that all was not well with her, she asked anxiously, 'What's wrong, Miss Violet?' She placed a protective arm about the old woman's shoulders, feeling the shaking of her body, noticing the seepage of tears from her blue eyes. 'Please tell me. I'll help you in any way possible.'

'I know, my dear, and I'm more than grateful to you for all you've done so far,' Vi said tearfully, deriving comfort from Thea's compassion, 'though it could be a wasted effort if my son has his way.'

'Your son?'

'You sound surprised.' Vi wiped her eyes with a cotton hanky. 'But I *was* married. Not very successfully I'm afraid. Oh dear. It's a long story, and I don't want to burden you with my troubles.'

'A trouble shared is a trouble halved,' Thea reminded her gently.

'Yes, I know' – Vi shook her head – 'but talking about it won't help much. You see, there's nothing to be done about it now. It's too late.'

Realising the limitations of a garden shed as a confessional, Thea suggested a walk round the garden, which appeared to upset Violet even more. 'I never thought we'd come to this,' she said despairingly. 'What dear Father would say if he were alive now, I can't bear to think.

'He loved this garden, and it was very pretty in those days, with neatly trimmed lawns and herbaceous borders. He called it his haven of refuge after busy days in the surgery, visiting patients and attending the hospital two evenings a week. Such a caring man, and to think I let him down the way I did. I'll never forgive myself for that.

'I married against his wishes,' she tearfully confessed. 'He warned me against marrying a man I knew little about – of "low breeding and intelligence" – his very words. I wouldn't listen. I loved Morris Hastings, and wouldn't hear a word against him. For the first time in my life I defied my father. Of course I was very young and headstrong at the time. I said terrible things, called Father a snob; accused him of not wanting me to be happy.'

'How did you meet – Morris?' Thea spoke quietly, not wanting to pry, simply to understand the cause of Violet's unhappiness.

Violet explained: 'A seasonal job. His home was in London. That made matters worse somehow. I couldn't bear the thought of losing him when the season was over. Oh, it all started quite innocently. He asked me to meet him on his afternoons off. Father didn't know about it at first. When he found out, he tried to put a stop to our friendship. And that's all it was to begin with.

'Morris was the first boyfriend I'd ever had. The first man to notice me, to seek my company, to tell me I was – pretty. And I *was* pretty then, believe it or not.'

Thea *did* believe her. Violet Hastings, despite her age, still retained traces of her youthful beauty in the softness of her skin and those blue eyes of hers. Drawing a picture in her mind's eye, Thea imagined an innocent young girl, at the height of her youth and beauty, beguiled by the flattery of a young man with whom she had fallen deeply in love, he presumably feeling the same way about her. Thea's heart went out to the old lady, robbed by time of her youth and prettiness.

The rough, uncut grass beneath their feet caused Violet to stumble now and then, and she would have fallen had it not been for Thea's sustaining hand beneath her elbow. Possibly walking in the garden had not been a good idea after all? She said, 'Perhaps you should go indoors now, Miss Violet? Your sister will be wondering what's become of you.'

'Yes, I dare say she will,' Violet said bleakly. 'The truth is, I scarcely know how to face her. Abby's no fool. She will guess that something is wrong, and she won't rest until she finds out about the letter.'

'What letter?' Thea asked intently, sensing trouble.

'The one I received from my son this morning. He'll be here soon to discuss the sale of the Laurels. So you see, my dear, when that happens, there'll be no need for you to bother about the garden. When the house is sold, likely as not the new owners will turn it into a car park.'

Talking to Thea had unleashed a host of memories for Violet, some happy, others too painful to dwell on. But life was made up of memories, each one adding to the sum total of experience, and the mistakes she had made along the way were beyond redemption. Never would she forget those harsh words she had spoken to her father at the height of their quarrel, nor the blow she had dealt him in leaving home to marry the man she loved, and going to London with him as his wife.

The marriage had taken place in South Bay Register Office early one September morning, a secret, hastily planned hole-and-corner affair, with strangers called in to witness the ceremony. Morris had tried to persuade her to get married in London, when at least his family would be present to celebrate the occasion. Stubbornly, Violet had turned down that suggestion. Asked why, she said, 'It would seem wrong to go away with you as a single woman.'

Tossing and turning in bed, unable to sleep, she recalled that guilt-ridden wedding day, and the long journey that followed. Truth to tell, she had not felt properly married, wearing an everyday coat and hat, and carrying a prayer book instead of flowers. The ceremony had been over in no time at all. Even the gleaming gold wedding ring Morris had placed on her finger seemed strange to her, and so had Morris, in his best suit of clothes, sitting beside her in the railway carriage.

London had seemed terrifying, bewildering to a girl who had seldom been away from home before, especially the Underground journey from King's Cross to Edgware. Despite Morris's assurance that his family would make her welcome, she had dreaded meeting her in-laws, spending her wedding night beneath their roof when she desperately needed to be alone with him. If only he had booked a room at the station hotel, had given her time to get used to the idea of being married, before taking her to meet his family.

Money had been a consideration, of course. She had none of her own apart from a few pounds in a Post Office savings account, and Morris had saved next to nothing from his wages and gratuities. Moreover, he had no job in prospect, although he appeared confident of finding something soon. Waiters were always in demand in the big London hotels, he'd told her, adding that as soon as he got fixed up, he'd rent a little flat somewhere. Meanwhile, they'd muck in with his folks for the time being.

The term 'mucking in' had conjured up a hovel in Violet's imagination. Thankfully her fear of living in a pigsty had proved groundless. Morris's home, one of a terrace of houses a stone's throw from the tube station, though small and cramped, had clean starched curtains and venetian blinds to the windows, and a sandstone edging to the front step.

Morris's mother, a plump middle-aged woman, wearing her best bib and tucker in honour of the occasion, had set the front room table with a starched white cloth, her best china, and a bewildering array of sandwiches, cakes, jellies and blancmanges.

'You shouldn't have gone to all this trouble, Ma,' Morris laughed, obviously as pleased as punch to be home again, when she had finished hugging him.

'Trouble? For my son on his wedding day! Don't talk so soft!' She turned her attention to Violet. 'And this must be your bride. Not that I'm best pleased with the pair of you, I must say, getting wed in such a hurry. Why all the rush?'

Reading Mrs Hastings's mind, Vi had blushed to the roots of her hair.

Morris's father had appeared on the scene at that moment, a heavily built man, ruddy-complexioned, wearing carpet slippers, braces, and a striped shirt with the front collar-stud showing. 'Hello, son,' he said, smiling broadly, clapping Morris's shoulder, 'so you're a married man now, are you?

About time too, if you ask me! And this is the lass you've married? Well, she's a bonny little thing and no mistake.'

In no way had Morris's parents been unkind or dismissive towards her, but Violet had felt ill at ease in their company. A natural enough reaction considering the strangeness of the situation, she thought: marrying a man she scarcely knew, ending up in a house she would have to share with her in-laws, sleeping in a room next to theirs.

How could she become closer to her husband, feel at ease with him in such unnatural circumstances? Inured to the spaciousness of the Laurels, she had felt trapped in that narrow house in Edgware with its poky, over-furnished rooms in which every available space, especially the back parlour, had been filled to overflowing with sideboards, whatnots, chairs and tables, gimcrack ornaments and family photographs.

On her wedding night, physically and emotionally exhausted, guilt-ridden, nervous and tearful, she had failed to respond to Morris's love-making, imagining his parents, in the room next door, hearing every movement.

In time to come, she would blame herself for the failure of a marriage based on nothing more than a summer-time romance. Soon would dawn the realisation that a brief wedding in a registrar's office, however clinical and unromantic, was as binding as a church ceremony, once the necessary legal documents had been signed. Then had come the daunting realisation that having made her bed, she must lie in it from henceforth.

In the early hours of the morning, in urgent need of the bathroom, Violet got up, albeit painfully, put on her dressing gown and slippers, and creaked along the landing, past Abby's bedroom. To her surprise, the door was ajar and Abby's bedside lamp was switched on.

On her return from the bathroom, Abby called out, 'Come in, Vi. I want to talk to you.'

'Yes, dear,' Vi said nervously, poking her head round the door. 'What is it?'

'Well, don't just stand there,' Abby said irritably, 'come in, sit down, and tell me what's going on. And don't pretend you don't know what I'm talking about.'

Vi's face crumpled. She said tearfully, 'I didn't want to worry you.' Feeling like a guilty schoolgirl summoned into the headmistress's office, she entered the room and perched on the end of her sister's bed. 'I meant to tell you yesterday, when the letter arrived, but I just *couldn't*. I'm sorry. Please forgive me.'

Abby, sitting upright in bed, propped up with pillows, wearing a flannelette nightgown which had seen better days – and nights – said calmly, 'A letter from your son, presumably, wanting to meddle in our affairs? Did he say when he's coming?'

'The week after next,' Violet admitted shakily.

'Alone? Or is he bringing that ghastly wife of his with him to bolster his ego?'

'Alone, I think. I'm not sure. He didn't mention Hester in his letter,' Vi confessed, miserably aware of her own shortcomings, her lack of courage in the face of adversity. She had suffered a mental and physical breakdown following the collapse of her marriage, provoked by her discovery of her husband's affair with another woman. She had been seven months pregnant at the time.

Abby said, 'No use raking over old embers. The past is done with. What matters now is the future. *Our* future.'

'I can't imagine a future without *you*, Abby,' Violet sobbed.

'Nor I without you.' Abby gathered her sister into her arms, holding her close, smoothing back her hair from her tear-stained face. 'Even so, there are certain facts to be considered. We both know the score. This house is worth a great deal of money so far as property developers are concerned, and half its sale value is yours by right. After all, Peter is your son, and I assume I'm right in thinking that he wants his share of your inheritance sooner, rather than later?'

Withdrawing from her sister's embrace, Violet murmured brokenly, 'A son I abandoned soon after he was born! What kind of a mother was I, to leave my son in the care of his grandparents in my absence?'

'You were very ill at the time,' Abby reminded her, 'far too poorly to look after yourself, let alone a baby. All credit due to Morris's parents for sending you back to South Bay to recover from your nervous breakdown. No doubt they felt it their duty after the way their son had mistreated you!'

She smiled grimly. 'Mind you, I tend to mistrust the human race as a whole. Selflessness is a rare commodity. In my view, no such thing exists in this day and age, apart from a few, a very few exceptions.

'In case you've forgotten, Father sent regular sums of money to the Hastings towards the upkeep of his grandson until his dying day, which they were more than happy to accept. Hence my belief that so-called human kindness has to do with financial gain, in the long run.'

Violet knew what her sister was driving at, and perhaps she was right in believing that Peter's forthcoming visit to South Bay was motivated by greed, not love or concern for his mother's well-being, his intention being to gain control of her half-share in the Laurels.

She said wistfully, 'You never cared much for Peter, did you? Even as a little boy, when he came to South Bay on holiday.'

'You are quite right, I didn't,' Abby admitted. 'I made no secret of the fact, so why bother to deny it? I thought him a sly, unattractive child. Ageing has brought about no appreciable improvement in his characteristics. So far as I'm concerned he has grown into a sly, unattractive man.'

Inured to her sister's uncompromising attitude towards

her son, Violet said, 'Even so, he has done quite well for himself, in rising to his present position.'

'As the under-manager of a tuppenny-ha'penny building society, you mean?' Abby spoke scornfully.

'Not just that, but other things too. He's happily married with three children and a comfortable home. Quite a large house, judging from the photographs he sent me two Christmases ago.'

'Huh! In which case, why not make room for you in that large house of his? Why condemn you to a future in expensive sheltered accommodation, reliant on the sale of the Laurels to pay for your upkeep? As for being happily married, I very much doubt it!'

Too tired and confused to continue the conversation, Violet returned to her own room, got into bed, lay flat on her back and stared up at the ceiling lit by blobs of light from the promenade below. Still unable to sleep despite her weariness of mind and body, she thought about her son's wife, Hester, whom she had met only once, seventeen or eighteen years ago. On their way to Scotland after their wedding for a short honeymoon, Peter and his bride had briefly broken their journey north for afternoon tea at the Laurels, at Violet's invitation. The least she could have done, since she had not felt well enough to attend the wedding.

Recalling that occasion, Violet remembered having taken an instant dislike to her daughter-in-law, a smartly dressed, self-confident young woman, dark-haired and brown-eyed, who had made all too obvious that she considered taking tea with Peter's erring mother a complete and utter waste of time. Nor, apparently, had she taken to Abby, a participant in that unfortunate tea party, who had told her succinctly that, if she wished to smoke, she'd best do so outdoors, in the back garden.

Dear, uncompromising Abby, Violet thought gratefully, who saw through people as easily as other folk saw through glass, and who had proved more than a match for Peter's high-handed bride.

Violet had long realised that she could not contemplate living beneath the same roof as Hester. As for her three grandchildren, Pippa, Damien and Jules, whom she had never even seen except in photographs, how could a woman of her age possibly relate to an up-and-coming generation of teenagers who, for all she knew, might well be into drugs, tongue piercing and tattooing? In which case, she'd be far better off in an old people's home.

In the dark watches of a restless, sleepless night, Violet reached the conclusion that her own – and Abby's – future depended entirely upon her imminent meeting with her son.

In the hinterland between wakefulness and sleep, she hazily remembered her first meeting with Morris Hastings, in a shelter overlooking the sea. She recalled their first kiss, the way she had felt at the touch of his lips on hers, as if her heart had taken flight to an undiscovered world of romance and love. Now she wondered how could she have deluded herself into thinking that her feelings for Morris could ever outweigh the love she felt for her father and Abby. Yet when she had returned home after Morris's betrayal and the birth of a baby she had not wanted, she had been welcomed with open arms, without a word of reproach. She had been nursed back to health as tenderly as a wayward child who had been hurt through no fault of its own.

Closing her eyes, she remembered her father's words. 'You are safe now, my child; safely home where you belong.' *Home . . .*

Ten

True to her promise, Bunty had made up a parcel of beauty products for June, saying she'd give her a run-down on the contents that evening, make certain she didn't go to bed wearing foundation cream instead of skin food.

'I'm not daft,' June said scornfully, handing over the thick end of thirty pounds which she could ill afford, at the same time thinking she must be barmy to have left herself skint for the rest of the week.

'Don't worry, it'll be worth it, you'll see,' Bunty assured her in her lilting Scottish accent. 'Och, ye'll not know yourself when you look in the mirror.'

'That's what I'm afraid of,' June muttered, wondering what she had let herself in for.

'Now, lie back and relax,' Bunty advised her. 'I've brought a bath towel to put round you, and a crepe bandage to keep your hair out of your eyes. Have you any cucumber, by the way?'

'In the fridge. But I'm not hungry; I've already eaten,' June demurred.

'I don't mean to *eat*; to put over your eyes while you've got the mud-pack on,' Bunty explained, scraping back June's hair and draping her with the towel.

'*Mud pack?*' June wailed. 'Why a mud pack?'

'To draw the impurities out of your skin.'

'*Impurities*? I didn't know I had any!'

'Everyone has impurities! For heaven's sake, girl, stop talking in italics! Far better, just stop talking and sit still. Let the organ grinder see the monkey!'

'*Monkey?*'

'A figure of speech!' Bunty burst out laughing.

June giggled nervously as Bunty began her administrations, though secretly she was a little worried about the impurities lurking beneath her smooth young skin, which, if allowed to fester, might well erupt in spots of volcanic dimensions – a veritable Vesuvius on her chin, for instance.

She was lying prone in an armchair, her face smothered in fuller's earth, her eyelids covered with cucumber slices, when someone knocked on the door.

Warning her not to move a muscle, Bunty answered the summons. Stella was on the landing, a shadow of her former self since the breakdown of her relationship with Brian Felpersham.

'Come on in,' Bunty said warmly. She had never been one to hold grudges. 'Welcome to the Villa Marina beauty salon. June's having her impurities removed at the moment, so why not make yourself useful? Put the kettle on for a cup of coffee.'

'Well, if you're sure I'm not intruding,' Stella said uncertainly.

'Of course not,' Bunty assured her. 'I was just about to remove the gunge from my client's mug, anyway.'

June sat up, and the cucumber slices went flying. 'Mug?' she said indignantly. 'If that's what you think of my face, I'm surprised you're wasting your time on it.' She heaved a sigh. 'Perhaps what I need is a facelift.'

Bunty said, 'Don't talk so daft. All you need is some new clothes to enhance your new personality.'

'What new personality?'

'The one you'll have when I've done with you. Now lie back and let me get rid of the mud.'

'About time,' June grumbled. 'I must be well purified by now.'

'All right, keep your hair on – for the time being, at any rate. You *have* made an appointment for a short back and sides, haven't you?'

'No, I haven't, if you must know. My hair will have to wait till next payday. I'm stony broke after shelling out for all that make-up you talked me into buying.'

Stella laughed, enjoying the badinage between Bunty and June, knowing it was all in fun. 'The kettle's boiled,' she said. 'Shall I make the coffee now?'

'Yes, please,' June said eagerly, 'I could do with a – mug.' She was delighted that Stella had decided to come. The poor girl had had a rough time of it recently. Nice to think that she had knocked on her door in search of company.

Waiting for the kettle to boil, Stella said, '*I* could cut your hair, if you like. I trained as a stylist before I switched to beauty therapy.'

'Really? Thanks Stella, I'd like that. I'd feel out of place in one of those posh salons in town.' June smiled blissfully, relieved at being spared the ordeal of some high-flown assistant snipping away at her locks, looking down on her, making her feel even more inferior than usual.

Walking slowly along the promenade, thoughts centred on the plight of the two old ladies at the Laurels, Thea realised how awful it must be for them, facing the loss of their home. Not that she knew the whole story; she had simply gleaned, from Miss Violet's distressed state of mind, that pressure of some kind was being brought to bear by her son, coming soon to discuss the sale of the property.

Thea understood, to some extent, the advisability of selling the Laurels, in view of its state of disrepair. It would ensure the sisters' future welfare in a much smaller house, a cottage perhaps, where they could spend the rest of their lives together in peace, tranquillity, and financial security. What was wrong with that?

Suddenly she *knew* what was wrong with it! Guessed the underlying reason for Miss Vi's distress. Once the Laurels was sold, the sisters would be forced to part company. Hence Violet's dread of Abigail's finding out about that letter from her son. What other explanation was possible? And if it were true, what, if anything at all, could a comparative stranger, an outsider such as herself, do about it? And why should she care about the fate of two old ladies who she scarcely knew?

Gazing out to sea, hands resting on the promenade railings as evening shadows fell and the first stars appeared in a turquoise-coloured sky, Thea recalled the words of John Donne, 'No man is an island', and knew that she was coming to care a great deal for Violet Hastings and her seemingly indomitable sister, Abigail Ashcroft.

On the landing near her room, Thea heard the sound of laughter, of girlish voices. There was no mistaking Bunty's Scottish accent or that rich, warm laugh of hers. She and June must be having a get-together, Thea decided, wishing she might join in the fun but not wanting to intrude uninvited. As she was about to unlock her door, however, Stella suddenly put in an appearance from the room next to hers.

'Oh, *there* you are,' she said brightly, 'we wondered where you'd got to. Bunty's giving June a facial, and I'm about to give her a haircut. Go in and make yourself a cup of coffee. The kettle's just boiled. I'm off to fetch my scissors. Shan't be a sec!'

'Sure you don't mind?' Thea demurred.

'Mind? Of course not!' Stella laughed. 'What price the Three Musketeers without d'Artagnan?'

This was a Stella Thea had never seen before, a far cry from the nervous wreck involved in a no-win liaison with a married man; robbed of her self-confidence until pride and common sense had prevailed and she had ended the affair.

Now, having put the past behind her, Stella was bound to meet, sooner or later, a decent man who really cared for her, Thea thought contentedly. A man who would give her the happiness she so richly deserved.

And so Thea's evening had ended on a high note, after all, despite her deep, underlying concern for the two lonely, embattled old ladies in the house next door.

Visiting the town's most prestigious jewellers, Philip Gregory had spent ages in choosing a ring for his wife which, hopefully, she would wear with pride on the occasion of their fortieth wedding anniversary.

A ruby ring was essential, he had told the manager, sotto voce, feeling rather like a criminal about to hold a sawn-off shotgun to the man's head. Nothing too ostentatious or flashy: his wife was not fond of gaudy jewellery in any case, he explained, so what he really wanted was something quite small and neat to suit her personality.

Finally, with the manager's help and advice, he had settled on a Victorian dress-ring, an engraved band studded with rubies.

Afterwards, the ring paid for and safely ensconced in his jacket pocket, he had walked into the reception area of the Mirimar to book a table for six for the following Saturday evening, making certain that the central adornment would consist of red rosebuds, and that there would be red, not white, linen napkins, if possible.

'But of course, sir,' the receptionist assured him. 'Any other special requests?' She smiled charmingly. 'Champagne, for instance? Possibly you have a personal preference?'

'No, not really,' Philip floundered, unwilling to admit he loathed and detested the damn stuff, would settle for a glass of lager any day of the week, 'just as long as it's – expensive!'

When everything had been arranged to his satisfaction, he

went to a florist in the town square and ordered a bouquet of red roses to be delivered to Ruth early on their anniversary morning, before she became too embroiled in domestic matters to even notice them. He wondered if he should take the day off in honour of the occasion. No, better not, he decided; Ruth would be far too busy making last-minute preparations for the arrival of their offspring and spouses to want him under her feet. He would only be getting in the way of bed-making, cooking and opening the presents the guests had brought with them which, he felt, would far outshine the ring he had bought her, the dinner party at the Mirimar, or the weekend in Paris come September.

If only he could spring a real surprise on her; give her something she would really like and appreciate, to inject a much-needed touch of romance into their mundane relationship. He could think of only one gift likely to outshine all the rest, to bring a sparkle to her eyes, a smile of satisfaction to her lips.

Gritting his teeth, entering a sports shop, he bought her a new set of golf clubs, complete with bag and a lightweight trolley. How romantic could one man get? he wondered, leaving the shop.

The following Friday morning, up to her eyes in customers queuing up to purchase scarves, jewellery, tank tops and Bellino blouses, stuffing goods into paper bags and taking money as fast as she could, Thea's heart sank to her shoes when Bess Hardacre entered the boutique, calling out to her not to worry, that all she wanted was a word when she, Thea, could spare a moment or two, during her lunch break. Meanwhile, she would wait outside on the promenade.

'I really thought you'd have been in touch with us before this,' Bess said chidingly when Thea emerged from the shop, having hung up a 'Closed for Lunch' sign on the door. 'You *did* promise, remember?'

'Yes, I know I did, Aunt Bess, and I'm really sorry. It's

just that I've been rather busy, what with one thing and another.'

Waving a be-ringed hand dismissively, as if shooing away a wasp, Bess continued, 'The thing is, it's Hal's birthday tomorrow, and I've planned a treat for him. Dinner at a nice little restaurant in town where Spanish cuisine is a *spécialité de la maison*, or so I've been told. So do say you'll join us. In fact, I refuse to take no for an answer. We'll pick you up at seven o'clock, have a few drinks in the bar first by way of a celebration. Wear something nice, dear, won't you? Sorry, must dash now. I've simply loads to do. Until tomorrow night, then. Bye, darling.'

Typical of Bess Hardacre, Thea thought crossly, taking everything for granted, crashing her way through life with the insensitivity of a bulldozer. On the other hand, she was fond of poor old Hal, and a birthday was a special occasion, even if it meant eating paella in some 'nice little restaurant' or other, the walls of which would probably be covered with blown-up pictures of bullrings and matadors.

Accepting the inevitable and missing her planned Saturday night visit to the theatre seemed a small price to pay compared to missing Hal's birthday celebration. In any case, she could afford to be generous-minded, with her afternoon meeting with Ross Drummond to look forward to . . . if he hadn't forgotten about it! But what if he *had*? What if she turned up at the art gallery and he wasn't there? The thought was unbearable.

'Hello, Thea,' he said quietly, smiling down at her.

'Hello, Ross.' She smiled up at him. 'I – I thought you might have forgotten.'

'No, I hadn't forgotten, but I thought that you might have. Tell me, did you enjoy the theatre?'

'Oh yes. It was brilliant. Not just the play but the theatre itself. I loved the red plush, the brasswork, and the boxes. One imagined evening gowns, elegant hairstyles, sparkling jewels, long gloves, women wafting lace fans, flirting outrageously with their escorts.'

He laughed. 'You have a wonderful imagination.'

'My mother would agree with you. She once accused me of acting like a character in a Victorian melodrama, and she was right. I was being a pain in the neck at the time.'

'I find that hard to believe. You appear to me extremely level-headed, not prone to temperamental outbursts.'

'I'm not as a rule,' she admitted, pulling a face. 'But I'd just been dumped by a boyfriend of mine, which I found hard to accept. Being dumped is not a pleasant experience.'

'No, it isn't,' he replied thoughtfully. 'But then any kind of rejection is hard to take, in my experience.'

Thea wondered what he meant by 'in his experience'. About to ask, she changed her mind abruptly, thinking it best not to pry into his past life at this early stage of their relationship – if indeed a relationship *did* exist between them? Common sense warned her to bide her time, not to take too much for granted. Above all, not to reveal her depth of feeling towards him, her overwhelming sense of joy and relief when, entering the art gallery, she had seen him standing near the reception desk, awaiting her arrival.

Now, standing side by side, renewing their acquaintance with John Atkinson Grimshaw's luminous painting, Ross said quietly, 'Tell me to mind my own business if you like, but are you any closer to a decision about your future?'

Thea smiled. 'Oh yes! Everything came into focus all of a sudden. Sitting in the theatre that night, I knew I wanted to be a designer: to learn everything possible about set designing, lighting, even costume design. The scope is unimaginable, tremendously exciting, involving not just the theatre but film design.'

She paused. 'There I go again, letting my imagination run away with me! What if I fail the course? What if I'm not talented enough to pass the exams with flying colours?'

Understanding her need of reassurance, Ross said firmly,

'Failure is scarcely an option in your case, I'd say. My best advice is to go full steam ahead, with success, not failure, in mind.'

Briefly, memory drew him back to a day, long gone, when his tutor at L'Ecole de Musique, in Paris, had advised him to give up hope of becoming a world-renowned concert pianist. 'You are an excellent pianist,' the old maestro had told him sadly, shaking his head, 'but not a *great* pianist, alas. You lack the drive and dedication to become a truly great artiste. Understandable, perhaps, in your circumstances.'

Ross had lived with the pain and humiliation of that rejection ever since. His failure to achieve either fame or success in his chosen profession was due to one insurmountable obstacle in his life, that one mistake which still coloured his existence with deep, underlying feelings of sadness, failure, and regret.

Now, having met Thea Bellamy, a lovely young girl with her future before her, he wished to imbue in her a spirit of independence, far removed from his own problems and downfalls in life.

Above all he had no wish to hurt her, to lumber her with the ghosts of his past, and so he must tread warily, bearing in mind that nothing could come of a brief, summertime liaison, destined to end when September came. The best he could hope for was a warm, continuing friendship with a girl whose fresh young beauty and charm had made him feel alive again, as he had done in his student days in Paris, a long time ago.

In any event, he had no reason to believe that Thea regarded him as more than a friend. How could she be attracted to a man so much older than herself, greying slightly at the temples? A private, self-centred man, guarding the secrets of his past, deeply aware of his status as a piano player, not a classical pianist. A world of difference lay between the two.

'Is anything the matter?' Thea asked concernedly, breaking into his reverie. 'You look tired. Would you rather be alone? Is that it? If so, I'll go away, get on with my shopping.'

'No, Thea, please don't go! It's just that I slept rather badly last night.'

'So did I, come to think of it,' Thea confessed. 'Perhaps what we both need is a breath of fresh air to blow away the cobwebs?'

Leaving the art gallery, turning their footsteps in the direction of the promenade, they stood for a while looking out to sea, noticing the slow passage of ships on the horizon, not speaking, yet deeply aware of the strong tide of emotion running between them.

Suddenly, breaking the silence, Thea said haltingly, 'That boyfriend of mine, who dumped me – I wasn't really in love with him. It was all a ghastly mistake.' She paused. 'Mother sent me here to get over him, to make up my mind about the future.'

'I like the sound of your mother,' Ross said, thinking how lovely Thea looked, deeply touched by her youth and innocence, wishing that he was twenty years younger, his future before him, the past behind him. 'Tell me about her.'

'Fliss is wonderful,' Thea told him, 'tall and elegant, very beautiful in an old-fashioned way; growing old gracefully, not caring a damn about clothes or make-up, knowing what suits her best, and sticking to it. Ageless, in a strange kind of way, taking everything in her stride, appreciative of the good things in life: music, books, art, the theatre.'

'All of which has rubbed off on to you,' Ross said quietly, 'apart from growing old gracefully.' He smiled. 'That's a long way off.' He paused, then said ruefully, 'My mother never grew old, gracefully or otherwise. She died soon after I was born.'

'I'm sorry. How awful for you.' Thea could not imagine

anything more dreadful than a child growing up without its mother. 'Then what happened?'

Ross shrugged dismissively. 'My father remarried in due course, a perfectly nice woman, not at all a "wicked stepmother" figure, who treated me kindly, on a par with my half-brothers and sisters to whom she later gave birth – and yet I was always conscious of being the odd one out, a kind of misfit.'

Caught up in a web of memories, Thea said wistfully, 'Things were the other way round for me. My father left Fliss for another woman when I was seven years old. Don't ask my why. He was there one minute, an integral part of my life. The next minute he was gone, without even bothering to say goodbye to me. I just figured that he didn't love me any more; had never loved me. I've never seen him from that day to this.'

Tears filled her eyes. 'But Fliss never uttered a word against him; she simply explained that such things often happen when, growing older, people fall out of love with one another. But how any man could fall out of love with Fliss, I can't begin to imagine, and I know, deep down, that she has never, for one instant, fallen out of love with my father.'

Laying a sympathetic hand on hers, Ross said softly, 'I'm certain that your father loved you a great deal, and still does. The trouble with life is that nothing seems to make sense at times.'

Blinking back her tears, Thea smiled up at the man she now knew she had fallen in love with. She knew, too, that he was not in the least bit in love with her. Bravely, light-heartedly, she said, 'So how about a sandwich and a cup of coffee at that snack bar near the harbour? Don't know about you, but I'm so hungry I could eat a – horse!'

'Come on, then,' Ross laughed, clasping her hand. He was aware that he had come dangerously close to holding her in his arms and kissing away her tears when she had spoken about her father, running the risk of losing her friendship, her trust in him as a confidant. God help him, possibly even as a substitute father figure.

Finding the snack bar, they had salad sandwiches and coffee, then, because it was such a lovely day, they walked along the beach, pausing to examine shells washed up by the tide, playing at 'ducks and drakes', laughing as if they hadn't a care in the world.

Happiness such as this, rare in Ross's life, reminded him of his student days in Paris, when the world had been his oyster. Each day, each passing hour had been lived in the joyous anticipation of evenings spent with carefree fellow students in the bistros of Montmartre, drinking lukewarm beer or café au lait from thick white cups. They had talked nineteen to the dozen, laughing at nothing, putting the world to rights, never for one moment harbouring doubts about their future happiness and success in life, until one night a waif of a girl had come in search of a student, Paul Gaston, who had quit the academy earlier that day and gone away without telling her.

The girl's name was Colette. It might as well have been – Nemesis.

Eleven

Joan and Eva and their respective husbands had arrived and taken root when Philip came home. As he had anticipated, the girls were in the kitchen talking nineteen to the dozen to their mother while his strapping sons-in-law were sprawled in armchairs in what Ruth referred to as the lounge, watching Grandstand.

Looking animated, Ruth was cutting up egg and cress sandwiches amid a welter of home-made cakes and scones and melba glasses containing strawberries and cream arrayed on a kitchen fitment in readiness for afternoon tea.

'Oh, here's your father,' she said, as if a half-forgotten stranger had appeared out of the blue.

'Hello, Father,' the girls said dutifully, planting perfunctory kisses on his cheek. 'Happy Anniversary.'

'Thanks. How was your journey?'

'Oh, you know,' Joan supplied, sounding bored, 'the usual build-up of holiday traffic on the coast road. *Why*, I can't begin to imagine. What I mean is, why would anyone in their right senses want to come to a backwater seaside resort like South Bay?'

'To visit the old folks at home?' Philip suggested drily, disliking his elder daughter intensely at that moment, wondering how it was possible for a once charming child to have developed into such a toffee-nosed snob.

Ruth butted in quickly, 'Just wait till you see the marvellous presents they've brought us. A case of champagne – Veuve Clicquot, no less! A dozen red crystal Waterford wine goblets! Above all, come September, tickets for a trip to Venice aboard the Orient Express!'

'The Orient Express?' Philip's heart sank.

'Yes. Isn't it marvellous? I've always wanted to travel in style,' Ruth enthused. 'And the lounge is like Kew Gardens with all the flowers the children brought with them. Two huge bouquets of red carnations, Madonna and stargazer lilies, and of course the roses you sent me.'

No mention of the golf clubs. Philip wondered if they had arrived – or had they been overlooked in the excitement of the 'children's' arrival?

He said, trying to inject enthusiasm into his voice, 'My word, champagne, flowers, wine glasses, a trip to Venice?'

'Well don't just stand there, Philip,' Ruth advised him, 'go through to the lounge while the girls and I set the tea table.'

'Yes, of course. But don't eat too much. Remember we're dining out tonight.'

Wondering if he looked as dull and stupid as he felt, and dreading the thought of making polite conversation with John and Daniel, Philip made his way to the lounge, noticing the golf clubs and trolley propped up in the hall near the front door. The card attached to the golf bag had not even been opened.

John Barratt and Daniel Smith had been at university together. Both were tall, beefy, sporty, well-heeled, laid back and clever. Philip had never quite decided which of them he most disliked. Ruth, on the other hand, thought the sun shone out of both of them. Thankfully, so did their respective wives, whom they had met some time ago at a Conservatives' dance in South Bay's Spa Ballroom, after which addresses and phone numbers had been exchanged, and the courtships had begun, resulting in a double Christmas wedding in the parish church eighteen months later.

It had been a 'stroke of fate', according to Ruth, who had

managed the nuptials with the flair of a West End director of stage musicals, leaving nothing to chance, including the brides' gowns and bouquets, the church decorations and the hymns. The reception had been held at the Mirimar, with roast duck, plum pudding and brandy sauce on the menu, plus twin wedding cakes, silver vases of trailing ivy and enough champagne to float a battle cruiser. He, Philip, had later stumped up a cheque in the region of two and a half thousand pounds to cover the cost of his daughters' wedding bonanza.

Two and a half thousand pounds had been a hell of a lot of money in those days so far as he was concerned. It was probably nothing more than a drop in the ocean compared with the present half-a-million annual turnover of his son-in-laws' jointly owned computer factory in the Midlands. Now, here were the pair of them, two self-made men, lacking the courtesy to acknowledge him when he entered the room.

'I hear you've done us proud,' Philip said cuttingly, not that they noticed. 'Champagne, goblets, flowers, a trip to Venice; two brand new cars cluttering up the driveway. Business must be brisk in the computer industry.'

'We're not complaining.' Barratt glanced in his father-in-law's direction. 'Why? Got a problem with that?'

'Not at all. I'd just rather you removed your feet from the coffee table, if you don't mind.'

'Whoops! Sorry, Squire.' Barratt laughed unpleasantly. 'Feet off the furniture, Danny Boy. We're not at home now; think on!'

Ruth popped her head round the door. 'Tea's on the table,' she called out in a high-pitched voice, pink-cheeked and flustered with excitement. 'Come through to the dining room. Philip, where are you going?'

'Upstairs,' he said briefly, 'to take a shower.'

'But tea's ready!'

'Thanks, but I'm not hungry.'

'Well, really!' Ruth's face darkened with anger. 'Must

you be so churlish? This *is* a family celebration, remember? What the hell's got into you? Have you looked at the presents the children brought us?'

'No, as a matter of fact I haven't! It slipped my mind, just as my present to you slipped *your* mind, apparently.'

'Present? *What* present?'

'The golf clubs and the trolley near the front door! Not the most romantic present in the world, I admit; nothing compared to a case of champagne and a trip to Venice! You might at least have bothered to read the card I sent you, though. Now, if you'll excuse me!'

Sick at heart, Philip went upstairs to shower and shave in readiness for the dinner party at the Mirimar, wishing to God the whole bloody charade was over and done with. He knew now that under no circumstances whatever would he present Ruth with the measly ring he had bought her, or the tickets for a piddling weekend in Paris. What point was there in risking further humiliation, aware as he was of his daughters' lack of affection, their husbands' obvious contempt of him and his inability to please his wife, no matter how hard he tried?

'Happy birthday, Uncle Hal,' Thea said, getting into the car, kissing him and handing him the present she had bought him earlier that day: a gold-plated fountain pen which, in all probability, he would use to fill in his bridge score card in Spain.

'Thank you, my dear, and may I say how very nice you look. Is that a new dress you're wearing?'

'No, just an old favourite of mine. You know, that "little black number" no girl should be without, according to fashion magazines.' She laughed. 'I added the red Spanish shawl and matching earrings as an afterthought, and these high-heeled shoes are giving me gyp, if you must know, so don't expect me to dance the tango, will you? I'd probably fall flat on my face if I did!'

'Hal's dancing days are over,' his wife said huffily, jealous of Thea's spectacular appearance in the figure-hugging, long black dress, the colourful Spanish shawl, the dangling earrings and the black, high-heeled shoes. Bess wished that she had worn her black lace dress and jacket, instead of the white satin number with the diamante shoulder straps.

'So where are we heading?' Thea asked light-heartedly, as Hal settled himself behind the steering wheel of the car.

'Darned if I know,' he confessed. 'Bess wouldn't say where. Just told me to follow her instructions. So best start instructing, old girl, otherwise we might well end up in the middle of a traffic island!'

As the journey progressed according to Bess's directions, Thea realised with a sinking heart that they were en route, not to some tucked-away Spanish restaurant, but to the Mirimar.

Philip and his entourage arrived at the hotel via a 'London' taxi, spacious enough to accommodate five passengers by way of its let-down seats in the rear compartment, with Philip himself seated next to the driver. They were in the reception area when Hal and Bess Hardacre walked in. Bess was in the forefront as usual, closely followed by her husband and Thea Bellamy.

Philip detached himself from his wife and family and, walking forward in a kind of dream of delight, extended his hand to greet her. 'Oh, Thea,' he murmured, 'you can't imagine how pleased I am to see you right here and now! I'm dreading this evening.'

'The same goes for me, frankly,' she assured him, sotto voce. Then, conversationally, 'Oh, I believe you've already met Mr and Mrs Hardacre.'

'Don't be silly, darling, of course we've met,' Bess said archly, claiming Philip's attention. 'Thea appears to have forgotten that she has me to thank for her job in that dear little boutique of yours. Honestly, young girls nowadays;

head in the clouds and their feet scarcely touching the ground.'

Some little distance away, Joan said coldly, 'Trust Father to leave us standing here like lemons. Who *is* that ghastly old hag he's talking to?'

John asked eagerly, 'More to the point, who is that stunner wearing the Spanish shawl? Do *you* know, Ma-in-law?'

'No, I do not,' Ruth said coldly, having witnessed the joyous expression on her husband's face when, with a hurried, 'Excuse me,' he had rushed to greet the girl in the Spanish shawl. 'And I wish you wouldn't refer to me as "Ma-in-law" again, John. You know how much I dislike it!'

John had that coming to him, Joan thought, referring admiringly to another woman in her hearing. The insensitive brute!

Eva said irritably, 'Oh, here comes Father now. High time too, if you ask me.' She was aware that Daniel's eyes also were fixed on the girl wearing the Spanish shawl, and felt far from pleased with him. 'Some fine celebration party this is, I must say. Whose idea was it in the first place, I should like to know!'

Rejoining the family party, Philip's light-hearted, 'Sorry about that,' seemed a slap in the eye to Ruth, who had expected an abject, not a carelessly uttered apology.

'You might have done your socialising later,' she said waspishly. 'Who are those people, anyway?'

'Oh, of course, you weren't at the Lamberts' dinner party, were you? The couple are the Hardacres, the young lady with them is Thea Bellamy.'

'You mean the girl in charge of the boutique?' Ruth's eyes flashed fire. 'Huh. She looks more like barmaid material to me!'

Biting his tongue, Philip said flatly, 'Well, shall we go through to the dining room?'

Joan said coolly, 'Why not, since that's why we're here? Not that I'm in the least bit hungry!'

Holding his anger in check, Philip replied levelly, 'Not to worry, Joan, you'll not be strapped into a high chair and force-fed, I assure you.'

'Hey, hang on,' John blustered. 'Joan happens to be my wife, in case you've forgotten!'

'She also happens to be my daughter,' Philip reminded him, 'and I've known her a lot longer than you have. She always was a picky eater, as I recall; inclined to throw unwanted food on to the floor. Hopefully she has learned better table manners now she's a grown woman, married into the bargain!'

What had come over him tonight? Philip scarcely knew – except that, for the first time, he had become clearly aware of the minor role he occupied, had always occupied, in the estimation of his family. Moreover, his brief encounter with Thea had endowed him with the courage to speak his mind for a change, to tell his wife, his daughters and their abominable, insensitive, mannerless husbands, if necessary, exactly what he thought of the lot of them!

No doubt the dinner party he'd arranged would not meet with their approval. There was bound to be something wrong with it. The Dom Perignon champagne would not be properly chilled, the menu not quite to the liking of his sophisticated in-laws. 'What, no caviar?' The table decorations he'd chosen with such care would appear to them as cheap and tatty – after all, what price a few red dinner napkins and a centrepiece of red rosebuds compared with flamboyant bouquets of crimson carnations, Madonna and stargazer lilies, a case of Veuve Cliquot champagne, a dozen wine goblets, a trip to Venice aboard a luxury train and everything else that was far above his own means to afford?

Not that he was a poor man, far from it, but neither was he rich enough to squander money like water. Nor had he any wish to do so, having worked hard all his life to achieve his present state of financial security, however modest it might seem to his high-flying sons-in-law with their fast cars and flamboyant lifestyles. Little wonder they looked down on him, Philip thought bitterly, as the maître d' ushered himself and his family to their table.

Glancing across the room towards the dimly lit bar area, discernible through gaps in the curved glass partitions, Philip's heart lifted suddenly, catching a glimpse of Bess Hardacre's dyed blonde hair and Thea's distinctive Spanish shawl, at the same time hearing an old favourite tune of his, 'All The Things You Are', played by the pianist seated at a spotlit grand piano.

This was the moment Thea had been dreading. She felt a strong urge to excuse herself on some pretext or other – a sick headache, perhaps – but realised that to do so would merely serve to draw attention to herself if Bess made a scene, as she was wont to do in an emergency, however small or insignificant it might be. The silly old thing, with her flair for the dramatic, had already turned heads in their direction when choosing a table. She had protested loudly that she couldn't see where she was going in the dark, whereupon Hal had grabbed her by the elbow and guided her towards a banquette in a corner of the bar, shushing her as he did so.

Poor old Hal, Thea thought; how he had managed to live with a show-off like Bess all these years without shaking her till her teeth rattled, she would never know. The attraction of opposites, she supposed. Sliding on to the seat next to Bess as Hal made his way to the bar to order their drinks, she felt thankful for small mercies – a seat in a dark corner of the room, close to the entrance, convenient to the dining room when their table was ready.

The last thing Thea wanted was Ross to know she was there, seeing him at work. She knew he would find her presence humiliating, akin to watching a circus animal performing tricks. It was something to do with the spotlights shining down on him, somehow highlighting his spiritual isolation amid a buzz of conversation, a drift of cigarette smoke, an occasional burst of laughter from the girls perched on bar stools, talking to the bartenders.

Thea knew the man she was in love with didn't belong here in this atmosphere of make-believe gaiety, any more than she did. It was very far distant from the quiet happiness of the afternoon they had spent together on the seashore, hearing the whisper of the waves coming in on the sand, revelling in the sunshine and fresh air. There had been a marvellous sense of freedom, of release from the niggling cares of life, Ross's far more deeply rooted than her own, she realised, when he had spoken briefly of his love of music, his failed ambition to become a concert pianist.

This had been his first reference to music, and she had listened intently, not asking questions, simply hoping that he would delve deeper into the subject; confide in her the reason for his failure to realise his ambition. Instead, he had bent down to pick up a scallop shell washed up by the sea. 'For good luck,' he had said, pressing it into the palm of her hand.

Then it seemed that a veil had been drawn between them, as gossamer-light as the mist which sometimes came in with the tide, and it had occurred to her how little she knew about him, even less than he knew about her. But perhaps it was better this way, getting to know each other gradually in the short space of time allotted to them, building up a warm, lasting friendship, not rushing headlong into an emotional relationship bound to end when September came.

Bess, who had been sampling the liquid fruits of the vine most of the afternoon, by way of celebrating Hal's birthday, was now in a state of intoxication, and in the mood for mischief making. Rising tipsily to her feet, she boomed: 'Young man. You at the piano. We have a birthday boy here! His name's Harold.'

Deeply embarrassed, Hal muttered sharply, 'For God's sake, Bess, sit down and shut up!'

'Huh? Why should I? We're here to enjoy ourselves, aren't we? And I intend doing just that!'

An uneasy silence had fallen momentarily on the room. Ross had stopped playing abruptly, his fingers still resting on the keyboard. To Thea's horror, a spotlight centred suddenly on their corner table, illuminating herself, Hal and Bess, causing an outburst of laughter and applause as the pianist began playing the well-known 'Happy Birthday' jingle.

Never, till her dying day, would Thea forget the blank expression on Ross's face when he caught sight of her in the glare of the spotlight. A look of total unrecognition, as if she had somehow betrayed his trust in her, had made a mockery of their relationship, delicately balanced between friendship and love.

Twelve

Philip was right in supposing that his carefully planned dinner party would prove a fiasco. If the saying, 'a house divided against itself cannot stand' was true, his seemed in imminent danger of collapse.

Ruth, he suspected, had not forgiven him for leaving her side to speak to Thea, hence her unkind remark about the girl's appearance. Joan was apparently at loggerheads with her mother over some ill-advised remark or other uttered during his absence from the family party. Eva was scarcely on speaking terms with her husband, heaven alone knew why. Finally, all of them appeared to be irked with him for reasons beyond his comprehension to understand. If anyone's behaviour had been unforgivable, it was certainly not his.

John Barratt's table manners had been lamentable, for instance. He'd complained loudly that the soup was cold, and the roast beef so tough he'd require a hacksaw to cut it, at the same time downing glass after glass of champagne until, rocking back in his chair, he was suddenly and violently sick.

Even Joan appeared shocked by her husband's lack of decorum in a public venue. Then she had realised the full extent of her husband's inebriation. 'Well, Father, don't just sit there doing nothing,' she adjured Philip sharply. 'Ring for a taxi! Can't you see John needs help? We must get him home as quickly as possible!'

Rising strongly to his feet, throwing down his table

napkin, angry beyond belief, Philip issued orders. 'You, Daniel, take John through to reception. Ruth, Joan and Eva, collect your belongings and come with me. The party's over!'

Ringing for a taxi, Philip caught a brief glimpse of a distraught young woman wearing a red Spanish shawl hurrying towards the street beyond the heavy glass doors of the restaurant.

'Well, of all the ungrateful, bad-mannered girls! Rushing away like that without a word of explanation,' Bess burst forth. The spotlight incident and the humiliating 'Happy Birthday' episode had precipitated Thea's hasty departure: half blinded by tears, and with a briefly uttered, 'Sorry, Uncle Hal,' she had abruptly quit the bar.

'Oh, come on, old girl,' Hal interposed, on Thea's behalf, 'she *did* apologise.'

'To *you*, not to *me*,' Bess bridled indignantly. 'But I shall make it my business to speak to her later; demand an explanation of her extremely rude behaviour.'

'The trouble with you, Bess,' Hal said, 'is that you never know where to draw the line! Speak to Thea if you must. Chances are she'll tell you to – get lost! And who could blame her? Not *I*, that's for sure! I think the world of that girl, more so for putting up with a couple of old fogies like us.'

'Speak for yourself, Hal! *I'm* not an old fogey, and I have no intention of behaving like one.' She added tetchily, 'Oh, come on! No use sitting here in semi-darkness, we might as well see if our table's ready. I just hope the chef has followed my instructions to the letter, that's all!'

So did Hal, for the chef's sake.

'In any case,' Bess continued, on her way to the dining room, 'what on earth did you mean by Thea telling me to "get lost"? Why should she? All I did was ask the pianist to play "Happy Birthday". What's wrong with that?'

She really hadn't a clue, Hal thought, and if he told her, she wouldn't believe him.

Seated beside the driver, leaving Barratt to the ministrations of Joan and Daniel, Philip could hear voices raised in dissension beyond the glass partition, in particular those of Ruth and Eva complaining anxiously at sharing a taxi with a member of the party who might be sick at any moment. Some party this had turned out to be, Philip thought grimly, at the same time wondering why Thea had left the Mirimar so abruptly, and alone. Had she felt suddenly unwell? In need of fresh air? But no, it went deeper than that, he realised. It appeared to him that she had been running away from something – just what, he could not begin to imagine, apart from that ghastly courtesy aunt of hers, Bess Hardacre, who had probably said or done something to upset her.

Tomorrow, Sunday, he intended to find out! Ruth would raise objections, of course, to his Sunday morning visit to the boutique. Frankly, he couldn't care less, just so long as his daughters and their respective husbands had packed up and cleared off on his return home. A more than likely scenario. After he had expressed his low opinion of the lot of them, they would probably refuse ever to darken his doors again. A consummation devoutly to be wished. This time, for once in his life, Philip intended to have his say. The sooner, the better!

Paying off the taxi, he opened the front door, switched on the hall lights, and stood aside as the disparate members of his family straggled past him, Daniel and Joan supporting the foolishly tipsy John, Ruth with a face like thunder, and Eva on the verge of tears.

'All this is your fault, Father,' she sniffed. 'If you hadn't gone off to talk to that girl, none of this would have happened! John said something to upset Mother, Joan was cross with John, I with Daniel. No wonder the evening turned out so badly!'

'Oh, I see,' Philip said grimly. 'I take it, then, that I am also to blame for your brother-in-law's appalling lack of good manners at table? Or do you condone his being sick at a dinner party as acceptable behaviour on the part of a supposedly well-educated man, who should have known better than to ruin what was meant to be a quiet celebration?'

'Oh, *I* don't know! Why ask *me*?' Eva replied huffily. 'And to think we came here, in good faith, to help you and Mother celebrate your anniversary. A complete waste of time, if you ask me!'

Inclined to agree with her, he turned his attention to the trio on the staircase, Joan, Daniel and the inebriated John. Philip called up to them abruptly to make use of the bathroom, as a matter of priority, before even attempting to put John to bed to sleep off his hangover.

Ruth interposed sharply, 'No need to adopt that tone of voice, Philip! Eva is quite right in saying that they came here in good faith. Why else would they have brought us such marvellous presents?'

She continued hoarsely, 'The trouble with you is that you've always been a little fish in a little pond, jealous of your daughters' marriages to men far more successful than you are, or could ever hope to be. Well, why not admit it? At the same time, I suggest you remember what you owe to me. Without my help and advice you'd have probably still been the manager of that common-or-garden clothing factory. Well, I'm right, aren't I?'

'And the trouble with you, Ruth, is that you've always been right, allowing me no margin of error to get things wrong, occasionally, in my own way.'

'What is that supposed to mean?' she flared back at him. 'Given your own way, you'd have squandered money on a tumbledown dream house, so-called! Well, all I can say is, you should thank your lucky stars that I talked you into buying *this* house, not some broken-down shack at the back of beyond! In any case, did you imagine that the bank would have sanctioned a mortgage on that sort of property? Did it ever occur to you that the bank manager, granting the loan, did so bearing in mind my headmistress's salary and the pristine state of the property *I*, not you, had in mind?'

'Yes, of course it did,' Philip admitted. 'And you were perfectly right, as always, in pointing out the error of my ways. The mystery remains.'

'*Mystery?* What – *mystery?*' Ruth demanded, in her hectoring, schoolmarm voice.

Philip said simply, 'The reason why you have put up with me for the past forty years. Now I suggest you take an unbiased look at our situation and tell me what you see. No, I'll tell you what *I* see for a change, a role reversal. No, don't interrupt, just sit down, Ruth, and keep quiet for once in your life. You too, Eva.

'Frankly, I've had it up to here with this house, this red brick box which you, Ruth, think of as home. You, too, Eva, and Joan, I suspect, since you were breast-fed here until you were old enough to attend an expensive nursery school for the offspring of middle-class parents such as your mother and me.'

'There's no need to be coarse, Father,' Eva protested. 'Oh God! I wish we'd never come here in the first place!'

'In which case, I suggest that you go upstairs and start packing your finery in readiness for your departure first thing tomorrow morning when, hopefully, your brother-in-law will have slept off his hangover sufficiently to drive his car back to Birmingham without undue mishaps on the way.'

Ruth butted in angrily, 'Have you taken leave of your senses? The children will be leaving tomorrow after luncheon. I have everything planned!'

Philip said impatiently, 'I had everything planned for tonight, and look what happened! Robbie Burns got it about right, I reckon, when he wrote "The best laid schemes o' mice an' men gang aft a-gley".'

Eva burst forth, 'No need to worry, Mother! I have no wish to stay where I'm not wanted. Daniel, Joan and John will agree with me when I tell them we've been given our marching orders!' So saying, she left the room abruptly and stormed upstairs.

Alone with his wife in the flower-filled lounge, Philip said, 'I'm sorry the party turned out so badly. I never meant it to happen. You must believe that. I'm not even sure what went wrong.'

'Well, if you are not, *I* am!' she retorted. 'The evening got off to a bad start when you left us to speak to that girl you're so fond of, making an exhibition of yourself! I've never felt so humiliated in all my life, the way you rushed to greet her.

'Oh, don't bother to deny it! No wonder you've been spending so much time at the boutique lately! Now I know why. Really, a man of your age making a fool of himself over a girl young enough to be your daughter takes some swallowing!'

'If you mean what I think you mean,' Philip said, disbelievingly, 'you're the one taken leave of your senses!'

'Really? Well, I hold her entirely responsible for everything that happened to ruin the evening. John and Daniel couldn't take their eyes off her; John asked me, point blank, and I quote: "Who is that stunner wearing the Spanish shawl?" Naturally Joan was upset, and so was Eva. Understandably so, in my opinion. Then, John said, "Do *you* know who she is, Ma-in-law?" and I told him, in no uncertain terms, that I disliked intensely that form of address! "Ma-in-law", indeed!

'Next thing I knew, you were talking nineteen to the dozen to some ghastly old harridan with bleached hair, the girl's mother, presumably, not caring tuppence about keeping me hanging about like a – spare part. Your own wife, on our wedding anniversary!'

Ruth's lips tightened to a thin line. 'I expected, at least, some special recognition of our anniversary, apart from flowers, a set of golf clubs and a disastrous dinner party.'

Philip withdrew from the pocket of his dinner jacket the box containing the ruby ring he had chosen for her. 'As a matter of fact,' he said, 'I intended giving you this at dinner. The reasons why not are obvious, I dare say. Your dislike of any of the other jewellery I've ever given you for one thing . . . your uncompromising attitude for another.

'There's something else: tickets for a weekend in Paris.' He smiled ruefully. 'No need to explain why I decided not to hand you that particular surprise packet! After all, a weekend in Paris compared with a trip to Venice, the dates coinciding! No contest, really. Just another mistake of mine, well-intentioned but futile, as usual. Symptomatic of the man you married, wouldn't you say?'

He continued levelly, 'I believe the time has come to evaluate our marriage, to question what the future holds for us. It seems fairly obvious to me that we can't go on the way we are.'

Ruth glanced up sharply. 'You could be right for once,' she said, slipping off the ring and putting it back in its box, 'especially since you appear determined to alienate your children's affection, giving them their marching orders so abruptly, with never a thought for *my* feelings. Or perhaps you simply don't care that they came home with the best of intentions, to bring some light relief into the boring monotony of our daily lives?'

'By way of Barratt's faux pas – being sick in public?' Philip suggested wryly. 'Well yes, I can see, in retrospect, what a relief that must have been, livening up a "disastrous dinner party" as it did. Your words, Ruth, not mine!'

Rising to his feet, he continued wearily, 'As for my daughters' affection, it doesn't exist. It never has done. So far as I'm concerned, you were far more necessary to the pair of them than a father figure. Think about it, Ruth! Ask yourself how important I am in *your* life!'

Sick at heart, he moved towards the door. 'I'll sleep in the spare room tonight; return the ring and the travel tickets on Monday. The last thing I want is to come between you and the girls.'

He smiled ruefully. 'Funny, isn't it? To think that, on our anniversary, I am about to give you the one gift you have wanted all these years? The gift of – freedom!'

Awake half the night, tossing and turning, wondering what to do for the best, he suddenly remembered the flat above the shop, a poorly furnished apartment used as a store place. Somewhat cramped, it was nevertheless habitable, comprising a bed-sitting room, kitchen and bathroom.

Up at the crack of dawn, he packed an overnight bag with a few personal belongings: his shaving gear, clean socks, shirts and underwear from the airing cupboard of the red brick box he was about to leave. Treading quietly downstairs to the hall and opening the front door to the sound of birdsong from the shrubberies, he drew the scent of fresh morning air into his lungs, then strode quickly, purposefully towards his old BMW parked in the driveway behind his son-in-law's brand new Mercedes. Philip's heart lifted to the awareness of a feeling of freedom, far distanced from an old, familiar pattern of life which had given him little pleasure of late, and certainly not joy.

He drove along the coast road into town, towards the shop and the flat on the top floor. Unlocking the door and entering the apartment, he knew that he would be happier alone than he would be in the company of a wife and children who had never really needed him.

The events of yesterday, culminating in that disastrous dinner party, had triggered a blinding awareness of his ineptitude as a husband and father, resulting in his decision to take control of his life before it was too late.

Money was the least important factor in the vaguely discerned future ahead of him. Just as well, he thought wryly.

Ruth would want her pound of flesh, would make him pay dearly for his desertion, and she would have right on her side, as usual. Strangely, the thought troubled him not at all.

The future he dimly envisaged in his present state of emotional turmoil included turning his back on the past; travelling, perhaps, to far-away places, finding, in his own place in the sun, the peace of mind long denied him as a prisoner trapped in a loveless marriage. He would escape what had become, in Ruth's own words, the 'boring monotony' of their daily lives.

This flat, he realised, was merely a temporary resting place, a much-needed caravanserai until he'd had time to consider the future more carefully, to plan his next step on the road to freedom.

In the note he had left for Ruth on the spare-room dressing table, he had told her of his intention to move into the flat over the shop for the time being – a bald statement of fact to prevent her ringing up the police and the local hospital or sending out a search party when he failed to put in an appearance later in the day. Though the thought of his daughters and their husbands scouring the countryside for a man they would be glad to see the back of held a certain grim humour.

Glancing at his watch, he saw the time was now seven a.m. Two hours to wait before Thea opened the boutique. He wanted to be there when she arrived. Thea, the innocent catalyst of last night's fiasco at the Mirimar, the cause of so much dissension, conjecture and jealousy. The one person he wished to see, the only one capable of providing the sympathy and understanding he needed so much at this crisis point in his life.

Thea was in the boutique, standing behind the counter replenishing the stock of scarves from a cardboard box, when Philip arrived at a quarter past nine. She looked tired, he thought, as if she also had slept badly.

Looking up, apparently surprised, she said, 'Gosh, you're early! Quite honestly, I didn't think you'd come at all. I thought you'd take the day off to be with your family.'

Commanding the moment, he said quietly, 'No, I'm afraid not. The fact is, I've left home. In the early hours of this morning, I moved into the flat above the dress shop, where I'll be staying, for the time being, until I have decided what to do about the future.'

Thea was appalled. 'Why? What happened?' She frowned disbelievingly, 'You seemed so happy last night, at the Mirimar, when we met in the foyer. Oh, I know you said you were dreading the evening, but I took that with a pinch of salt. I never dreamed, for one moment, that you really meant it!'

'You hinted as much to me,' Philip reminded her, 'before your aunt took over our conversation. Next thing I knew, you were running away from the hotel as if the devil was after you! *Why*, Thea? I'd really like to know.'

'It's a long story! A silly misunderstanding occurred, that's all, involving someone I happen to – to care about. But that's a far cry, surely, from your decision to leave home after a family party.

'I couldn't help noticing, last night, when you came to speak to me, how deeply your wife resented your departure from the norm, as if she had you, to coin a phrase, "hog-tied and branded"; had hung a "hands off, this man is mine" sign around your neck. Not really wanting you at all, I dare say, apart from appearances' sake, as the dutiful husband, father, and breadwinner. Or am I wide of the mark? If so, please forgive me for speaking my mind so bluntly!'

Ruth would have said not 'Or am I wide of the mark', but 'I'm right, aren't I?', Philip reflected. Ruth, his partner of the past forty years who, never during all that time, had possessed the humility or grace to admit that she might just have been wrong once in a while.

'This has been coming for some time now,' Philip said,

'the tension between Ruth and me. Nothing specific, no major dust-ups, at least not until last night, when I said things I'd wanted to say for a long time, to the extent of giving my children their marching orders and telling Ruth the time had come to take a long hard look at our marriage, that we couldn't go on as we were.'

'What did she say?'

'For once in her life, she agreed with me; admitted that I could be right, since I seemed hell-bent on alienating our daughters' affections, the reason why she was angry. That's when I decided to leave, to save her having to choose between us.' He smiled ruefully. 'So, in a sense, I took the coward's way out of a no-win situation.'

'There must have been more to it than that,' Thea said compassionately, aware of his underlying tension, completely on his side. Then, 'Sorry, that was insensitive of me. Just one thing, for what it's worth; I can't accept that you took the coward's way out. The exact opposite! I'd say you acted honourably in leaving when you did, for your wife's sake – and don't you forget it! She's a lucky woman, in my opinion, and she'll come to realise that one of these days.'

'Thank you, my dear. I'll try to remember,' he said softly, grateful for the warmth of words, her presence in his life. She was the kind of daughter he'd longed for, and never had.

She said briskly, 'Shall I make some coffee? Don't know about you, but I could murder a mug right now.'

'No, I have a better idea. Let's stroll along to the snack bar, shall we, for a full English breakfast? I'm so hungry I could eat a horse!'

'Lock up the shop, you mean?' she demurred anxiously. 'But what about the customers? They could be along at any minute, wanting to spend money hand over fist.'

'To hell with the customers,' Philip laughed, aware of a sudden easing of tension, the return of his sense of humour in this girl's company. 'Just hang the "Closed" notice on the door, and come with me.' He added more seriously,

'I've told you what happened to me last night. Now I want to know what happened to you. Why you left the Mirimar so abruptly.'

Walking beside Philip along the promenade to the snack bar, Thea said dejectedly, close to tears, 'I've made a fool of myself, that's all, in thinking Ross might be falling in love with me. Last night, I read contempt in his eyes when he caught sight of me under the damned spotlight. As if I had somehow betrayed our friendship, his trust in me as something more than a – bar-fly!

'It was my aunt's fault, I suppose. But no, that's not quite fair, is it? Blaming someone else, I mean. If only she'd told me beforehand, I wouldn't have set foot in the bar, even if it had meant upsetting poor Uncle Hal on his birthday.

'If only Aunt Bess had kept quiet. But oh no, she had to be the centre of attention, as usual. She actually called out to him to play that awful happy birthday jingle: then the spotlight centred on our table, and I just got up and – and ran away.

'Oh God, I felt so humiliated, so ashamed. He didn't look at me at all, you see. He looked through me, as if I didn't exist – and I knew why, because he, too, felt ashamed and humiliated that I had seen him, not as a free spirit, but a – a slave. A bit like a dancing bear in a circus, performing to please the onlookers. So now you know, don't you, the way I felt when he saw me, last night, at that spotlit table alongside Bess Hardacre.'

Philip frowned, attempting to make sense of Thea's stream of consciousness without admitting that he had scarcely understood a word of it. Then, bringing his common sense to bear on a subject obviously distressing to the girl beside him, he suddenly realised that she was referring to Ross Drummond, the bar pianist at the Mirimar. God help her! Drummond, of all people! A man of mystery, once involved, if he was not mistaken, in a scandal concerning the murder of a child.

* * *

Alone in the house, Ruth found herself looking anxiously at the clock, expecting to hear the crunch of tyres on the drive, the opening of the garage doors as Philip put away the car for the night. But there was no sound apart from the ticking of the carriage clock on the mantelpiece, the hands of which stood at twenty minutes to nine.

Really, this was ludicrous, she fumed inwardly, and she would tell him so in no uncertain terms when he did put in an appearance. A man of his age behaving like a silly schoolboy, going off without a word apart from that stupid note on the spare-room dressing table, placing her in the invidious position of telling the family, when they came down to breakfast, that her husband of forty years had taken it into his head to move into the crummy flat-cum-store place above the shop.

'Why, for heaven's sake?' Joan asked crisply, helping herself to orange juice from the fridge.

'You know why! I told you last night that Father was behaving badly; saying dreadful things to Mummy and me; actually ordering me out of the room; telling me to go upstairs and start packing.' Eva sniffed audibly. 'But you took no notice, as usual!'

'I had more important things on my mind at the time,' Joan reminded her.

'Oh yes, I know! Listening to John being sick in the bathroom!' Eva said scornfully. 'Lumbering my husband with the responsibility of putting yours to bed to sleep off his hangover! And don't bother to deny it because I heard you issuing orders to Daniel, as if he was to blame for John's beastly behaviour at the Mirimar.'

'If you ask me, the entire evening was a disaster from start to finish,' Joan replied heatedly. 'The food was rubbish, so was the champagne!'

'Huh,' Eva flared back at her sister, 'not rubbishy enough to prevent John getting plastered.'

'That's enough. Be quiet, the pair of you!' Ruth interrupted sharply, deeply shocked at the underlying hostility between her offspring. 'Your father has left home, and all you can do is stand there arguing about who's to blame for last night!'

She added grimly, 'I thought I knew – now I'm not so sure! Well, don't just stand there doing nothing. Make yourselves useful. You, Joan, set the dining-room table for breakfast. You, Eva, hand me the bacon and sausages from the fridge, then go upstairs and tell Daniel and John that breakfast will be on the table in half an hour and I'll expect them to be down on time to eat it. Is that perfectly clear?'

'Yes, Mother.' The girls scattered at her behest.

News of Philip's defection had scarcely registered with the menfolk, and nobody had seemed in the least concerned about *her* feelings, Ruth thought. Neither Joan nor Eva had expressed sympathy or wanted to know what had really happened to cause their father to leave home so abruptly. Joan, in particular, had treated the episode as a storm in a teacup.

'I shouldn't worry unduly if I were you,' she had said off-handedly. 'Father enjoys his creature comforts too much to pig it alone in that ghastly apartment over the shop for very long.'

At that moment, for the first time, Ruth had realised Joan's inability to care unduly about anything or anyone apart from herself, her husband and her appearance, clothes, jewellery and money.

Eva, tarred with the same brush, but less forceful and domineering than her sister, said sanctimoniously, 'You mustn't blame yourself, Mother, for what's happened. I'm sure it wasn't your fault. Father behaved abominably.'

'He wasn't the only one,' Ruth said grimly, making preparations for the roast beef luncheon that possibly no one wanted or would enjoy eating. Especially not John, still green about the gills, whose appalling behaviour had been the root cause of Philip's decision to leave home. Ruth knew that now. And to think she had, hitherto, thought the sun shone out of her son-in-law.

After coffee in the lounge had followed lunch, John had glanced at his Rolex, risen to his feet and said, stretching, 'Well, time we were off!' And that was it. No mention of helping with the washing-up. Simply a carrying downstairs of luggage and an air of confusion at the sorting out of their various items of Louis Vuitton baggage prior to their departure, leaving behind them a mess of unmade beds, crumpled sheets and pillowcases, a mass of unwashed pots and pans in the kitchen sink and a stained lavatory in the bathroom.

First of all, Ruth had stuffed the soiled bed linen into the washing machine. Next she had scrubbed and bleached the tainted lavatory pan. Last of all, she had tackled the washing-up, refilling the sink repeatedly with hot soapy water until every trace of grease had been removed from the roasting tins in which she had cooked the sirloin of beef and the Yorkshire puddings, and the dinner plates on which she had served a meal that nobody, including herself, had appreciated.

Finally, she had repaired to the lounge to watch television. Not that there was anything worth watching. And so, switching off the set, she simply sat there, in the lamplit room, listening to the ticking of the clock, expecting to hear the sound of car tyres on the drive and Philip's key in the front door, his voice calling out to her: 'I'm home! Sorry I'm late!' But the silence remained unbroken apart from the monotonous ticking of the clock.

When Philip came back, Ruth thought she would demand an explanation. Make it abundantly clear to him that she was not prepared to put up with his foolish behaviour.

She sat up till midnight, expecting the phone to ring, to hear a message from the girls to say they had arrived home safely, to ask how she was feeling. Eventually, switching off the lights, she went upstairs to bed. The phone had not rung. And Philip had not come home.

Thirteen

'You might as well come clean,' Bunty said in that forthright way of hers. 'I can tell something's wrong. Has that aunt of yours said something to upset you? I couldn't help hearing her having a go at you the other evening. What I mean is, there was no mistaking that booming bittern voice of hers. I'd just bumped into her on the landing and she nearly deafened me. "I'm Mrs Hardacre," she bellowed, "come to see my niece, Thea Bellamy. Is she in?"'

Bunty giggled, recalling the incident. 'Know what I did? I cupped my hand to my ear and said, "Pardon?" She wasn't best pleased about that, I could tell. She went all pink, and puffed up like a turkeycock!'

Thea smiled briefly. 'It wasn't a very pleasant encounter,' she admitted. 'I'd behaved badly, and she wanted an explanation; demanded an apology.'

'Hmm, sounds intriguing.' Bunty perched on the end of Thea's bed. 'And did you explain, and apologise?'

'I apologised, of course.'

'But you didn't explain?'

'No. I couldn't. What happened was my own business. I simply offered a lame excuse, said I'd felt unwell, but she kept on poking and prying until I lost patience with her, and asked her to leave.'

Bunty frowned. 'That's not like you, Thea: losing patience; behaving badly, telling fibs, drooping around the place like a lost soul the way you've been doing this past week – and Stella's just as bad. Or hadn't you noticed?'

'Stella? No. Why, what's wrong with her?'

'How should I know? Nobody tells me anything any more! She's gone all broody again for no apparent reason, unless that beastly Brian has started pestering her again. Now you're giving me a hard time, looking as if you'd lost a tenner and found a quid. So why don't you tell me what's really the matter? Or don't you trust me? Is that it?'

'Of course I trust you. It's just that I'm not thinking very clearly at the moment.'

'Has it anything to do with that birthday party at the Mirimar last Saturday night?' Bunty asked.

'Everything to do with it,' Thea confessed. 'We were in the bar when Bess called out to the – the pianist – to play "Happy Birthday".'

'God, how embarrassing.' Bunty pulled a face, imagining Mrs Hardacre's voice booming across the room, shattering the indigo atmosphere as surely as a well-aimed stone would have splintered one of the softly lit mirrors behind the bar counter.

'Yes, it was.' Thea shuddered slightly, recalling the moment when, caught in the beam of a spotlight illuminating their table, she had apologised briefly to her Uncle Hal, run out of the building into the fresh air, and walked all the way home in her high-heeled shoes and the ridiculous Spanish shawl she'd been wearing at the time.

Bunty said sympathetically. 'How rotten for the pianist too. How did he react?'

'Rather badly, I'm afraid. He is a very private person,' Thea replied unthinkingly.

'You speak as one who knows,' Bunty replied shrewdly. 'You haven't fallen for him, by any chance?'

'If you mean am I in love with him, well, yes, I am. So now you know!'

Along with half the young female population of South

Bay, herself included, Bunty thought. Well, not in love exactly, but intrigued by his mature good looks and air of mystery. How well did Thea know him? she wondered, not daring to ask, knowing she'd find out in the fullness of time.

Getting up, she said, 'June's been late-night shopping this evening. I'm off to take a peek at her new wardrobe. You coming?'

'Yes, sure.' Thea smiled, interested in her neighbour's efforts to discard her old dowdy image. The beauty routine had done wonders for June's skin, despite her initial misgivings about the mud pack and the use of cosmetics. These plus her shorter, more casual hairstyle had given a much-needed boost to her self-confidence.

'Well, come on, let's have a look-see at your new clobber,' Bunty said cheerfully, by way of encouragement, once June had ushered them into her room. 'No pleated skirts and embroidered blouses, I hope?'

'No, of course not,' June giggled. Opening the wardrobe, she withdrew a sleekly tailored skirt and jacket, silver-grey in colour, a black wool cocktail dress with a scooped-out neckline and three-quarter-length sleeves, a pair of black high-heeled shoes, a plain white silk shirt, a smart black handbag, and two pastel-coloured sweaters, one pink, the other green. 'Well, what do you think?'

'Ye gods! How much did that lot cost you?' Bunty stared admiringly at June's new clobber.

'An arm and a leg, if you must know,' June replied jauntily, 'but who cares? I'm not saving for that hi-fi system now – besides which, I've been given a pay rise and a bit of a bonus – well, a hundred pounds as a matter of fact. So I went in at the deep end for once in my life.'

Thea said light-heartedly, 'You went in at the deep end when you came here to South Bay to live. That couldn't have been easy for you. Now look at you, all bright-eyed and bushy-tailed, the captain of your soul, master of your fate. Well done, June. Your new clothes are lovely.'

Glancing at Thea, perched beside her on June's bed, Bunty noticed tears were close to the surface, and knew that, despite her pretended gaiety, the girl was deeply troubled and unhappy. Well, that figured. A love affair between an uncomplicated individual like Thea and a man of mystery such as the pianist stood little or no chance of success in her view. One would float on the surface, the other would sink without trace. Just as she had sunk, without trace, when her mother had sent her those newspaper photographs of her ex-boyfriend on his wedding day.

Desperate to see Ross, the following Saturday afternoon Thea entered the art gallery, hoping, praying he'd be there, knowing, deep down, that he would not. And she was right. There was no sign of him.

To add to her distress, John Atkinson Grimshaw's painting had been replaced by a Landseer depicting dead animals and birds.

'All alone today? Where's that young man of yours?' Tom Fenby, the attendant, asked when she came down from the upper gallery.

'I wish I knew,' Thea said. Then, taking a chance, 'I need to speak to him urgently. You don't happen to know where he lives?'

Tom scratched his head. 'Not the number of the house, but I know whereabouts. He rents a flat not far from here, in Lissom Grove.'

He added reflectively, 'A quiet sort of bloke, a bit of a loner, I'd say. Still, it can't be an easy job, playing piano for a living, working every night that God sends during the summer months, having to dodge them flighty young lasses waiting for him when he leaves work, like he was some kind of pop star or other. I dunno, girls these days! Out till all hours; skirts like pelmets; made up to the nines!

One thing's for sure, he's not the kind to take advantage of that kind of come-on.'

'I'm sure you're right, Tom,' Thea said. Then, changing the subject, 'What has become of *Liverpool from Wapping*, by the way?'

'Oh that?' Tom sighed regretfully. 'It's gone to Newcastle. Now we're stuck with a bloody Landseer! Huh, why any artist would want to paint a load of dead creatures beats me. Talk about depressing!'

Bidding Tom goodbye, Thea went in search of Lissom Grove. The house she was looking for turned out to be a neat Victorian villa with an iron gate, a privet hedge, bay windows, and a row of bell-pushes near the front door, denoting that the house was carved up into flats. Pressing the bell marked 'Drummond', Thea awaited a reply to her summons with a rapidly beating heart.

More than likely he'd be out on this fine Saturday afternoon, she thought bleakly. And if he was not, what then? Chances were, seeing her on the doorstep, he would send her away, making some excuse or other to get rid of her unwelcome presence in his life.

Suddenly, the door opened, and he was there, looking down at her, not speaking, simply holding out his arms to embrace her, holding her close to his heart. There was no need for words. Words would come later, upstairs in his flat; words she had longed to hear. 'Oh Thea, my darling, thank God you came! I love you so much. So very much!'

Later, in the bay-windowed sitting room, Thea said, looking out at the thickly clustered laburnum and lilac blossoms in the gardens of the houses across the way, '*Liverpool from Wapping* has gone to Newcastle, did you know? I felt bereft, as if I'd lost a well-loved friend.'

'Yes, I knew. Tom Fenby told me when I went to look at it, the other day,' Ross said quietly, standing beside her, his arm about her waist. 'The picture had just been crated in readiness for its journey.' He added gently, reflectively, 'Who knows? Perhaps other lovers will fall under its spell, as we did. You see, my darling, I fell in love with you the moment I saw you standing there, in the gallery, all alone, looking at the painting. I think I knew, even then, that we were destined to meet again.'

'Despite last Saturday night?' Thea asked uncertainly. 'The way you looked through me, without a sign of recognition?'

'Despite everything,' Ross said. He added honestly, 'The truth is, I felt ashamed of my profession. A bar pianist, of all things!'

'But I already knew,' Thea confessed. 'I'd been in the bar before, with a friend of mine.'

'Then why didn't you say so?'

'For the same reason, I imagine, that you didn't tell me what you did for a living,' Thea reminded him. 'Not that it matters a damn. Why should it? I fell in love with you that night; you looked so lonely, I longed to comfort you. Was that wrong of me?

'I couldn't get you out of my mind afterwards. Then, when I met you in the gallery, it seemed like a miracle; actually being with you, talking to you as a friend. What you did for a living seemed unimportant. If it had cropped up in conversation, I'd have told you I already knew. Something told me you didn't want to talk about it, though, and I didn't want to pry.' She said softly, 'Fliss taught me to respect other people's privacy because of my father. She would never discuss what had happened between them with anyone. Not even me. She simply said what I told you before: that, growing older, people often fall out of love with one another. She's always left it at that.'

Resting her hand on his arm, turning to look up at him, she said, 'I don't want to know about your past. The here and now is enough for me; knowing that you love me. What else matters?'

Smoothing back her hair, tracing her features with sensitive fingertips, he gazed at her tender young face, her gently smiling mouth. Her features were suffused with happiness, those clear blue-grey eyes of hers expressive of a love which he knew, deep down, he did not deserve and could never hope to repay. He said, 'A great deal else, I'm afraid. You see, my darling, I shouldn't have let this happen. I should have sent you away before the damage was done.'

'*Damage*? I don't understand.' She looked bewildered. 'What damage? Are you saying you lied when you told me you loved me? That it was all a pretence? A form of punishment for having made a fool of myself?'

'For God's sake, Thea. How could you even think such a thing? Do you really believe me capable of cruelty towards someone I love? Because I *do* love you! More than I have loved anyone in my life before. More than I thought possible.' Despairingly, he pulled her into his arms, holding her so tightly she could feel the trembling of his body, the drum beat of his heart close to hers; knew, by the intensity of his emotion, that what he said was true. He really did love her. Joy flooded through her, tears ran down her cheeks unchecked, sweet, cleansing tears of relief at being held by him; loved by him.

In a little while, releasing her from his arms, he said quietly, 'Please forgive me. The last thing I intended was to cause you a moment's pain or unhappiness, to damage your life in any way. If I have already done so, I shall never forgive myself for keeping you in the dark about my past. I should have told you from the beginning about – Colette.'

'Colette?' Thea stared up at him uncomprehendingly.

'Yes, the girl I married in my student days, in Paris, to whom I am still married, God help me. So now you know what I meant by damaging your life. You see, my darling, as much as I love you, we have no hope of a future together, you and I.'

Feeling as if the world had suddenly stopped turning,

thinking that if she looked out of the window at the gardens across the way she would see that the bright lilac and laburnum blossoms had withered and died within the space of an early summer afternoon, Thea said dully, 'Yes, I see.' She paused. 'Just one thing before I go: no matter what the future holds in store for us, I shall never stop loving you, wanting to be loved by you.'

Turning at the door, looking about her at the flat, she said, attempting a smile, 'Next Saturday, perhaps, I'll go by train to Newcastle, to visit a well-loved friend of ours.' She added, 'No, don't bother to come downstairs with me. I can find my own way out.'

Bunty said, 'Might as well give that cocktail dress of yours an airing, so how about a night out at the Mirimar?'

'Yes, fine,' June replied eagerly, anxious to present her new-look image in the most glamorous garment she'd ever owned, though what her mother would say if she ever clapped eyes on it, she shuddered to think.

Yesterday, recklessly perhaps, she had bundled her old clobber – pleated skirts, embroidered rayon blouses complete with Peter Pan collars, several pairs of flat-heeled shoes and a couple of catalogue summer dresses – into a bin liner, which she had taken, in her lunch hour, to a charity shop in the town centre.

'Good, that's great,' Bunty declared cheerfully. A thought occurred. 'Shall I ask Stella to come, too? An evening out would do her good; buck her up a bit.'

'Yes. She has seemed a bit down lately,' June observed, frowning. 'You don't suppose that boyfriend of hers has started his old tricks?'

'The thought had crossed my mind. If so, it's time someone put a shot in his locker,' Bunty said grimly.

'How do you mean?' June looked worried. 'You're not planning to blow him up, are you?'

'As if! No, I shall simply have a word in his shell-like.

Tell him that if he doesn't stop pestering Stella, I'll make damn certain his wife finds out what he's up to! That should take the oil out of his diesel engine.'

June knew, by the determined expression on her friend's face, that Bunty meant what she said.

In the event, Stella turned down their invitation, pleading a headache, saying she'd just taken a couple of painkillers and intended to spend the evening listening to the radio. She'd answered the door in her bathrobe, looking like death warmed up, the way she had done before she'd given Felpersham his marching orders.

When Bunty had gone, Stella lay face down on her bed, wetting the bunched-up pillows with tears of despair. It simply couldn't be true, she told herself. There must be some mistake. She couldn't be pregnant. But she knew she was. The pregnancy test she'd taken a few days ago had proved positive. She was carrying Brian's child.

What to do about it, she hadn't decided. In a state of shock, she couldn't think clearly. Her mind in turmoil, the options open to women in her situation seemed equally odious – abortion, adoption, or, worst of all, single parenthood, struggling to make ends meet, tied hand and foot to a child she didn't want.

One thought emerged from her muddled thought processes. Brian must shoulder the financial responsibility towards her. An abortion at a good private clinic would cost money. Money she hadn't got.

Eventually, when the painkillers she'd taken had lifted her throbbing headache to some extent, she realised that abortion was the only option open to her in her present predicament. No way was she prepared to carry the child full term, to end up in some council flat or bed-and-breakfast accommodation, reliant, as a single parent, on minimal hand-outs from South Bay's Social Services.

First thing Monday morning, she would contact Brian; tell him she wished to see him as soon as possible. Arrange a meeting; coerce him, if necessary, into providing the financial aid she needed to abort the child he had so carelessly fathered.

At the Mirimar, Bunty saw with amusement the admiring glances shooting June's way from a clique of young executive types at the far end of the bar. 'Play your cards right, and you could end up on the back seat of a taxi,' she said teasingly.

June looked stricken. 'Don't you dare leave me alone with one of that lot,' she hissed. 'They're not my type at all! I wouldn't have a clue what to say.'

'How about, "Are your intentions honourable?" Though I'm pretty sure they wouldn't be. Not with you in that dress!' Bunty chuckled, sipping her dry martini. 'So what *is* your type, exactly?'

June said, sotto voce, 'That boy sitting alone at the corner table looks rather nice. The one with the glasses.'

'Huh? You mean that bloke with the elbow patches on his jacket and the long hairdo? Strewth, he's probably a student without a mobile phone to his name. The kind who probably prefers girls in pleated skirts and flat-heeled shoes anyway!'

'Yes, I know. That's why I like him.' June sighed deeply. 'He looks nice and ordinary, just like me.'

'Now see here, my girl, there's nothing in the least ordinary about the way you look tonight, thanks to me,' Bunty reminded her. 'Are you telling me I've gone to so much trouble for nothing? Here you are, looking like a million dollars, attractive young blokes fairly drooling over you, and all you can do is make sheep's eyes at a drop-out in horn-rimmed glasses!'

'I don't care about the way I *look*! It's how I *feel* that matters,' June protested. 'Right here and now I feel *common*!'

'Hey, come on, love, I was only teasing,' Bunty assured

her, wishing she'd kept her mouth shut. 'You couldn't look common if you tried. You look drop-dead gorgeous. A fact that "Jack Horner" has already registered, if I'm not mistaken.'

She smiled mischievously. 'Wanna bet he'll sidle up to the bar any moment now, offer to buy us a drink, and the pair of you will end up, not on the back seat of a taxi, but walking, hand in hand, by the light of the silvery moon!'

'Do you really think so?' June asked uncertainly, wishing she hadn't dumped her old clothes so unceremoniously at that charity shop in the town square. The kind of clothes she felt at home in, which best suited, she imagined, her lacklustre personality.

'Sshhh,' Bunty whispered intently as blue spotlights hit the grand piano and the pianist, dressed all in black, taking his place at the keyboard, began playing the theme tune from *The Way We Were*. He smiled faintly in recognition of the spontaneous ripple of applause greeting the opening bars of the music.

No wonder Thea had fallen in love with the man, Bunty thought wistfully. He was – magnificent. All male: charismatic, with a finely honed body and a remarkably handsome – if careworn – face beneath a mane of hair that was greying slightly at the temples, brushed back from a high, intelligent forehead. A man whose hands on the keyboard of a grand piano held his audience enthralled.

A girl without a jealous bone in her body, she thought how perfectly matched, in looks, he and Thea were. Both were tall and slender, he handsome, Thea beautiful. Not pretty, but beautiful, with that abundant shining brown hair of hers, clear complexion and warm, outgoing personality.

The pianist, she reckoned, needed a girl like Thea to break through his barrier of reserve, to bring a smile to his lips, to lift the air of reserve about him, the innate sadness somehow reflected in the tune he was playing.

Memories! Bunty recalled the words, 'What's too painful

to remember, we simply choose to forget.' The way that she was trying hard to forget painful memories of her ex-boyfriend who had married someone else. Her own fault entirely, she realised, thinking that she might have been the one in that wedding photograph if she hadn't been so pig-headed and choosy when he'd asked her to marry him. She'd turned him down flat in the mistaken belief that someone better would come along. But no one had.

For the first time, Bunty admitted to herself that she was lonely, living on the periphery of other people's lives.

Fourteen

On Monday, unable to contact Brian by phone, Stella went to his office in her lunch hour. There she encountered his secretary, a tall blonde girl who told her that Mr Felpersham had gone out.

'Then why is his car on the forecourt?' Stella tapped her foot impatiently. 'I know he's in, and I intend seeing him. Don't bother to announce me; I want to surprise him!'

'Hey, hang on, you can't go in there,' the girl called out to her, but Stella was already in.

'Hello, Brian,' she said sarcastically. 'Don't bother to get up. What I have to say won't take long.' She paused. 'I'm pregnant. You are the father, and I want to know what you are going to do about it.'

'My God, keep your voice down, can't you? Coming in here, shouting the odds. Well, I won't stand for it! Now go on, clear off before I call the police; have you arrested for trespass!'

'I shouldn't bother with the police if I were you. Why not call your wife? Or shall I do it for you?'

Felpersham muttered hoarsely, 'That's blackmail! What the hell do you want?'

'I want money for an abortion. Unless you'd prefer me to keep the child and name you as the father.' She was speaking recklessly and she knew it, deriving grim satisfaction from the fact that he had begun to sweat profusely; beads of perspiration were gathering on his forehead. Filled with contempt for the man's cowardice, she continued, 'It's make your mind up time, Brian!'

'Why, you rotten little tart,' he flung at her. 'Coming here, accusing me, without a shred of proof. Tell me, Stella, how many men have you slept with since I gave you the brush-off?'

'None, as it happens! As for proof, there's such a thing as DNA testing these days, in case you hadn't heard. A bit of a long-drawn-out, messy procedure, I imagine, of interest to the gutter press in particular. Not that I'm interested in spinning out this sordid little drama. I want rid of your child as much as I wanted rid of you.'

Stella knew she had won when, with a muttered curse, Brian got out his cheque book and pen, 'All right. How much?' he snarled.

Strangely enough, quitting his office, his cheque safely stowed away in her shoulder bag, Stella felt no sense of elation. She felt – cheap, sullied, unclean.

Thea had never been to Newcastle before, but she liked what she saw. The Tyne with its many bridges, and the river traffic butting through greyish water, reminded her of the Thames, though not so wide or handsome. Even so, there was a feeling of vitality about the town, despite the steadily pouring rain.

Truth to tell, she liked rain, the cleansing feel of it, the sound of it plopping on her umbrella, the sight of it scurrying the gutters. If only she could paint rain as consummately as John Atkinson Grimshaw had painted moonlight.

With a tug of pain in the region of her heart, she remembered that she was here to renew her acquaintance with *Liverpool from Wapping*. It was a necessary step in the wake of an abortive love affair, if only to prove to herself that she remained a person in her own right, responsible for her own actions, capable of facing the inevitability of a love affair that had ended before it had fairly begun, when Ross had spoken briefly of Colette, had told her that, despite his love for herself, there was no hope of a future together.

Ross would never know what it had cost her to walk away from him that day, too hurt and bewildered to stay. Too proud to question him about Colette, registering only the fact that he was married, remembering her mother's past advice to respect other people's privacy, she had made no attempt to plead with him, to beg him to reconsider. To what purpose? Nothing she could have done or said would alter the fact that he was another woman's husband.

Hazily she recalled walking away from him, her head held high, to the theatre box office, to book a ticket for the evening performance of *What Every Woman Knows*. Despite her heartbreak, she was, after all, her mother's daughter.

The week before that had come the shocking news that Philip had left home. She remembered his words, that he had taken the coward's way out of a no-win situation. She, apparently, had done the same thing.

But what other choice had she? A love affair with a married man was a no-win situation if ever there was one, Thea had realised, every bit as devastating as the ending of a long-standing marriage must have been for Philip Gregory.

Finding a snack bar, she shook the rain from her umbrella and stepped across the threshold. She pushed a fibre tray along the rail fronting the counter, choosing a jacket potato with tuna and cucumber and a cafetière of coffee. Seated at a table near a rain-washed window overlooking a busy main thoroughfare, Thea wondered how she would feel paying homage to *Liverpool from Wapping*.

Inevitably, she realised, memories would flood back to her of the first time she had seen the painting in the South Bay gallery. Memories of the man she loved standing beside her; the sheer delight of his company; his quiet charm and erudition as they had talked together across a table in the cafeteria, and she had confided in him her hopes for the future, her indecision over taking up art or design as a career.

She had at least reached a decision regarding her future and, come September, she would return to London to begin her studies. Some day South Bay, the boutique, the Villa Marina, the Mirimar, the pianist, would all be behind her. The memories of her brief sojourn in a little seaside town she had come to love would be blurred by the passage of time.

Perhaps one fine day, when she was older and wiser, she would forget the pianist, the two old ladies, Abigail and Violet, her friends Bunty, Stella, June and Philip Gregory, in pursuit of success in her chosen career. Except that she would never wish to forget, even if she could, any one of the people whose lives had somehow become inextricably entwined with hers, for better or worse. Fliss had never forgotten Charles Bellamy, the man she had loved and would go on loving to the end of her days. So would Thea go on loving Ross Drummond, even if they were destined never to meet again.

The rain had eased a little when she entered the art gallery. At the custodian's request, she left her umbrella in charge of a cloakroom attendant before making her way to the John Atkinson Grimshaw collection in an upstairs room.

The picture she had come to see caught her eye immediately, but there were other paintings by Grimshaw also on display, canvases never seen by her before except in photographs at the London College of Art. Wonderful paintings of moonlight on water, on cobblestones and rooftops. Enchanted, Thea wandered about the room, pausing to fill her senses with the magic of the Master of Moonlight, thinking that if ever she became rich, she would part with every last penny she owned to possess an original painting, however small, by an artist whose genius surpassed all the rest.

Keeping the best till last, tears filled her eyes as she gazed at *Liverpool from Wapping*, remembering the first time she had seen it, wishing she could turn back the hands of time to the day when, stepping back a pace, she had literally bumped into the man she loved. But nothing in earth or heaven came as it came before. Magic moments in life could never be reprised or relived, except in memory.

Turning away from the painting, eyes blurred with tears, she dimly discerned the figure of a man standing close behind her. A tall man who, stepping forward, clasped her hands in his and said quietly, 'I knew I'd find you here.'

'Ross?' Thea stared at him disbelievingly. 'But *why*?'

'Because I love you,' he said simply. 'Because, however short the time left to us, I want to spend that time with you.'

'And when September has come and gone, what then?' Thea asked bleakly. 'Shall we go our separate ways, never to see each other again?'

'I can't answer that question. There are so many imponderables.'

'But you will be going back to your wife?'

'Not in the way you imagine,' he said gently. 'I shall return to Paris to be near her, to visit her whenever possible, depending on whether or not she wishes to see me, or if it is expedient to do so. I have to check with the – the authorities – first.'

He paused. 'You see, Colette has been confined in the psychiatric wing of a hospital for several years now; kept under constant surveillance for her own safety.'

'Oh, dear God! I'm so sorry.' Thea's tears brimmed over. 'If only I'd known!'

'You mustn't blame yourself,' Ross said wearily. 'I should have told you the truth from the beginning. But old habits are hard to break. I've never spoken of this to anyone before. It's just something I've had to live with in my own way, all these years.'

'Shall we go home now?' Thea asked gently.

Ross nodded, holding her hand. 'Yes, let's.' Turning on

the threshold of the room, looking back at *Liverpool from Wapping*, he said, 'The magic never fails.'

Knowing exactly what he meant, entwining her fingers in his, smiling, Thea said, 'Pray God, it never will.'

Fifteen

They took a taxi from the station to Ross's flat. The time was seven o'clock, which allowed him an hour to shower, shave and change, and walk to the Mirimar for his stint at the piano. 'I wish I didn't have to go out again,' he said, drawing her into his arms. 'I hate the thought of leaving you on your own.'

'Don't worry about me.' She smiled. 'While you're getting ready, I'll rustle up some sandwiches and coffee, shall I?'

'What a wonderful idea! Thanks, darling. Shan't be long.'

Pottering happily in the kitchen, she heard him whistling softly in the bathroom next door; caught the scent of citrus soap, heard the swish of the shower curtain on its rail. She imagined the lean strength of his naked body emerging from the shower, the mirror above the washbasin clouded with steam, Ross rubbing it clear to begin the shaving ritual, and remembered the many times when, as a little girl, she had peeped round the bathroom door to watch her father shaving. She clearly recalled how she had giggled when he'd dotted the end of her nose with foam.

Making the sandwiches and coffee, she heard the opening of the bedroom door as Ross went in to put on his 'working clothes'. She wondered whether he did his own laundry, ironed his evening dress shirts, cooked his supper when he came home from the Mirimar, realising, as she carried the tray to the sitting room, how little she really knew about his lifestyle, his likes and dislikes.

His living quarters gave little away apart from his passion for neatness and order by its lack of clutter or of extraneous objects such as ornaments, photographs, flowers and pot plants. It was as if he had deliberately shut himself away from the fripperies of existence apart from books, music, and lamplight, witness a well-filled bookcase on the far side of the room, a hi-fi system and piles of records near one of the two armchairs flanking the fireplace, and two attractive green-shaded lamps, one on the occasional table near the chair opposite, the other on the bookcase.

She had just set down the tray on the coffee table occupying the space between the armchairs when Ross entered the room, dressed all in black, wearing not his usual evening dress regalia but a lightweight black polo-neck sweater, his hair still damp from the shower.

'What do you think? Will I pass muster?' he asked.

'You look—' About to say 'wonderful', she changed her mind and said, 'You look fine. Very smart indeed.' Pouring the coffee, she hoped he wouldn't notice the slight trembling of her hands.

'These sandwiches taste good,' he said. 'Thanks, darling. I'm not used to being spoiled. It's something I could get used to, given the chance.'

Glancing at his watch, he remarked, 'Lord, is that the time?' He rose quickly to his feet. 'A quarter to eight! Mustn't keep the punters waiting, I suppose, for their nightly dose of nostalgia.' He added, 'I've a damn good mind to ring up, cancel tonight's performance! I want to be here with you, Thea, not at the Mirimar.'

'You'll do no such thing,' she said calmly. Making up her mind in an instant, she offered, 'I'll wait up for you, if you like, cook you a bite of supper, an omelette or whatever. Then you can walk me back to the Villa Marina, if you're not too tired.'

'But I shan't be home till around midnight,' Ross reminded her. 'Are you sure you won't mind being left here alone for the next four hours?'

'Not at all,' Thea assured him, 'granted permission to make use of your bathroom, to "wash away the cares of the day", so to speak! The fact is, I am feeling a bit grubby after the train journey.'

'Permission granted,' Ross said tenderly, bending down to kiss her upturned face, first her forehead, then her cheeks, finally her lips. Then, on the threshold of the room, turning back for an instant before hurrying downstairs, he blew her a kiss, as light as thistledown, which she pretended to catch, as a wayward butterfly, in the palms of her hands.

When he had gone, Thea first washed up the contents of the tray in the kitchen. Then, going to the bathroom and stripping off her clothes, she stood naked beneath the shower, revelling in the benison of the hot water laving her slender young body, wanting to be clean and fresh for Ross when he returned to her at midnight.

Stepping from the shower, she discovered a quantity of towels in the airing cupboard, one of which she wound turban-wise about her wet hair, another of which she wore as a sarong as she padded to the living room to choose Beethoven's 'Moonlight Sonata' from the pile of records stacked beside the hi-fi system.

Listening to the music intently, she wondered if this time, this place, this love affair with a man she scarcely knew was nothing more than a moonlit dream, lacking in substance or reality, as fleeting as moonlight, as ethereal as starshine.

She wanted Ross with every fibre of her being, but at what cost to her pride and self-respect? Taking another woman's husband as surely as Carol Lindsay had robbed she and Fliss of a husband and father would be every bit as mean and despicable, even more so in view of Colette's mental illness.

Colette! Impossible to imagine what she looked like. Was

she dark or fair? What had caused her mental breakdown? Was Ross still in love with her? Had she borne him a child – children? Had he a home in or near Paris? A wintertime occupation? And who, apart from the hospital nurses and doctors, cared for Colette when Ross was in South Bay? Had she relatives, friends, who visited her in his absence?

The flat was compact but not cramped. Doors led from the main room to the well-equipped kitchen and bathroom and Ross's bedroom, so far unseen. Tempted to open the door, Thea put the urge behind her, not wanting to pry. Instead, returning to the bathroom, she dressed quickly and gathered together the damp towels, which she bundled into the washing machine. Then, having dressed, she opened the fridge and took from it a bowl of eggs, a slab of butter and a punnet of mushrooms in readiness for the omelette she had promised to cook for Ross's supper.

Nervously, she awaited his homecoming, his key in the lock of the street door, his footsteps on the stairs, his presence in the room, the moment she would hurry into his arms to be held by him, kissed by him . . . and yet by what right? He belonged to another woman, not herself, but Colette.

She had set the kitchen table in readiness for supper. When he came home, she was standing at the cooker, her back to him, melting butter in an omelette pan. She said lightly, not daring to look at him, 'Supper is almost ready.'

He said, 'I was afraid of this, that you'd have second thoughts. I'm right, aren't I? Oh God, I should have stayed with you, told you the whole story, not left you alone to put two and two together and come to the wrong conclusion.'

'About you and – Colette?'

'Of course. Who else?' His face a mask of pain, of utter weariness, he said, 'We need to talk, to get things straight between us. Switch off the cooker, and come with me. I'm taking you home, Thea, back to the Villa Marina.'

'But I—'

He pressed a fingertip to her lips. 'Please do as I ask. I have my reasons.'

They walked along the seafront. It was a lovely night, fresh and clear after the rain, the sky pinpricked with stars. Ross had placed a hand in the crook of her elbow. Even so, Thea was conscious of the tension between them, the weight of unspoken words which, once uttered, might irretrievably alter their delicately balanced relationship. When Colette emerged from the shadows as a flesh and blood person, not as a pathetic, mentally ill woman confined to the psychiatric unit of a faraway hospital, but as Ross's wife, she would become a force to be reckoned with.

Sick at heart, Thea acknowledged inwardly her jealousy of the woman Ross had loved enough to marry in the dim and distant past. And perhaps it were better if that past remained a secret?

Ross said quietly, 'In here,' leading her towards a shelter overlooking the sea, a Victorian shelter massed about with burgeoning fronds of wisteria, clematis and rambling roses. 'Please sit down, darling, and listen. What I'm about to tell you is the truth, the whole truth, and nothing but the truth, in the well-worn words of the British judiciary system.'

He smiled grimly. 'The French system of justice is somewhat different. Even so, I was called upon to utter a similar oath at the trial of my wife for the wilful murder of a two-year-old child, her son, Louis, of which crime she was found guilty and sentenced to life imprisonment in a jail on the outskirts of Paris in which, God help her, she still remains.'

He continued, clasping Thea's hand, 'Louis was not my son. Colette was already pregnant when we met. I was a penniless student at the time, she a pitiful, half-starved creature crazy with grief that the man she loved had gone away, leaving no address.

'She had come to Paris to find him, to tell him about the

baby. I had two rooms on the top floor of students' lodgings on the Left Bank. Colette came into the bistro where we students would gather most evenings for a cheap meal and a couple of beers. I could see she was faint from hunger so I bought her a bowl of soup, some bread and cheese.

'Afterwards, I took her to my lodgings. The poor kid had nowhere else to go, so I took pity on her. She was in a terrible state, in need of a good night's sleep, so I gave her my bed and slept on the sofa in the other room. Except that I didn't sleep, thank God, otherwise she'd have died that night.'

He brushed a hand across his forehead. 'In the early hours, I heard the opening of the bedroom window, a window overlooking a stone parapet and the courtyard below. Realising something was wrong, I went to the bedroom to find the bed empty. Colette was standing on the parapet staring down at the courtyard, plucking up her courage to jump.

'I haven't a doubt that she would have done so if I hadn't been there to prevent her. Don't ask me how. It all happened so quickly I scarcely remember climbing out of that window. All I clearly remember is the way she fought and struggled as I caught hold of her and dragged her back into the room.'

'Please don't go on, Ross, if you'd rather not,' Thea said compassionately, laying a hand on his arm. 'I think I understand now why you – fell in love with one another. Why you married Colette.'

Ross shook his head. He said impatiently, 'It wasn't like that at all. I married Colette to legitimise the child she was carrying, to make possible her return home to her family. I didn't love her. She certainly did not love me. The marriage was never consummated. She was, and always has been, my wife in name only. The only woman I've ever loved in my life is – you.'

Standing up, offering his hand, he said, 'We'd better go now. It's getting late and you have to be up in time for work.

The rest of the story can wait.' They walked the rest of the way in silence.

At the steps of the Villa Marina, cupping Thea's face in his hands, Ross said, 'I told you I had my reasons for wanting to bring you home tonight. You see, darling, had you stayed a moment longer at the flat, I would have wanted to make love to you, and I believe you would have spent the night with me had I begged you to stay.

'You know how much I love you, far too much to have risked a far deeper, more intimate relationship before you were ready. You must be the one to decide if and when it happens. You understand?'

'Yes, I understand,' Thea said bleakly. Then, turning away from him, she ran up the steps to the front door, not looking back, not wanting to see his tall figure striding away towards the starlit esplanade.

Sundays were becoming increasingly busy at the boutique, for which Thea was more than grateful. Serving customers, restocking shelves, disrobing and rerobing the wicker dummies, taking cash and giving change took her mind off her own troubles for a while. Yet Ross lay at the back of her mind no matter how hard she tried not to think of the strange events of yesterday: the train journey to Newcastle, the art gallery, their return to Ross's flat, the interlude in the shelter and their leave-taking when he had said it was up to her to decide whether or not she wished to become his lover.

No wonder she had scarcely slept last night, playing tug-of-war with her conscience, getting up in the middle of the night to look out at the town lights clustered about the harbour, imagining what would have happened if Ross had begged her to stay with him. Of course she knew. Inevitably they would have slept together. But, she reminded herself over and over again, he was a married man. How would she have felt in the cold light of morning knowing she had flouted the rules of decent human behaviour?

At the boutique, having served a contingency of day trippers with scarves, jewellery, sun-tops, Bellino blouses and sun-tan lotion, she took advantage of a brief lull between their departure and the next influx to replenish the stock. When the doorbell pinged, she turned to see a woman whose face seemed familiar to her standing on the threshold.

'May I help you?' Thea asked politely. 'Or would you prefer to browse?'

The woman said coldly, 'It's you I came to see. I am Ruth Gregory. In case you've forgotten, my husband and I were at the Mirimar, the other evening. When you appeared on the scene, he left me to talk to *you*!

'Tell me, Miss Bellamy, how long has the affair between you and my husband been going on? You know that he has left me, I suppose? I hold you responsible for that. Well, don't bother to deny it! I want the truth! How long *has* the affair been going on?'

Thea stared at the woman disbelievingly. '*What* affair?' she asked, with an upsurge of anger. 'I like and respect your husband enormously, but your suggestion of an affair between us is utter rubbish! How dare you come here to accuse me of a figment of your warped imagination?

'I know, of course, that Philip left you. I'm beginning to understand why. Just you listen to me, Mrs Gregory, I took this job as a stop-gap! Come September, I'll be leaving South Bay to pursue my career as a set designer. I certainly shan't be running off with your husband, if that's what's on your mind! Now, if you'll excuse me, I have work to do, a living to earn – not, I assure you, as your husband's mistress, but as the manager of his boutique!'

The encounter left a sour taste on Thea's tongue. Serving the next influx of customers after Ruth Gregory's departure, at the back of her mind lay the thought, why wait till September? Why not pack her belongings and return to London, to Fliss, tomorrow or the day after? But she knew she could not.

How could she turn her back on the man she loved? Her friends, Bunty, Stella and June? How could she desert the two old ladies next door, at a crisis point in their lives, with Violet's son on the verge of taking control of their finances and putting their home on the market? How could she let him whisk Violet away to Norfolk and condemn his proud, feisty Aunt Abigail to an old people's home here in South Bay?

How could she possibly stand by, doing and saying nothing to prevent this happening? But what, if anything, could she do – unless . . . ? An idea occurred to her, a crazy idea perhaps, but worth a try. Any idea, however crazy, was worth a try in a crisis. In this instance, to prevent the separation of two old ladies who lived for one another, who, robbed of each other's company in the twilight of their years, might not want to go on living.

Returning to the Villa Marina that Sunday evening, her mind in a turmoil, physically and emotionally exhausted by the many dilemmas confronting her, the last thing Thea had envisaged was yet another problem to add to the list.

She had just made herself a cup of strong black coffee and sunk down in a chair near the window to drink it when a knock came at the door.

'Come in,' she called out wearily, 'it's not locked.'

Stella entered the room, looking distraught. 'I'm sorry, Thea,' she blurted, 'but I really need to talk to you! I'm in such a hell of a mess, I don't know which way to turn! I'm pregnant, you see? Planning an abortion, but frankly, I'm scared stiff. I thought I wouldn't care tuppence about condemning a child to death, but I do. At least I *think* I do, but how can I be sure? If only I had more time to think about it.'

'Then you should *make* time,' Thea said, appalled by the news. 'Take a few days off work, go somewhere quiet – a place in the country, perhaps? There must be plenty of country hotels, not too far away, where you could stay to think things over. Preferably somewhere off the beaten track. Or possibly a retreat? You know the kind I mean. A spiritual sanctuary?'

'What? A – *nunnery*? You must be joking,' Stella uttered scornfully. 'I'd feel like a fish out of water!'

'It was only a suggestion, but I do think you should think things over from every angle before taking a step you might live to regret.'

Stella bit her lip. 'Yes, you're right,' she admitted. 'Sorry I snapped your head off. I just feel so rotten, so disgusted with myself. You were the only one I could turn to. Brian didn't want to know.'

'What about your family? The aunt you told me about?'

'She'd throw up her hands in horror. Tell me I should be ashamed of myself. Well I *am* ashamed, so I don't need her to rub it in.'

Getting up, she said, 'You won't tell anyone else, will you? I'll just take a few days off work; tell Bunty and June I'm going to stay with a friend in the country. They probably won't believe me, or if they do they'll assume I'm having another affair!'

Sixteen

Hester Hastings, thin, shrewish, dark-haired, sporting a mannish hairstyle and outsize gilt earrings, as if to establish some claim to femininity despite the severely tailored black trouser suit she had on, had made it abundantly clear to her husband that the sooner the 'South Bay business' was concluded, the better it would be for all concerned.

Not that she was looking forward to being lumbered with her mother-in-law for the foreseeable future. What Hester cared about most, however, was the financial aspect involved when the Laurels was sold and Violet's half-share from the sale of the property was safely tucked away in her own and her husband's joint bank account.

Today was the first Saturday that she and Peter had had a chance to travel up from Norfolk. They had set off at the crack of dawn with a view to arriving in South Bay mid-morning for a pre-arranged meeting with the estate agent who, acting on their behalf, would come up with an accurate appraisal of the value of the property, despite its present state of disrepair. More positively, its worth as a house in a prime position overlooking the whole of South Bay.

Drawing up the car near the steps of the Laurels, Peter Hastings noticed immediately the tidiness of the front garden. The straggling laurel bushes had been neatly clipped and the wilderness of weeds, groundsel, nettles, convolvulus and willowherb had been dug up and replaced with salvias, pansies and antirrhinums.

'That's odd,' he commented, frowning, lingering to stare at the garden.

'Oh for God's sake, Peter, get a move on. We haven't got all day!' Hester said irritably. 'The sooner we get this visit over and done with, the better!'

With a hurried glance at her wristwatch, she continued, 'The time is now eleven fifteen. So where's the estate agent? He said he'd be here to meet us between eleven and half-past!'

'Perhaps he's waiting for us indoors,' Peter suggested unhappily.

'Then why not ring the doorbell and find out?' Hester flung back at him.

Obediently, Peter did as he was told, wishing devoutly that his wife looked and behaved more like a stereotypical woman than a man. Romantically inclined, he possessed a penchant for long-haired women.

Seconds later, to his amazement, he found himself gazing at a slender, long-haired young woman who smiled and said, 'You must be Mr Hastings. My name is Thea Bellamy. I volunteered to answer the bell. The others are having coffee in the parlour. Please, do come in.'

Pushing her way forward, Hester snapped, 'Just who do you think you are? We scarcely need a stranger to invite us into our own property!'

'No, of course not. I'm sorry,' Thea said. 'I'll leave you to find your own way, then. I'll just go through to the kitchen and make more coffee. I'm sure you could do with a cup after your journey?'

'Thanks very much,' Peter muttered suspiciously. 'Er, what "others", by the way?'

'Oh, Mrs Hastings and Miss Ashcroft, a Mr Slade from the estate agents, and Mr Bill Cumberland.'

'*Bill Cumberland*?' Hester butted in rudely. 'Who's he when he's at home? And what the hell is he doing here, I should like to know!'

'I'm sure you'll find out in due course. Now, if you'll excuse me, I'll make a fresh pot of coffee.'

Seeking sanctuary in the kitchen, Thea refilled the kettle and put it on an ancient gas jet to boil. Oh God, she thought guiltily, what if she had gone too far, meddling in other folks' business the way she had done? On the other hand, there was no way she could have stood by doing nothing to prevent the separation of two old ladies who virtually lived for one another. And so she had turned to Mr Cumberland for help.

She remembered feeling nervous, a little out of her depth that Sunday evening she'd gone down to Bill Cumberland's private quarters to say – what, exactly? She scarcely knew what. She would have to play it by ear.

He'd seemed surprised to see her standing there outside the door leading to his ground-floor apartment. Surprised but not, apparently, displeased.

'May I have a word?' she'd asked, feeling foolish. 'I could come back later, if you're busy.'

'No, not at all. Come in, Thea.' He led the way to his bay-windowed sitting room overlooking the promenade. 'Sit down. What's on your mind?'

'It's the house next door,' she said bluntly, not beating about the bush. 'It's coming up for sale soon, and I think you should buy it.'

Intrigued, Bill frowned slightly, pouring out and handing his visitor a glass of sherry. 'And here was I thinking you'd come to complain about the plumbing!' He paused, then, sitting down in the armchair opposite, 'Right then, fire away. Give me one good reason why I should even consider buying a broken-down property like the Laurels!'

'For that very reason. Because, the state it's in, it will probably go for a song,' Thea said earnestly, putting down her glass of sherry before she spilt it. 'Think of the extra space it would provide as an annexe to the Villa Marina, for instance. Or the profit from a block of self-contained flats.'

Bill Cumberland regarded her thoughtfully. 'Fair enough,' he conceded. 'What you say may be true. What puzzles me is your interest in the matter. What's the snag? There must be one! I wasn't born yesterday. So hadn't you best come clean? Tell me what's really on your mind?'

'Very well, then. It has to do with the present occupants of the Laurels, Miss Ashcroft and her sister, Mrs Hastings. I just can't bear to think of them being separated, that's all! Oh, I know it sounds crazy, and it's really none of my business, but they surely will be parted if Mrs Hastings' son has his way. You see, the property is jointly owned by the pair of them, and when the house is sold, Peter Hastings intends to demand his mother's share of the proceeds, take her to Norfolk to live in sheltered accommodation; and put his Aunt Abigail into an old people's home here in South Bay.'

'Does he, by God,' Bill Cumberland said grimly. 'So what you're really saying is that I should buy the Laurels, stump up Mr Hastings' half-share of the sale price, and allow the two old ladies to go on living together in part of the building? Am I right?'

'Well, yes,' Thea admitted, biting her bottom lip, close to tears. 'I just happen to think they wouldn't live for very much longer, robbed of their home and one another's company, after all the years they've been together.'

Mr Cumberland said levelly, 'So you have appointed yourself their guardian angel? Very commendable of you, I'm sure. And you wish me to take up the cudgel on their behalf, and yours? May I ask, why me?'

Thea said simply, 'Because you are the only person likely to be interested in the Laurels as a business proposition. If I'm wrong, I'm sorry. Perhaps I shouldn't have come, so if you'll excuse me, I'd best be getting back to my room.'

Switching on the table lamps as evening shadows invaded the room, Bill said, 'No, don't go just yet! Sit and tell me more about Mrs Hastings' son, Peter. Why, precisely, should he anticipate a half-share of his mother's property during her lifetime?'

He frowned. 'In my experience, most beneficiaries are called upon to wait until the reading of the last will and testament of the dear departed to claim their inheritance. Now, and this is very important, to the best of your knowledge and belief, has Mrs Hastings signed legal documents, relevant to the sale of the Laurels, appointing to him her half-share in the property prior to her death?'

'No – at least, I don't think so,' Thea replied thoughtfully. 'You see, Mr Cumberland, Violet Hastings is just a confused old lady torn between loyalty to her son and her lifelong devotion towards her sister.'

'Yeah, I get the picture.' Mr Cumberland smiled briefly. 'A case of coercion, of emotional blackmail, I suspect; that of a greedy son intent on claiming his inheritance during his mother's lifetime. Well, Mr Peter Hastings might well be in for a shock if I decide to put in a bid for the Laurels – and if my offer is accepted, it will be on my terms, not his.'

'You mean . . . ? Oh, Mr Cumberland, how will I ever thank you!'

'Now hang on a minute, young lady. I make no promises apart from looking into the matter more fully. Meanwhile, I want you to have a word with the two old ladies; make certain there is no binding legal agreement re the half-share nonsense between Mr Hastings and his mother. Get Mrs Hastings to consult a good solicitor as a matter of urgency, with a view to making a will, ensuring that her son shall receive his share of the money after, not prior to her death.'

Thea said, 'I'll try, but it won't be easy. You see she's already been brainwashed into believing that her son has her best interests at heart in taking her to Norfolk to live closer to himself and his family. And blood *is* thicker than water.'

Bill Cumberland nodded sympathetically. 'I know. Old folk can be difficult to handle, at times. On the other hand, she may well be open to gentle persuasion when she realises that by the simple expedient of drawing up her will in the way I've suggested, she and her sister will likely remain together for the foreseeable future.'

'I can't thank you enough, Mr Cumberland,' Thea said mistily. She added, rising gracefully to her feet, 'Now it really is time for me to leave. It's been a long day, and I could fall asleep on a clothes line!'

Escorting her to the door, Mr Cumberland said, 'It's I who should thank you for coming here tonight. Not only have you managed to alert me to a worthwhile business proposition, more importantly, you have taught a self-centred man a much-needed lesson in concern for the plight of individuals in need of help. So goodnight, Thea. Sleep well!'

It hadn't been easy to speak to Violet and Abigail on so delicate a matter as family relationships. Thea had spent long hours wondering how best to broach the subject. In the end she had decided to say what must be said simply and straightforwardly, laying all the cards on the table and leaving the old ladies to reach their own decision.

Pushing her own problems to the back of her mind for the time being, she had centred her thoughts on the more immediate problem confronting her, finding an unexpected ally in Abigail whose mind was far sharper and less muddled than that of her sister.

In the long run, it was Abigail who had talked Violet into making a will bequeathing her half-share of the Laurels to her son after, not prior to her demise. It was Abigail who, taking the reins in her capable hands, had visited Mr Cumberland to clarify the situation regarding his intentions.

Calling Thea into his office one evening when she returned from the boutique, Bill told her about his confrontation with the formidable Miss Ashcroft.

'I felt like a naughty schoolboy caught hiding a mouse

in his desk,' he admitted, 'when she marched in, for all the world like a headmistress in charge of a modern version of Dickens' Dotheboys Hall! But you know what? When I'd stopped being scared of her, I liked her enormously. What's more, I think she liked me. Actually, we got on like a house afire once we'd got down to the nitty-gritty of the business in hand.'

'Then what happened?' Thea asked anxiously.

'She gave me the go-ahead to make a bid for the Laurels,' Bill said cheerfully. 'A piece of cake, really, once we had got our act together, when I knew for certain that Mrs Hastings had made a will, and my bid for the Laurels would meet with her sister's and her approval.'

Now, making a pot of fresh coffee, Thea wondered how Peter Hastings and his wife would accept the news that their journey to South Bay had been in vain, and winced slightly on hearing Hester Hastings' voice raised in altercation. Deciding that discretion might be the better part of valour in face of the sounds of verbal battle from the front room, she stayed in the kitchen while the main protagonists carried on their slanging match in the hallway near the front door.

Hester screeched, 'Mark my words, you haven't heard the last of this! Coercing a dotty old woman into changing her will, offering peanuts for a house this size in a prime position on the seafront. Well, we'll see what our solicitor has to say about it! We'll get a restraining order, a magistrate, a psychiatrist to prove the old girl was out of her mind when she made that will!'

Thea guessed that the diatribe was directed at Bill Cumberland. A quick glance round the kitchen door proved her assumption to be correct. Bill was absorbing the shocks like the Rock of Gibraltar, in no way perturbed, allowing the vitriolic flow to wash over him like bathwater. Peter Hastings was simply standing there, like a spare bridegroom at a wedding, letting his wife have all the say. Not that he could have got a word in edgeways, even if he'd tried. Thea felt almost sorry for the man, married to a harpy like Hester Hastings.

Suddenly the tall figure of Abigail Ashcroft appeared on the scene, her gaunt, aristocratic face framed untidily with stray wisps of iron-grey hair, eyes blazing, thumping her walking stick on the threadbare hall carpet. 'Enough of all this!' she bellowed in a voice like thunder. 'I want you, Hester, and that wretched husband of yours out of this house *now*. At once, is that perfectly clear? The person in need of a psychiatrist is yourself! Now, clear off, the pair of you, and don't come back! The Laurels has already been sold to Mr Cumberland, and there's nothing you can do about it!'

She added fiercely, 'I trust Mr Cumberland implicitly. As for you two' – she stared contemptuously at her nephew and his wife – 'I wouldn't trust you as far as I could throw you!'

Thea felt like applauding the old woman's stand as, with a muttered curse, grabbing her husband by the arm, Hester marched down the front steps to the wheel of their car, looking more like Peter's brother than his wife with her black trouser suit and mannish hairstyle.

When they had gone, with much slamming of doors, unnecessary revving up of the engine and tyres churning up the dust as the car sped away out of sight along the esplanade, Abigail called out wearily, 'Thea, are you there? If so, I'm sure we'd all appreciate a fresh cup of coffee.'

'Just coming,' Thea sang out cheerfully. Coffee pot in hand, she entered the front parlour to find poor Violet in tears. It could not have been easy for her to draw up that will in her own and her sister's favour, rather than that of her son and his family.

She said compassionately, setting down the coffee pot on a side table, 'If you'll allow me, Miss Violet, I'll take you upstairs to your room, tuck you into bed and draw the curtains. You'll feel much better after a nap. And I'll bring you a boiled egg, bread-and-butter soldiers and a pot of tea afterwards. Would you like that?'

'Oh yes, indeed I should,' the old lady replied mistily. 'Just like my dear Mama used to do when I was a little girl.'

Helping Miss Violet upstairs to her room, Thea drew the curtains, took off the old lady's shoes and settled her down to sleep beneath a puffy, rose-coloured eiderdown. Thea's heart went out to her, a vulnerable old lady in need of love and understanding – along with the rest of the human race. That included not only herself, but also the man she was in love with, who was right now awaiting her decision regarding their future lives, either together or apart.

Try as hard as she might, Thea remained uncertain of the future. She was desperately afraid of reaching a wrong conclusion, of handing her life into the care and keeping of a man already committed to the upkeep and welfare of another woman. His poor, demented wife Colette.

Seventeen

Philip listened intently to Thea's account of the Laurels interlude. 'Bill Cumberland's a decent man,' he said approvingly. 'He'll take care of the old ladies just fine when the time comes. It wouldn't surprise me if he moved them into the Villa Marina, pro tem, until the alterations are complete.'

'That idea has already been mooted,' Thea said. 'Mr Cumberland mentioned the possibility after the Hastings' dramatic departure.' She smiled, pleased that things were working out well for her friends. 'Miss Abigail didn't even demur. It seems that she and Mr Cumberland have a mutual admiration "fan club" which helps enormously. Miss Abby isn't the easiest person in the world to get along with, as I discovered the day I offered her a helping hand up the front steps, when she told me in no uncertain terms that she didn't accept help from strangers!'

'But you went ahead and helped her anyway,' Philip commented drily, 'the way you have helped me here at the boutique. You've been a tower of strength, Thea, you really have, and I'm grateful, believe me.'

She brushed aside his thanks. 'I only wish I could have done more. Tell me how you're coping at the flat. Are you eating properly? Getting enough sleep? Has your wife been in contact? Have you reached a decision about your future?'

Philip smiled grimly. 'No to all four questions. I appear to be living in limbo land at the moment. Food is the last thing on my mind; I haven't had a decent night's sleep for weeks. Ruth hasn't been in touch. As for the future, what lies ahead for a man incapable of even coming to terms with the present?'

Thea's heart went out to him. She said, 'As Fliss would have it, "It's always darkest before the dawn."' Fliss, that beloved mother of hers whose wise counsel and enfolding arms Thea desperately longed for at this, her own fraught moment in time. A refuge against a world of emotional upheaval centred on her 'affair' with Ross Drummond.

Thea knew, deep down, that Fliss would never countenance cowardice. Asked for advice, she would say, 'Only you can decide how you feel about Ross, and whatever conclusion you reach, you must be honest and truthful with him. Meanwhile, go on seeing him. Talk to him. Weigh up the pros and cons and base your final decision on what seems best for all concerned.'

That evening, Bunty came to Thea's room for coffee and a chin-wag. 'Whaddayou know,' she blurted, 'Stella's just sprung it on me that she's off on a week's holiday in the country! Asked where, she wouldn't say. Sounds fishy to me! If she'd said she was off to London, I might have believed her. But a week in the country? No way! Stella hates the country! She's a townie, not a – cow-girl!'

Plumping down in an armchair, she continued, 'Know what *I* think? Stella's found herself a new boyfriend! Another married bloke, I shouldn't wonder, who daren't show his mug in a crowd for fear of being recognised. What do *you* think?'

'Quite frankly, it's none of our business,' Thea said. 'Stella's been through a rough patch recently. Possibly what she needs is a bit of peace and quiet to come to terms with the past and make decisions about the future.'

Bunty sniffed. 'You're right. Sorry. Me and my big mouth! I guess, living on the same landing, with nothing much going for myself at the moment, I tend to get involved too deeply in other folks' lives.' She grinned. 'It's what's known as "living vicariously".'

'I can't think why,' Thea frowned. 'To hear you talk, anyone would think you were past your sell-by date. With your looks, you should have a list of admirers a mile long.'

'If only!' Bunty blew out her cheeks despairingly. 'One look at me, and men dive for cover. The decent types, that is. The rest of them I wouldn't touch with a bargepole.

'Huh, would you believe it?' she continued, self-deprecatingly. 'Even June has managed to find herself a boyfriend! We were in the bar of the Mirimar one Saturday night when this chap in glasses, with elbow patches on his jacket, offered to buy her a drink. Next thing I knew, they'd gone off together like Romeo and Juliet, and I was left there on my tod – as usual!'

Thea said, 'Has it occurred to you that in clinging to the memory of your ex-boyfriend you're denying yourself the right to a new romance?'

'If that meant taking aboard a long-haired student with horn-rimmed glasses and leather elbow patches on his jacket, or a smug young executive with a mobile phone, highlighted hair and a bulge the size of Ben Nevis beneath his embroidered waistcoat, you can bet your life I would,' Bunty said forcibly.

She added, tongue in cheek, 'The only man I really fancy is the pianist at the Mirimar! But he's already spoken for. More's the pity!'

Knowing that Bunty was dying to find out how her affair was progressing, Thea said, 'I haven't seen much of Ross lately. I'm working during the day, he works at night. The only time we're free to meet is Saturday, my day off.'

'Well, that's better than nothing,' Bunty said wistfully. 'Quite romantic, really. A bit like that old film, *Brief Encounter*, though Celia Johnson and Trevor Howard only ever managed to meet in that station buffet, except when they went to a cinema matinée, or for a row on the lake. Still, they managed to pack a lot into their relationship before conscience got the better of her.

'Huh, a bit daft when you come to think of it. I mean real life isn't like that, is it? Not these days anyway. Nowadays, no way would a woman stick to a boring old fart of a husband. No way would a man find himself a job in South Africa, lumbered with a delicate wife, to distance himself from the woman he loved! More than likely they'd have got divorced and gone off somewhere to start a new life together. Honestly, I can't think why I bother watching black and white British films on late-night television, with all those cut-glass accents and everyone being so boring and stiff-upper-lipped.'

So saying, Bunty got up, stretched, yawned, and declared her intention of having an early night. Turning at the door, she said sagely, 'At least you haven't got a boring old fart of a husband to worry about, and Ross isn't lumbered with an ailing wife. So take my advice, make hay while the sun shines!'

If she only knew, Thea thought despairingly, how closely her own love affair resembled that of the couple in *Brief Encounter*. Fraught, short-lived meetings not in a station buffet but in art galleries, tea-rooms and cafés, Ross's apartment, a public shelter in the early hours of one Sunday morning. Moreover he *did* have an ailing wife to contend with, in dire need of his support, and when September came, he would go back to Paris to be near Colette.

Stella saw that a great many changes had occurred in a short space of time. The broken-down veranda had been repaired and painted and the mantle of overgrown clematis had been cut back to reveal new shoots and buds apparently revelling in their new-found freedom.

Also, many of the crowded-together trees that had once cluttered the slopes of the valley had been removed to create a less claustrophobic atmosphere and to give open views from the windows of The Inn Thing.

Entering the hotel, she wondered if she had acted wisely in returning to the scene of that humiliating weekend she had spent here with Brian Felpersham. A bit like entering the eye of a hurricane, she thought, paying off the taxi driver who had driven her from the station.

It seemed ludicrous that the taxi fare had cost her more than the rail fare had done. Even more ludicrous that she had chosen to return to a place she had not merely disliked, but loathed intensely the first moment she had set eyes on it. And what on earth had possessed her to book the same suite that she and Brian had occupied a matter of a few weeks ago?

Was there a deeper reason why she had chosen to return to The Inn Thing?

Somehow, she had never been able to forget the hotel owner, Grant Edwards, who, knowing that she was not a 'lady' in the true meaning of the word, had nevertheless treated her as such. His gentlemanly behaviour towards herself and her pig-ignorant lover had fuelled in her a sense of shame that he might believe her also to be ignorant or incapable of decent feelings and behaviour.

There was no one in the reception lounge, but she could hear sounds of sawing and hammering from the kitchen region, and she had noticed vans and a contractor's lorry parked in the drive. Apparently alterations were still under way. She hoped, for Grant's sake, that the improvements would bring an increase in business when his plans came to fruition.

Leaving her luggage near the reception desk, Stella walked across to the dining room and looked inside. The tables, set for dinner, were immaculate with pristine napery, polished silverware and gleaming crystal. She was heading towards the kitchen in search of Grant Edwards when, abruptly changing her mind, she returned to the reception area and rang the bell on the desk.

Eventually, a young, flustered-looking girl appeared. 'Ever so sorry to keep you waiting,' she said. 'I were sorting out the files, leastways trying to. This ain't really my job, you see. I usually work in the kitchen, but there's workmen everywhere, fixing new units, so Mr Edwards told me to tidy the office.'

She continued nervously, ''Ave you a booking, or are you here on the off-chance?'

Stella said impatiently, 'I do have a booking, but I've changed my mind. Something important has cropped up. I must leave immediately. Please ring for a taxi. I need to get back to the railway station as quickly as possible.'

The girl – 'Rosie', according to her name tag – looked stricken. 'Sorry, miss,' she said, 'but the phone's out of order. There's a line down somewhere or other.' Trying her best to be helpful, 'I could ask Mr Edwards to ring up on his mobile. If you'll hang on a sec, I'll nip to the kitchen and ask him.'

'No, that won't be necessary,' Stella said wearily, feeling suddenly unwell, drained of energy, in need of a hot bath, food and rest. 'I'll stay the night. Leave first thing in the morning.'

'Are you all right, miss?' Rosie asked anxiously. 'You don't half look pale.'

'I'll be fine,' Stella said tautly. 'Just give me the key to my room. I can find my own way.'

'Can I get you anything? A pot of tea and a sandwich?' Rosie said concernedly. 'I could bring it up to you.'

Stella felt ashamed of her curtness. 'Thanks, that would be nice.' She smiled faintly. 'Room Fourteen. The key's on the board behind you.'

'Oh, so it is.' The girl looked relieved. She said, 'I can't quite get the hang of this job, and we ain't got a proper receptionist. Mr Edwards has interviewed lots of lasses, but they all say the same, this place is too far off the beaten track. Daft of 'em really, since there's a nice bedsit an' bathroom what goes with the job, an' the food's great.'

She added sagely, 'I live in, so I should know. Mind you, I have to share a bathroom with the chambermaid, but that don't worry me none. An' Mr Edwards is ever so nice to work for. A proper gent.'

Stella was in her bathrobe when a knock came at the door. 'Just a sec,' she called out, turning off the bath taps. Hair loose about her shoulders, face devoid of make-up, she unlocked the door, expecting to see Rosie, not Grant Edwards, holding the tea tray.

'Hello, Stella,' he said, 'it's good to see you again. Rosie said you weren't feeling too well, so I came to find out if there's anything I can do to help.'

'Thanks, but there's nothing much anyone can do for me, right now.'

'May I come in?'

'Yes, of course. Sorry, I'm not thinking very clearly at the moment.'

'A cup of tea might help,' he said, putting down the tray on a table near the fireplace and thinking how much she had changed in appearance since their last meeting, on the half-landing, when she had thanked him for the champagne and told him that she and her florid, overweight escort were not married. Not that he had believed for one moment that they were. Hardly likely that a smart, attractive young woman would have willingly saddled herself, for life, with an oaf of a man who treated her like dirt.

Pouring the tea and handing her a cup, Grant said, 'Sit down and drink this. I understand you are leaving here tomorrow morning. Frankly, I'm surprised that you even thought of returning, especially alone. May I ask why?'

Stella's face hardened. 'Without Brian Felpersham, you mean?' Sitting on the edge of the chair, slopping tea into the saucer, unaware that she had done so, she said bitterly,

'That's all over and done with. I never want to set eyes on him again for as long as I live!'

'I see.' Grant frowned slightly. 'But that doesn't answer my question. Unless, of course, you are still in love with him.'

'No, I'm not, if it's any of your damn business. I came because I was gulled into believing that I needed time to think things over. A country holiday. Somewhere off the beaten track. This was the only place I could think of.

'Oh, I know my friend meant well. She didn't want me to rush into something I might live to regret later on. But she was wrong. I know what I want, and no amount of thinking things over will change my mind. That's why I'll be leaving here tomorrow morning – to do what needs to be done!'

Grant decided to take a calculated risk. 'Have an abortion, you mean?' he said quietly, having put two and two together and drawn the obvious conclusion.

'Well, yes,' Stella admitted, deeply shocked by his plain speaking, 'but how the hell did you know? How could you possibly have guessed?'

Grant said, 'I wasn't born yesterday. There's a certain look about a pregnant woman. I've come across it many a time in my line of work – and elsewhere. Nice young girls getting pregnant, scared stiff of telling their parents, afraid of facing the music, in nine cases out of ten taking the apparently easy option of abortion, not taking time to think things through.'

'Just like me, you mean?' Stella said hoarsely, standing up to face him. 'Except that I am not "a nice young girl", am I? More of a tart, wouldn't you say? In any case, why should you care one way or the other?'

Grant pondered the question, knowing that he did care a great deal for Stella Johnson, and what became of her and the child she was carrying.

She said angrily, 'If it's money you're worried about, forget it! I'll pay for a full week's board and lodging. My ex-lover was quite generous, you see, when it came to giving me the brush-off. A cheque for a thousand pounds, no less, for the sheer pleasure of getting rid of me and his child. If that's not generous, I don't know what is!' Her voice rose hysterically. Tears poured down her cheeks.

'Stop this nonsense at once, do you hear me?' Grant said forcibly, gripping her shoulder. 'In my opinion, you should have stuffed that cheque in Felpersham's mouth and made him swallow it! I certainly don't want any part of it. So far as I'm concerned, you don't owe me a brass farthing for your board and lodging. And never, ever have I thought of you as a "tart". Quite the opposite, as a matter of fact. Rather as a decent, well-educated young woman in search of the good things in life. And why not? Join the club!

'Why, do you imagine, I bought this hotel in the first place, if not to make money? Not that I've made much, so far, but hope springs eternal. You see, Stella, I also want the good things in life, but not at any price, certainly not at the sacrifice of an innocent human being.

'All I'm saying is this, take your friend's advice to think things over before going ahead with an abortion. Now, if you'll excuse me, I have dinner to see to. I'll have yours sent up to you, if you wish. Rosie will bring you the menu beforehand.'

'No,' Stella said quickly, decisively. 'I'll come down to dinner, and I'm sorry I said what I did about – money. I've behaved badly, I know. Will you forgive me?'

'There's nothing to forgive,' Grant assured her. 'Why not have your bath, then sleep for a while?'

His heart went out to her. She looked so young, so vulnerable, standing there in her bathrobe, a scrap of a girl in need of help and support, kindness, tolerance and understanding. Above all, love.

It was then he knew that what he had long suspected concerning his feelings towards her was true. He had fallen in love with her that day on the half-landing, when she had told him the truth about her relationship with Brian Felpersham, and thanked him for the champagne.

Seldom, if ever, since then had he stopped thinking about her at some point during his busy daily routine. At night, too, standing alone on the veranda looking up at the moon or stars, he would find himself worrying about her, wondering where she was and what she was doing, whether or not she was happy as the mistress of a fat, ignorant bastard unfit to even tie her shoelaces.

Now here she was, apparently alone in the world, a forlorn little creature faced with a soul-shattering decision. There was no easy solution so far as the emotional after-effects were concerned. He wondered if she had thought of that. Probably not, but he had seen the devastating effects of abortion on many of the young women he had worked with during his years in the hotel trade: their overwhelming feelings of guilt, depression, incompleteness and loss. And it was not just his colleagues and employees whose turmoil he had witnessed.

All these things he wanted to tell Stella, but now was not the time or place. He had work to do, dinner to cook for the dozen or so other guests staying in the hotel.

He said kindly, 'I'll get Rosie to give you a call around seven. Here' – he gave her the hanky from his breast pocket – 'dry your eyes, and don't cry any more.'

Obediently, she did as she was told. 'Thank you,' she murmured, attempting a smile, 'you've been good to me. Kinder than I deserved.'

He said, 'You haven't touched your sandwiches. Will you eat them now?'

With a hint of her old sparkle, she said, 'No, I don't think so. I don't want to spoil my appetite for dinner.'

Eighteen

The change in June since her meeting with Luke Carter was nothing short of remarkable.

Luke had proved to be kind, perceptive, intelligent and romantic. He, also, was 'into' music, particularly that of Giacomo Puccini – to the disgust of Bunty, who told Thea she'd probably throw up if she heard 'Lovely Maid in the Moonlight' one more time.

'Oh, come on, Bunty,' Thea laughed, 'the pair of them are head over heels in love. You only have to look at June to see how happy she is.'

'Yeah, I guess you're right,' Bunty admitted grudgingly. 'I just have the feeling she could've done better for herself if she'd waited a bit longer; found herself a smarter-looking bloke with a decent haircut and—'

'An embroidered waistcoat, a mobile phone and highlights?' Thea interrupted, tongue in cheek. 'One of those smart executive types with whom June would have had nothing at all in common? I think she's lucky to have found a man of Luke's calibre.'

'Calibre? He looks more like a dropout, a layabout, to me.'

'Then his looks belie him,' Thea said impatiently. 'He happens to be a brilliant student with a great future ahead of him, from a stable family background. Would it surprise you to know that his father received an accolade several years ago, in respect of his contribution to medical research?'

'What's an accolade when it's all there?' Bunty scoffed.

Thea sighed. 'A knighthood, in this case.' Really, there were times when Bunty's downbeat attitude towards life tried her patience to breaking point. What on earth was wrong with the girl? What had become of her old charm and sparkle, her joie de vivre?

'Huh, on the side of the underdog, as usual,' Bunty commented grumpily.

'If you mean Luke, he's no underdog, believe me.'

'There you go again. Always putting me in the wrong. Well, I'm sick and tired of it!'

'I don't believe this. When have I tried to put you in the wrong?' Thea asked, seriously worried about Bunty's frame of mind, her recent mood swings, caustic comments, her general air of self-pity that was so far removed from her former carefree attitude to life. 'If I've upset you in any way, I'm sorry, but I think I deserve an explanation. Tell me, what's wrong?'

'Just about everything! I'm piling on weight, for starters. Then it turned out to be June who found herself a boyfriend that night at the Mirimar, not me. Now, my ex-boyfriend is married to someone else. Can't say I blame him! I mean, who the hell would look twice at a fat frump like me?'

So that was it. Thea had suspected as much. Why Bunty's mother had sent her those newspaper cuttings, she would never know. Possibly she hadn't realised the damaging effect they would have on her daughter's morale? She said, 'You are neither fat, nor a frump, just as Luke Carter is not a dropout. In any case, what do looks matter, in the long run?'

'Oh, you would say that, wouldn't you?' Bunty said huffily. 'You with not a spare ounce of fat on your body and with a handsome bloke in tow to boot. Miss Perfection personified! Well, excuse me for living.'

'Bunty, come back!' But she had already flounced back to her room, slamming the door behind her.

Thea had tried her best to placate Bunty, but she had her

own problems to cope with: the continuation or severance of her affair with Ross Drummond, her concern for Philip Gregory's welfare and that of the two old ladies at the Laurels, and Stella Johnson's decision about the future of the child she was carrying.

If only, she thought, there was someone she could turn to for help and advice. Someone dear to her to hold her close. To wash away all her worries, to tell her what to do next to make sense of her seemingly muddled existence.

Darkness had fallen almost completely when a knock at the door dredged Thea from the outskirts of sleep to the reality of the living world once more.

'Come in, the door's open,' she called out hazily, half expecting to see Bunty on the threshold. But it *wasn't* Bunty!

Thea would have known anywhere, even in half-darkness, the tall, slim silhouette of her mother adumbrated against the light of the landing beyond, arms spread wide to enfold her in a long, silent embrace.

Fliss had arrived in South Bay earlier that day, booked a room at the Mirimar, settled herself in and contacted Bess and Hal Hardacre, whom she had invited to dine with her the following evening. Tactfully refusing Bess's suggestion that she should cancel her room at the Mirimar and stay at the Hacienda, Fliss explained that this was just a flying visit to spend a little time with her daughter and to reacquaint herself with the delights of South Bay – a kind of trip down memory lane.

'Well, it does seem rather a pity,' Bess retorted in a put-out tone of voice. 'With a little more notice, Hal and I could have laid on a party, invited our golf and bridge club friends to meet you. Shown you a good time. Still, we'll look forward to seeing you at the Mirimar tomorrow evening. I just hope the food and service are a damn sight better than the last time Hal and I dined there. That occasion, Hal's birthday, was a disaster from start to finish, believe me!'

Hanging up the phone, Fliss had gone downstairs to reception to book a table for four the following evening, in the hope that Thea would join them for dinner – though that would have to be her own decision entirely. No excuses or explanation necessary if she decided not to.

The booking made, Fliss walked from the Mirimar to the esplanade where she stood for a while looking out to sea, reliving memories of happier times when she, Charles and Thea had spent long, lazy summer days on the beach below. Revelling in the fresh air and sunshine, she and her husband had watched their sturdy-limbed little girl building castles in the sand, paddling in the waves washing in on the beach, shrieking with pleasure as the waves tickled her ankles.

Now that sturdy little girl was no longer a child but a woman, confronting her own problems in life – and that was the reason why Fliss had decided upon this flying visit to South Bay, to help and support Thea in any way possible. Not to pry into her affairs, to offer possibly unwanted advice, but simply to listen, to sympathise, to provide a shoulder to cry on, if necessary.

Making her way to the lower promenade, Fliss treated herself to a parcel of fish and chips, which she ate seated on an iron bollard overlooking the harbour. She was a striking figure in her normal garb: long skirt, checked cotton shirt, hair drawn back from her warm-skinned, angular face into a loose bun at the nape of her neck, a holdall containing a loose-fitting cardigan, books, newspapers, purse and reading glasses, at her sensibly clad feet. Fliss remained totally unaware of the admiring glances of passers-by, particularly those of younger women envious of her air of calm detachment despite the heat of the August afternoon.

Her meal completed, she deposited the remains – paper, polystyrene tray and plastic fork – in the nearest litter bin, and walked along the beach by the sea's edge, past the Spa complex with its Victorian concert hall and row of shops, to a slipway leading back to the upper promenade, formulating her plans for the evening. She was hoping for a meeting with Thea in the privacy of her room at the Villa Marina, when the girl had had time to recover from her day's work at the boutique.

The thought of paying Thea an unexpected visit during working hours had never entered Fliss's mind. She was not and never had been a 'Hello! Surprise, surprise' kind of person. She preferred the softer, more meaningful approach: a quiet embrace, no fuss, no bother; no questions asked, simply a tender reunion with the person she loved best in all the world, apart from her child's father, Charles Bellamy, whom she would never stop loving till her dying day.

'Oh, Mum! Is it really you? Are you really here?'

Clinging to Fliss, inhaling the familiar womanly fragrance of her, clasping her hands, Thea led her mother into the shadowy room, lit by the street lamps on the promenade beyond. 'How did you know – how did you guess how much I needed you right here and now?'

Fliss chuckled softly. 'You could call it a mother's instinct. No, darling, don't switch on the lights. Let's sit here together in the gloaming, shall we? How lovely the sea sounds coming in on the shore, the way it used to sound, long ago, when I came upstairs to tuck you into bed, in this very room, remember?'

'Of course I remember. How could I possibly forget? But things are not the same any more. This room, the Villa Marina. You must have noticed the changes when you came upstairs?'

'Yes, darling, I'd have been blind not to, but the essence of the place, the memories contained within these walls, will remain intact, inviolable, just as long as we keep them fresh and vibrant in that storehouse we call memory.'

Thea said haltingly, 'The fact is, I'm in a bit of a mess at the moment.'

'Because of this man you're in love with?' Fliss suggested.

'Yes. But it's all so complicated. You see, he's already married.'

'If you want to talk about it, I'm listening,' Fliss said, leaning back in her chair, eyes half closed, fully aware that secrets of the heart could never be coerced or demanded in any shape or form, even from a person as close to her as her daughter.

Darkness had fallen completely when, an hour later, she kissed Thea goodnight and walked slowly back to the Mirimar to watch the pianist in action from a tucked-away table in a far corner of the bar.

Prepared to mistrust the man for the harm he had caused her daughter, Fliss watched his hands on the keyboard of the spotlit piano intently. She witnessed his handsome, careworn face bathed in sweat from the relentless spotlights, listened to the old familiar tunes of yesteryear streaming from his fingertips on to the keys of a Steinway Baby Grand, and suddenly she knew, beyond a shadow of doubt, why Thea had fallen so deeply in love with him.

Of necessity, she also knew that she must speak to Ross Drummond. Despite her inborn dread of interference in other people's affairs, she needed to know more about him, to satisfy herself that his feelings towards Thea were genuine.

When, at midnight, Ross rose from the piano, bowed briefly to his audience and went through to his dressing room, Fliss slipped unnoticed from her corner table, following him by a more devious route. Imbued with common sense, she realised there must be a door leading backstage via the dining room, which was fairly empty at this time of night, now that the diners had drifted away to their rooms and the tired waiters were busily engaged in removing soiled tablecloths and empty wine bottles and glasses, preparatory to re-laying the tables for breakfast next morning. And she was right.

Finding the pianist's dressing room along a narrow passage leading to the street beyond, she knocked resolutely on the door, and entered when he called out, 'Come in, it isn't locked.'

Drawing in a deep breath, she stepped into the room, heart pounding. Seeing the pianist stripped to the waist, towelling moisture from his upper torso, face and hair, she said quietly, drawing together the shreds of her dignity in face of this somewhat bizarre situation, 'Please forgive this intrusion on your privacy, but we really need to talk. You see, Mr Drummond, I am Fliss Bellamy, Thea's mother.'

His response to her announcement startled her somewhat. He said intently, 'Thank God you're here, Mrs Bellamy! If you wouldn't mind waiting until I've finished dressing, perhaps you'd care to come back with me to my flat? We can talk much better there than here.'

Impressed by the neatness of Ross's flat, Fliss settled herself in an armchair while he made a pot of coffee. Glancing about her, she realised that here was a man who cared deeply about his environment.

When he returned with the coffee things, she said, 'I enjoyed your performance tonight. Tell me, do you ever feel the urge to launch into Chopin's Revolutionary study?'

He laughed, pouring the coffee and handing her a cup. 'You'll never know how much I long to do just that.'

'Then why don't you?'

'Because it's not what I'm paid to do. I'd probably lose my job if I stepped out of line, and I happen to be rather fond of South Bay in summertime.'

'And what happens when summertime is over?' Fliss asked quietly.

'Then I'll go back to France to be near my wife,' he

said levelly, 'but I'm sure that Thea has told you all about that.'

'I'm not certain that she has,' Fliss said thoughtfully, 'which begs the question, how much does she really know about your past life, apart from the fact that your wife is a sick woman, confined in the psychiatric wing of a prison hospital? Forgive my speaking so bluntly, but I can't help thinking there's a great deal you've kept hidden from my daughter.'

'Perhaps, but unintentionally, I assure you,' Ross replied, brushing back his hair distractedly from his forehead. 'She knows, of course, that I married Colette to spare her the disgrace of returning to her strictly Catholic family as an unmarried mother. Naturally they assumed that I was the father of her child. Not that they ever accepted me, an Anglican, into their close-knit family circle.'

He shivered slightly, as if a goose had walked over his grave. 'But at least, when her child was born, it was not as a bastard, thank God. He was christened Louis Paul Drummond – to all intents and purposes, my son, my own flesh and blood, though never at any time had Colette and I felt inclined to consummate our marriage. She was then, and has remained ever since, my wife in name only.

'Eventually, when Louis was six months old, I drifted away to pursue my career as a second-rate concert pianist.' He smiled ruefully. 'You see, I'd been told by my tutor at the Academy of Music, in Paris, that I lacked the dedication, the talent, the ability to ever become a world-renowned pianist in the same league as Alfred Brendel, for instance. Even so, in my capacity as a "second-rater", I managed to earn a decent living for myself, my wife and her son.'

He continued, 'Can you possibly imagine my feelings when, out of the blue, I received an urgent message from Colette's father, informing me that his daughter, in a fit of madness, had strangled the child to death? Moreover, having confessed to the crime, that she had been arrested on a charge of murder!'

'Oh, Ross,' Fliss murmured, 'how dreadful for you. And you, I gather, have stood by Colette all these years?'

Ross said quietly, 'How could I have done otherwise? She is my wife according to French law.'

Fliss said quickly, 'But what about English law? Your marriage was never consummated. Worth consideration, don't you think? Unless, of course, you are not in love with my daughter and don't wish to marry her.'

Ross said quietly, 'Thea is, and always will be, the only woman in the world for me.'

Rising to her feet, Fliss said warmly, 'You know, Ross Drummond, you are exactly the kind of man I'd envisaged as my future son-in-law.'

'Oh, really?' He smiled. 'Well in my wildest dreams, I never ever envisaged a mother-in-law like you!'

'I'm not sure how to take that.'

'Take it as a compliment, Mrs Bellamy.'

'Call me Fliss.'

'Thank you. Now I'll walk you back to the Mirimar. You are staying there, I take it?'

'Yes. I've invited friends to dine with me tomorrow night. I hope to persuade Thea to join us. Or would you rather I didn't?'

'You are a remarkably perceptive woman,' he said, taking her hand to guide her downstairs, aware that a strong bond of friendship had been forged between them.

Walking back to the Mirimar, looking up at the moon riding high amid a constellation of stars, Fliss said softly, 'What a glorious night this is. You and Thea should be together on a night like this. Life is so short, so precious, you shouldn't squander a moment of it. Love is even more precious, and summertime ends all too soon.

'If you love my daughter as much as she loves you, you

must let nothing stand in the way of your happiness, your future together.'

Ross smiled wistfully. 'If only I knew how.'

At the door of the Mirimar, he said quietly, 'Please, Fliss, will you come through with me to the bar?'

'But it'll be closed,' she demurred, 'at this time of night.'

'Not to worry. I work here, remember? Trust me.'

'Yes, of course, but . . .'

Pressing a light switch to illuminate the piano, Ross guided her to a chair in a dark corner of the room. 'Please, sit down and listen,' he said. 'There is something I wish to play, especially for you.'

Sitting down at the piano, he began playing, very softly, Debussy's 'Clair de Lune', each and every note a jewel of perfection.

Listening intently, Fliss's eyes filled with tears at this, a magical melody played in her honour. A gift worth more than gold, which she would remember, with joy, all the days of her life.

Deeply moved, when the music died away, when Ross closed the piano keyboard and came towards her, she said, 'For what it's worth, that tutor of yours was mistaken in his assessment of your talent. You belong to the great concert halls of the world. To Paris, Milan, Madrid, New York's Carnegie Hall!

'Believe me, Ross, you must not let anything stand in the way of your success.'

'Not even Thea?' he asked quizzically, expecting a rebuttal.

'No, not even Thea,' Fliss said unexpectedly, 'if she hasn't the sense she was born with. Just one thing, before we say goodnight: you have my blessing, but the future is hers to decide. You understand?'

Ross understood completely.

Nineteen

Next day at ten o'clock Ross was outside the Villa Marina when Thea emerged, pin-neat in navy slacks, a tailored white silk shirt and navy sandals, her hair tied back with an Italian scarf.

'Ross? What are you doing here?' She hurried down the steps to meet him.

He said, 'I need to talk; there's something rather important I want to say to you. Shall we walk along to the shelter?'

Thea frowned, reluctant to discuss anything of importance at this time of day. 'Not now, Ross.' She glanced at her watch. 'Later, perhaps? My mother arrived unexpectedly yesterday. I promised to meet her for coffee at ten thirty, and I'll be late if I don't get a move on. It's just a flying visit, you see, and I want to spend as much time with her as possible.'

'Yes, of course Thea, I understand.' He masked his disappointment. 'Later, you said? Shall we say seven? What I have to say to you won't take long.'

'Very well, then, seven o'clock it is. I'll meet you in the shelter. Just one thing, Ross: I'd rather not continue our last conversation, if you don't mind. I still haven't reached a – conclusion.' She smiled faintly. 'Now, if you'll excuse me, I mustn't keep Fliss waiting.'

The promenade was already crowded when Thea and Fliss arrived there, having walked arm in arm down the cliff path from the esplanade, pausing now and then to admire the brilliantly coloured flowerbeds along the way, the yachts fluttering like white moths on the blue expanse of the bay.

Thea had suggested the snack bar at the end of the promenade for morning coffee, knowing that Fliss would enjoy pushing a tray to the checkout far more than being waited on in a town-centre hotel lounge where the coffee and milk came in silver-plated pots with red-hot handles necessitating the use of a handkerchief or a serviette to prevent burning one's fingers during the pouring-out process. Fliss had no patience with such fiddle-faddle.

Thea's heart lifted when she saw her mother coming towards their table carrying a fibre tray with mugs of coffee, cartons of cream, packets of demerara sugar, plastic spoons, paper serviettes, and two packs of bourbon biscuits in cellophane wrappers. Dear Fliss, so alive, charming and uncomplicated, possessed of the 'common touch' which drew people towards her like a warm fire in winter. Fliss reminded Thea of the central character, Mrs Ramsay, in Virginia Woolf's novel *To the Lighthouse*.

Glancing across the table at her daughter, Fliss thought that Thea looked tired, as though she hadn't been sleeping well lately, and guessed the reason why not. Playing tug-of-war with her conscience, night after night, had robbed her of the benison of dreamless sleep.

She gently said, 'Thea, darling, it is often better to make a wrong decision than no decision at all. Think about it and remember that I'll always be on your side, whatever conclusion you reach about the future. All I want, all I've ever wanted is your happiness.'

Thea said haltingly, 'I met Ross briefly this morning, promised to meet him again at seven this evening. Apparently there's something important he wants to say to me. But what's the use of listening? Prolonging the agony?'

Fliss said quietly, 'No use at all, if you're in love with him. Take my advice, listen to what he has to say to you, then forget about "prolonging the agony", simply follow your heart. And for God's sake stop acting like a prissy character in a Jane Austen novel!'

After coffee, they walked along the promenade past the Victorian concert hall towards the boutique. Fliss guessed that Thea was dying to show it to her, having told her so much about it.

'Did you do the window display?' she asked, pausing to browse. 'If so, you made a good job of it. I say, I rather like the look of that blouse on the dummy. Just the thing for my dinner engagement with the Hardacres tonight. Neat but not gaudy, as the devil said when he painted his tail pea-green. What do *you* think?'

'You're having dinner with Bess and Hal? At the Mirimar?'

'Yes, since that's where I'm staying. No need to look so startled. I'll make your excuses if you prefer not to join us. By the way, you never did tell me what happened on the occasion of Hal's birthday party, except that it ended disastrously.' Fliss paused discreetly. 'I gather, from Bess, that you stormed out of the bar in a huff?'

'I did,' Thea confessed, 'with good reason. But I'd rather not talk about it. I behaved badly, and I'm sorry.'

'Fair enough,' Fliss conceded, turning her attention to the Bellino blouse. 'I've a good mind to try that on, unless you'd rather I didn't drag you into the shop on your day off?'

Thea laughed. 'I'm not *that* sensitive! In any case, I'm sure Miss Mould would be chuffed to bits to add thirty-five quid to her day's takings.'

'Miss Mould? Your holiday relief, I take it?' Fliss commented drily. 'Let me hazard a guess: a tall, angular spinster in her mid-forties, self-contained, immaculately dressed and coiffed, charming in manner, with a thin smile belying the charm, but determined to keep it going at any price? Am I anywhere near the mark?'

'Spot on target as usual!' Thea chuckled deeply. 'I've often wondered, Mum, where you keep that crystal ball of yours.'

Pinging open the door, they entered the boutique. Thea's eyebrows shot up in surprise when not Miss Mould but Philip Gregory stepped forward to greet them. She said blankly, 'Mr Gregory, what on earth are you doing here?'

'Holding the fort,' he said wryly. 'Miss Mould is indisposed: a sick headache, according to her phone call earlier this morning. Someone had to stand in, so here I am.'

'Have you had any breakfast?' Fliss enquired, not waiting to be introduced. 'If not, I think you should pop along to the cafeteria. You can't possibly work on an empty stomach. My daughter and I will look after the shop.'

Philip looked bemused. Thea said, 'Mother's right, and she has a fetish about breakfast.' She laughed. 'I should do as she says, if I were you.'

'Oh Lord, Mr Gregory, I *am* sorry,' Fliss apologised. 'Whatever must you think of me, butting in like that? You may not want any breakfast – or perhaps you've already eaten?'

'No, I haven't, as a matter of fact. I've been skipping breakfast lately,' he admitted, remembering the reasons why – lack of appetite for one thing. Worried that Ruth had not even troubled to keep in touch with him personally, he had not been bothering to cook for himself.

He wondered fleetingly if Thea had told her mother about his present situation? Almost as quickly, he realised that she had not and never would have betrayed his trust in her, not even to her own mother.

Imbued with a sudden upsurge of hope and something akin to happiness in the company of Fliss and Thea Bellamy, and feeling hungry for the first time in ages, imagining a plateful of crispy bacon, eggs, sausages, tomatoes and mushrooms set before him, he said gratefully, 'I think I'll make it – the full mazuma!'

'What a charming man,' Fliss said thoughtfully when he had gone. 'But he doesn't look at all well. Has he been ill recently?'

'Not ill exactly. He's just had a lot of personal problems to contend with of late.'

'In other words, it's none of my business?'

'I didn't say that, *you* did!' Thea reminded her. 'Now, are you going to try on that blouse, or not?'

Fliss said, 'There's really no need. I'm having it anyway. I've discovered, from long experience, what's right for me and what isn't.' She smiled. 'I suppose that being selective comes with ageing, along with deciding what is important and what isn't.'

'Meaning what, exactly?' Thea asked uncertainly.

'In your case, harbouring too many secrets, perhaps? Becoming too deeply involved in other people's lives to the detriment of your own? The old folk at the Laurels, for instance; your friends Bunty, June and Stella; Philip Gregory. You're young, Thea, too young to assume responsibility for other people's problems.'

'It isn't like that at all,' Thea said. 'People confide in me; I can't very well break their confidences. *You* wouldn't, would you?'

'I don't know. I might. My name's Fliss Bellamy, not Mother Teresa.'

Conversation ended abruptly when a group of holidaymakers entered the shop: a dozen or so women of all shapes and sizes, wanting sun-tops, sun-tan lotion, cotton squares and bit and bobs of jewellery. Three of them were riffling among the hangers on the chromium rail, two hanging so far over the low wrought-iron grille backing the window that they seemed likely to take a nose-dive into it. The rest were trying on rings and other items of jewellery.

Quick as a flash, eyes sparkling with fun, Fliss removed her Bellino blouse from the wicker dummy and queued up at the counter to pay for it, as proud as Punch of her daughter's unflappable presence at the receipt of custom as she neatly folded goods into paper bags, totted up the amounts owing and handed over the correct change, at the same time keeping a wary eye on the jewellery and the window displays.

The invasion ended as quickly as it had begun, whereupon Thea flitted quickly about the shop, repairing the damage, reclothing the wicker dummy, replenishing the empty hangers with more sun-tops and checking the jewellery to make certain that nothing was missing.

'Is it always like this?' Fliss asked.

'Like what?'

'The D-Day Landings! Do customers always flock in in a body? Don't they ever come in singly?'

'Not if they're all members of the same coach party, they don't,' Thea said wryly. 'The next contingent should be along any minute now, when the Sun Court recital is over.'

She added suspiciously, 'Why? What's on your mind?' But she already knew. 'Oh, very well then,' she said resignedly, 'I'll give up my day off, if that's what you're driving at. For Philip Gregory's sake, you understand? But what will *you* do in the mean time?'

Fliss smiled mistily. 'Oh, a number of things. Hire a deckchair, perhaps sunbathe; tackle *The Times* crossword; read a book; wander along to the harbour for a fish-and-chip lunch. The possibilities are endless. I might even visit the art gallery, or the theatre for a matinée performance of *Night Must Fall*.'

Philip Gregory entered the boutique at that moment. 'Sorry I've been so long,' he said apologetically, 'but the snack bar was busy. I had to queue for a table, and the food was a long time coming.'

'Not to worry, Mr Gregory,' Fliss said kindly, feeling intensely sorry for the man, 'Thea is more than willing to give up her day off on your behalf, aren't you, darling?'

'Yes, of course,' Thea readily agreed, aware that Philip could not possibly have coped on his own on this, one of the busiest Saturdays of the South Bay season.

'But that would be totally unfair of me,' Philip demurred, 'robbing you, Mrs Bellamy, and Thea, of your precious time together. I'd far rather close the shop for the afternoon.'

'What? And miss out on the "Saga" bonanza?' Fliss reminded him, tongue in cheek. 'Can you imagine their disappointment if, having marshalled their forces, not to mention their spending money, they came up against a Closed sign on the shop door? No, that is out of the question. Make hay while the sun shines, is my motto! Isn't it, Thea?' Giving her daughter a mental dig in the ribs.

'*Huh*? Oh yes, of course,' Thea responded bemusedly, never having heard that particular cliché from her mother's lips before. She wondered what the hell Fliss was up to as, bidding her an airy farewell, she quitted the boutique with Philip Gregory in tow, eventually to take her place beside him in the passenger seat of his car, headed, with him, to heaven alone knew where. A matinée performance of *Night Must Fall*, more than likely, Thea surmised, as a fresh contingent of day trippers, with money to burn, invaded the shop, and she found herself stuffing goods into paper bags at a rate of knots.

As the afternoon wore on, she wondered if what Fliss said was true. Had she become too deeply involved in other people's lives? If so, she hadn't meant to. Or was she kidding herself? After all, it had been her idea to appoint herself gardener to the old ladies at the Laurels, against Miss Abigail's wishes. And by what right had she meddled in their affairs to the extent of eliciting Mr Cumberland's help on their behalf?

She had, moreover, advised Stella not to go ahead with an abortion until she'd had time to think things through, adding to the girl's confusion regarding the fate of an unwanted child. Why couldn't she have left well enough alone, recognised Stella's God-given right to reach her own decision concerning her pregnancy?

As to the breakdown of Philip Gregory's marriage, she

had never clearly understood her involvement in his domestic affairs, except that she had played a role, albeit an innocent one, in the drama beginning with that chance encounter with Philip in the foyer of the Mirimar, on the occasion of Hal Hardacre's birthday celebration.

Thea paused to draw breath between influxes of visitors entering and leaving the boutique. Had she been born stupid, she wondered, or, in her case, had practice made perfect?

Why the hell, she asked herself while replenishing stock, had she fallen madly in love with a face, a pianist seated at a spotlit piano in the bar of the Mirimar hotel? And why her misgivings about meeting him, later this evening? Was she afraid that he would break down the remaining shreds of her resistance towards him, that, in acknowledging her feelings of love, she might well relinquish her innate sense of decency in becoming the mistress of a man already committed to another woman?

Ross had been waiting for some time when Thea arrived at the shelter. The magnetism between them was as powerful as ever, she realised as she came towards him, as undeniable as it had been the first time she had seen him, and later when they had come face to face in the art gallery.

She said, 'Sorry I'm late.'

'Are you? I hadn't noticed.' He smiled. 'It's such a lovely evening, I came early for a breath of sea air.' He was standing near the open entrance of the shelter, looking out to sea, wearing dark slacks and an open-necked shirt which, she knew, he would later exchange for a black polo-neck sweater. Her heart went out to him. He seemed so vulnerable somehow, a decent, caring human being suffering the consequences of an act of folly committed so thoughtlessly in the flush of youth.

'You said there was something important you wanted to say to me.'

'Yes, there is.' Turning to face her, he took her hands in

his. 'I love you, Thea, and I think you love me, too. No, don't speak, not just yet. Let me finish.

'Believe me, I understand your reluctance to give yourself to a married man. That's the reason why I'm asking you to wait for me, to marry me one day – no matter how far away that day may be. You see, my darling, having found you, I could never bear to lose you, and I have reason to believe, thanks to a wise and dear friend of mine, that I shall be free to marry again in the fullness of time. And the only person I shall ever want to marry is *you*!'

Producing a morocco leather box, heart in mouth, he handed it to her, hoping to God that she would accept this token of his love.

Opening the box, Thea beheld a flawless solitaire diamond, flashing fire from its blue velvet pad. Lost for words, she stared at it in silence, understanding that her refusal to accept his gift would end the affair once and for all. Ross's pride would never allow him to beg her to reconsider. He would simply turn and walk away from her.

In her mind's eye, she imagined his leave-taking, his tall figure diminishing as the distance between them lengthened. He would utter no word of reproach; would not even look back at her. He would disappear from her life as if their love had ceased to exist.

Glancing up at him, she saw the lines of suffering about his eyes and lips as he silently awaited her decision, making no attempt to hurry her. He was offering her a lifetime of devotion, an engagement ring, hope for a future together, no matter how dim and distant that future might seem at this moment. What else could he have possibly done or said to prove his love for her?

Now it was her turn to prove her love for him, to chase away the shadows from his face, that haunted look in his eyes. Drawing closer to him, she smiled tremulously. 'I *will* wait for you, Ross. I'll wear your ring on our wedding day.'

Raising her hands to his lips, he kissed her fingers one by one, then, cupping her face in his hands, he kissed her cheeks, her eyes, her hair and finally her mouth, telling her again and again how much he loved her until, breaking away from his arms, she reminded him of the time, that he'd be late for work if he didn't hurry.

'Oh God, yes,' he said bemusedly, glancing at his watch. 'I'd forgotten all about it. Thanks, darling, for reminding me, but it isn't every day that a man becomes engaged to the most beautiful, adorable woman in the world!'

He added happily, 'Just a thought, darling: how about a midnight tryst? Same place? You see, I'd really love to kiss you goodnight.'

Watching his departing figure along the esplanade, waving to him when he paused to look back at her, Thea realised how different things might have been had she allowed her prissy 'Jane Austen' conscience to overrule her heart. And yet she still felt that she hadn't really proved her love for him at all.

The last thing she expected was the sound of raised voices when she entered the landing area of the Villa Marina, sounds issuing from behind the closed door of June's apartment.

Oh God, she thought, what on earth was going on in there? But she had a rough idea. June's mother had arrived unannounced, to read the riot act to her hapless daughter, not quietly, but in a coarse voice resembling a factory whistle.

Thea couldn't help overhearing. No one could have, with the possible exception of Ludwig van Beethoven, in advanced old age.

The woman was screaming, in a high-pitched voice, 'Well, that's it, young lady, I'm taking you back home with me on the next train to Batley! So just you pack your duds, wash that muck off your face, and get moving! To think that a daughter of mine could have stooped so low as to wear trousers and plaster her face with make-up!

'Well, I'll soon put a stop to that kind of nonsense when I get you back home where you belong, my girl, to help me with the housework and wear decent clothes once more. As for all this fakey equipment of yours, it'll bring a bob or two, I dare say, when it's advertised in the local paper. And for God's sake stop snivelling before I give you summat to snivel about!

'And who's this bloody fella you've got yourself mixed up with? A right little turd, I shouldn't wonder, taking advantage of an innocent young girl to his own ends. Huh, he wants castrating if you ask me!'

Bunty, ashen-faced, had joined Thea on the landing. 'Oh, this is dreadful, isn't it?' she murmured, shaking like a leaf.

'More than dreadful, it's intolerable,' Thea declared forcibly, 'and I intend to do something about it! That dreadful woman is threatening violence, causing a disturbance. I'm going in there to confront her. Meanwhile, you alert Mr Cumberland. And if the worst comes to the worst, send for the police.'

'Oh, please don't go in there,' Bunty begged her. 'She may attack you, the state she's in.'

'I know, but I must help June.' Pushing open the door, Thea entered the arena.

Mrs Blake gaped at her, open-mouthed. 'Who the hell are you?' she demanded hoarsely, eyes flashing fire. 'You've no right here, so get out before I throw you out!'

Placing a protective arm about June's shoulders, Thea said desperately, 'I strongly advise you to calm down and keep quiet. As for throwing me out, lay a finger on me and I'll have you arrested for assault. The same goes for June, whom you've already threatened with physical violence. And don't bother to deny it. There are witnesses. People outside on the landing heard every word you uttered!'

Agnes blurted, 'I never touched her. In any case, what's it got to do with you? I'm her mother, an' she'll do as she's told. Now get that muck off your face, my girl, an' pack your duds. You're coming home with me, if I have to drag you!' Her voice had risen shrilly once more.

'No, I won't! You can't make me!' June said bravely, clinging to Thea. 'My boyfriend and I are going steady. We're getting engaged.'

'Engaged? Over my dead body!' Agnes flung back at her.

Thea said levelly, stretching the truth a little, 'I may as well tell you, Mrs Blake, that the police have been sent for, so you'd best make yourself scarce before they arrive.' She was shaking inwardly. 'Take my advice: go now, and don't come back!'

Mr Cumberland and Bunty were outside on the landing when June's mother marched out of the room, muttering darkly that no jumped-up bit of a kid could tell her what to do and get away with it. 'I shall come back as often as I damn well please,' she declared stoutly.

Impeding her progress, Cumberland said forcibly, 'That you will not! Rest assured, madam, that if ever you set foot in this building again, I shall have you arrested for trespass. Now, clear off, and thank your lucky stars that you are not faced with a night behind bars.'

Thea registered subconsciously that Mr Cumberland had placed a protective arm about Bunty's shoulders, and that she was looking up at him as if he were a knight in shining armour come to the aid of a damsel in distress.

June had drifted on to the landing, her eyes red-rimmed with weeping. 'I think you might have told me about getting engaged to Luke,' Bunty said hoarsely. 'I thought we were friends.'

'We *are*,' June sobbed. 'You've been wonderful to me. I didn't tell you about Luke because I knew you didn't approve of him.'

'Whatever gave you that idea? I said I didn't think he was good enough for you, that's all,' Bunty protested. 'Well, apparently I was wrong, and I'm sorry. I was only trying to protect you.'

Mr Cumberland said easily, 'Let's leave it at that, shall we? Take my advice, June, go to bed and try to get some sleep. You've had an unpleasant experience, but you're safe now, and there'll be no repeat performance, of that you may rest assured.'

'Bunty and I will stay with you, if you like,' Thea suggested quietly, guiding the weeping girl back to her room. 'Won't we, Bunty?'

'Yes, sure we will,' Bunty said wholeheartedly. 'Thea will see you into bed, and I'll make you a nice cup of tea.' She added, shyly for a forthright Scot, 'Thanks ever so much, Mr Cumberland. I don't know what we'd have done without your help and support.'

Awarding Bunty the highest of accolades, he insisted, 'Call me Bill,' smiling contentedly as he went downstairs to his own quarters.

Twenty

Thea had helped the trembling June to undress and get into bed and Bunty had made her a cup of tea and was halfway across the room with it when someone knocked on the door.

June's eyes widened in terror. 'If that's my mother, please, *please* don't let her in,' she cried out in distress. 'I don't want to see her again. Not *ever*!'

'You leave her to me,' Bunty uttered grimly, setting down the cup and saucer. 'I'll frog-march her to the station, if necessary! The police station, that is!'

But it wasn't June's mother. Bunty flung open the door to find Luke Carter on the landing.

'Mr Cumberland rang me, told me what happened. I came as soon as I could. Is June all right?' he asked intently.

At the sound of his voice, June got out of bed. Uttering a cry of joy, she stumbled across the room and threw herself into his arms – 'for all the world like one of those soppy scenes in an old Hollywood movie', Bunty remarked later. 'All that was missing was the soundtrack from *Gone with the Wind*.'

Thea laughed. 'June's happy, and that's all that matters. You seem fairly happy yourself, come to think of it. Perhaps love is in the air tonight? Possibly the appearance of June's mother, however unpleasant, was heaven-sent so far as you and Mr Cumberland are concerned.'

'Don't talk so daft; Bill, I mean Mr Cumberland, is damn near old enough to be my father.'

'So? What has age got to do with it? It's how you feel about someone, not age that matters. It's feeling at ease, relaxed, happy and hopeful that really counts, with a future to look forward to.'

'It's funny,' Bunty said softly, 'I've known Bill for ages; ever since I came to South Bay to work, but tonight was the first time I'd really noticed him. It happened when I went down to fetch him – you know, when Mrs Blake was on the rampage.

'I was really scared she'd hurt you when you went into the room to stand up to her, the temper she was in. I don't remember what I said to Bill, I was so upset. But he was ever so kind and well, you know, somehow solid and dependable. He said not to worry, he'd sort things out. I must have been crying, 'cos he gave me his hanky, and I felt safe all of a sudden, the way I used to when my dad was alive.

'He took my hand, and we came upstairs together. Oh, I don't suppose it meant anything to him, but it did to me. 'Spect I'm making a fool of myself as usual. The truth is, I'm tired of being on my own. I need someone to care for me, someone to care for in return. But I guess I'm barking up the wrong tree.' Her eyes filled with tears.

Thea said, 'Somehow, I don't think so. I couldn't help noticing the way he looked at you. It may take him a little time to recover from the shock of seeing you, too, in a new light. My guess is that when you return his hanky, he'll ask you in for a drink, and well, the rest is up to you.'

'But what shall I say to him? What shall I wear?'

'Say as little as possible, and wear that kaftan thingy of yours, without the beads and the dangly earrings. Just be your natural charming self.'

'Huh! I haven't been my natural charming self for so long that I've forgotten how,' Bunty sighed forlornly.

'You were tonight,' Thea reminded her, 'when he gave you his hanky.'

* * *

Bess Hardacre had elected to wear a cerise lace dress and matching bolero for her dinner date with Fliss, whom she greeted effusively in the foyer of the Mirimar. 'Oh, darling,' she enthused, 'you haven't changed a bit – has she, Hal?'

'No, thank goodness,' Hal responded warmly, wondering whether he dare kiss her, deciding not to. Bess had been a bit edgy all day and had tried on one dress after another, finding fault with all of them until, late that afternoon, she had driven into town to treat herself to a new ensemble – this puce lace affair, which Hal had loathed on sight.

Now here was Fliss Bellamy, tall and slender, looking wonderfully elegant in a long black skirt and an Italian silk blouse in muted shades of brown and gold, reminiscent of autumn leaves. A simple outfit in which she appeared entirely comfortable and relaxed, unlike Bess, who seemed ill at ease and fidgety in her puce lace get-up, with good reason. The ill-chosen garment was far too small for her, and she knew it, hence her high-pitched laughter and ceaseless flow of verbal diarrhoea, to which Fliss listened patiently, unable, possibly unwilling to get a word in edgewise.

'Thea not with us tonight?' Bess had begun. 'Just as well, perhaps, after the last debacle. The occasion of Hal's birthday, no less.

'I've never understood what really happened that night, but there was something decidedly odd about it. Hal and I and Thea were standing here when suddenly Philip Gregory – Thea's employer – came across to speak to us.

'I remember thinking, at the time, that his wife and guests weren't too pleased. I can only think that his wife was jealous that he had singled me out for special attention. But after all, why not? I am a very good client of his.

'Well, to cut a long story short, we, that is Hal and I and Thea, went through to the bar for drinky-poos until our table was ready. There was a pianist at a spotlit piano, to entertain the public, I imagine, why else? So I called out to him to play "Happy Birthday". I mean why not, for heaven's sake?

That's when Thea jumped up suddenly and rushed out of the bar without a word of apology for her bad behaviour.

'Hal and I were devastated, as you can imagine. His birthday party was ruined. We ate alone, and quite frankly, the food was ghastly.

'Another strange thing happened that night. Apparently a member of Philip Gregory's party had been taken ill in the dining room. Drunk, more likely, if you ask me. The waiter made that the excuse for being kept waiting. Huh, any excuse for bad service in this country nowadays. They wouldn't stand for it in Spain.

'Well, as I was saying, there was something fishy going on that night. I heard afterwards that Mrs Gregory had given her husband his marching orders when she found out he was having an affair with a girl half his age.' Bess sniffed audibly. 'A woman of *my* age I could have understood, but to engage in a hole-and-corner affair with some brazen young floozy beggars belief. I mean to say, a man of his standing in the community, a family man to boot, with grown-up daughters married to respectable businessmen—'

'One of whom vomited at the dining table,' Fliss interrupted equably, keeping her anger in check. 'Scarcely the act of a respectable businessman, wouldn't you say?'

'Huh?' Bess's mouth sagged open momentarily in surprise. 'How could you possibly know that? Oh, I see. You're staying here, of course. I suppose one of the waiters told you?'

'No, Philip Gregory told me.'

'*Philip Gregory?* But how could he? You don't even know the man!'

'Wrong again,' Fliss said charmingly, aware of Hal's discomfiture and feeling sorry for the man, as she would have felt sorry for any man married to Bess Hardacre. 'I met Philip this morning, at the boutique, after which we spent the afternoon together. A delightful man whose company I enjoyed enormously, to the extent of inviting him to dine with us, this evening. He should be here any minute now.'

'*What*?' Bess's cheeks flushed a bright red – almost the colour of her gown. 'No way! If you think I'm prepared to spend an evening in the company of *that* man, you have another think coming! Hal and I are leaving right now!'

'I don't see why we should,' Hal protested. 'I've been looking forward to this evening, to seeing Fliss again. Besides, I like Philip Gregory, and I don't believe all that stuff about him having an affair. You should be careful what you say, Bess, or you'll find yourself in hot water one of these days, spreading silly gossip the way you do.'

'Hal's right,' Fliss said quietly. 'The affair, so-called, was a figment of Mrs Gregory's imagination. She saw him talking to Thea, put two and two together and came up with the wrong answer.'

'*Thea?* Oh, so that's it! That's why she left Hal and me in the lurch the night of his birthday party! A guilty conscience, I shouldn't wonder. I *knew* there was something fishy going on. I expect she was jealous at seeing Philip and his wife together!'

Fliss said levelly, despite her rising anger at the woman's stupidity, 'No, Bess, Thea left because of *you*! And now I know why. Because of your damned, mindless insensitivity when you called out to the pianist to play "Happy Birthday".'

'*What?* But that's a load of rubbish!' Bess bridled indignantly. 'I had every right to make a perfectly normal request on the occasion of Hal's birthday. Why ever not? In any case, why should Thea have taken umbrage the way she did? She was the mindless, insensitive one, if you want my opinion. At least I know now what you really think of me. Mindless and insensitive, am I? And to think I've kept in touch with you all these years because I felt sorry for you. Can't think why I bothered.'

'For God's sake, Bess, calm down, you're making an

exhibition of yourself,' Hal muttered, clasping her elbow. 'People are looking!'

'Yes? Well, let them look! I'm worth looking at, aren't I? A real flesh-and-blood woman, not some bloody monument like my so-called friend here! No wonder she hasn't changed! She's stuck in a time warp! Same old clothes, same old hairstyle, same old holier-than-thou attitude to life! No wonder her husband left her for another woman. As for that po-faced daughter of hers, I offered her a home from home, found her a job and what did she do? Flung my kindness back in my face, that's what! And why? For what reason, I should like to know!'

Thea's clear voice came out of the blue. 'Because, Aunt Bess, that mounted bull's head over your mantelpiece put the fear of God into me to begin with, but not half as much as you did. And if you befriended my mother because you felt sorry for her, you were wasting your pity on the wrong person. How about poor Uncle Hal? One of the nicest, kindest, most forbearing, misunderstood men on the face of the earth: how he has managed to survive a life sentence of marriage to a woman like you, I can't begin to imagine.'

'That's enough, darling,' Fliss said quickly. 'Bess and Hal were just about to leave, as Bess is reluctant to dine in the company of Philip Gregory. And so, since there seems little more to add to a wake, apart from the usual expressions of regret at the death, in this case of a worn-out friendship, the only thing left to do is say goodnight, and goodbye.'

'Oh, come on, Hal,' Bess uttered sharply. Brushing aside impatiently her husband's restraining hand on her elbow, she marched, head in air, towards the plate-glass doors leading to the promenade where he had parked their car less than half an hour ago.

'No, don't say a word,' she warned him. 'Just take me home! I want to go upstairs to my bedroom, to get out of this bloody awful dress. Why I bought it in the first place,

I can't imagine! I knew all along that it made me look fat! So why didn't you tell me?'

Driving carefully, intent on the road ahead, Hal held his tongue, inured to his role as his wife's whipping boy. He knew that whatever he said to her in her present, frenetic frame of mind would be utterly useless, in the same way that everything about him was considered useless nowadays – apart from his inherited wealth, which made possible the maintenance of the Hacienda, holidays in Spain during the winter months, and the vast sums of money squandered by his wife on entertaining, clothes and beauty treatments.

If only, like Fliss Bellamy, Bess had chosen to grow old gracefully. Too late now, he realised the die was cast. He was lumbered for all time, for better or worse, with not a woman but a trashy work of art, with a runaway tongue, dyed blonde hair, cellulitis, appalling dress sense and ingrowing toenails.

So why hadn't he left her long ago? The answer came pat: because, despite all her faults and failings, he still loved her; still remembered her as the pretty young girl he had married in the heyday of her youth and beauty.

Driving her home, Hal pretended not to have noticed that she was crying, her mascara running down her cheeks in rivulets. All he said was, 'Not to worry, old girl, we'll soon be home. What you need is a good night's sleep.'

'But what about all those dreadful things Fliss said to me?'

'What about the awful things you said to her?' Hal sighed deeply. 'It wasn't kind of you to comment on her appearance, to criticise her daughter and rake up her past life. To my way of thinking, Charles Bellamy was a damn fool to leave her for another woman.'

'Oh that's right! Blame me! Everything's my fault, as usual, I suppose? Now you've turned against me! Well, go on, tell me what I've done wrong apart from speaking my mind.'

'Not now. Tomorrow, when you've had a night's sleep.'
The time had come, Hal realised, to speak his mind. Had he done so earlier in their married life, the dire events of tonight might never have happened.

Fliss said, 'I thought you'd decided not to come this evening. What changed your mind?'
Thea said, 'Philip Gregory talked me into it. I think he felt in need of moral support when he knew he'd be dining with Bess Hardacre. But there were other reasons too: a bit of a shemozzle at the Villa Marina for one thing, but more importantly – *this*. Ross gave it to me. He asked me to wait for him, to marry him one day, and I said yes.'
'Oh, my darling. I'm so glad! It's a beautiful ring. I'm sure you've made the right decision. Ross is a wonderful person!'
Thea frowned. 'But you haven't even met him! Or have you?'
'Well, yes, I have as a matter of fact.'
'And?'
'I think he quite admired me. And that's all I'm prepared to say on the subject.' Fliss laughed. 'Ah, saved by the bell. Here's Philip!'

Ruth Gregory had decided to sell the red brick house, to institute divorce proceedings against her husband based on his defection from their marital home, plus irreconcilable differences of opinion between them which made impossible their future cohabitation as man and wife.
Her smart young solicitor had readily agreed with his client that, in view of her husband's desertion, a quick divorce should be easily attainable once the financial aspects of the affair had been resolved to the court's satisfaction, bearing in mind that her husband was entitled to his fair share of the proceeds from the sale of their home and its contents. This, unfortunately, was the law of the land,

which must be obeyed and adhered to as part and parcel of the divorce package nowadays.

In which case, Ruth thought darkly, let Philip dig his sticky fingers into the honey-pot if he felt so inclined. Happily, there would be more than enough money left over to pursue her dream of living in closer proximity to her daughters and their husbands.

She envisaged a small self-contained flat in the Midlands. Better still, a warm invitation to divide her time equally between Joan and Eva in their respective homes.

This was something she must settle immediately. She wanted her plans cut and dried when the time came to move away from South Bay.

Joan sounded less than enthusiastic on the phone when Ruth rang up to say she was coming down to Birmingham for the weekend. 'But isn't this a bit premature?' she asked. 'Why all the rush? Have you spoken to Father yet?'

'No, and I don't intend to. My solicitor is taking care of the details; the divorce settlement and so on.'

'So you intend going ahead with the divorce?'

'Of course. I thought you knew that. Your father has treated me shabbily, and I have no intention of staying on in a house far too big for one person.' A long pause, then, 'Joan, are you there? Are you listening?'

'Yes, I'm listening,' Joan uttered indifferently. 'I'll have a word with Eva.'

'About – what?'

'Putting you up. You can't stay here with John and me; we're having the house redecorated. I'll ask her to ring you later, all right?' The line went dead. Joan had rung off abruptly.

Eva, the kindlier of the sisters, had rung up later to say that she, Ruth, could spend the weekend with herself and Daniel, in their spare bedroom. An offer which Ruth accepted as an alternative to shelling out money on hotel accommodation.

At the back of her mind lay the appalling thought that

she wasn't about to be welcomed, with open arms, into the lives of her daughters and their respective husbands.

It was a bitter pill to swallow that they regarded her as an interloper, a kind of 'cuckoo in the nest', a presence in their lives they could well do without, rather than a venerated mother figure living, if not *with* them, then within a stone's throw away from them.

Sharing a table with Thea and Fliss Bellamy in the Mirimar restaurant, Philip Gregory realised that he had fallen in love with Fliss.

Whether or not she had fallen in love with him, he hadn't the faintest idea. He simply knew that here was a woman with whom, given the chance, he would gladly spend the rest of his life, come hell or high water. For richer or poorer, for better or worse.

Given his present circumstances, the latter would be the more likely, he assumed.

In retrospect, he realised that his marriage to Ruth had borne the hallmarks of failure from beginning to end. Needing love, he had been given common sense. Wanting a tumbledown beamed cottage with an orchard and outbuildings, he had been talked into buying a red brick house as charmless as a cement mixer. His children were as dull as ditchwater, and always had been; prissy facsimiles of their mother, totally lacking in charm, as if they had been born wearing straitjackets.

Turning his thoughts to other things, Philip said, 'The pianist plays remarkably well, doesn't he? His talent seems wasted here. He belongs to a wider public. Is he living in the hotel at the moment?'

'No, he rents an apartment near the art gallery,' Thea said. 'His permanent home is near Paris. He'll be going back there in September.' She shivered suddenly, remembering that September would soon be here. In a matter of weeks, she would have to say goodbye to him. Their summertime in South Bay would be over; then heaven knew how long it would be before their next meeting. Months, perhaps even years. Perhaps never.

Philip said wistfully, 'Paris in September. Falling leaves, twilight coming early, lights blossoming along the Champs-Elysées.'

'Why, Philip, you old romantic,' Fliss said softly, eyes shining, thinking how much she liked and admired him, how much she would miss him, despite the brevity of their acquaintance, when she went back to London.

He smiled. 'I suppose I must be. You see, I had planned a surprise weekend in September as an anniversary present for my wife. I meant to cancel the booking but, well, somehow I never got around to it.'

'Hoping she might change her mind?' Fliss suggested compassionately.

'Yes, but there's no hope of that now she's going ahead with the divorce.'

'Oh, Phil,' Thea said anxiously, 'I'm so sorry. I had no idea. But couldn't you go on your own? Better still, take someone else with you?'

'That idea had occurred to me,' he admitted. 'But who? One of the South Bay golfing fraternity? I never could stand the game anyway.'

'How about Miss Mould?' Thea suggested, tongue in cheek.

Fliss said unashamedly, 'How about me?'

Thea slipped away from the table almost unnoticed, saying she had a midnight appointment to keep. Philip rose to his feet. 'Oh, must you go?' he murmured.

Fliss simply smiled and said, 'Goodnight, darling, and God bless. See you tomorrow? Lunch at that café?'

'But I thought you were leaving first thing in the morning?'

Fliss said calmly, 'I've changed my mind. A woman's prerogative.'

Turning at the door of the restaurant, looking back at her mother and Philip clasping hands across the table, Thea's heart lifted at their obvious happiness in each other's company. High time, she thought, that Fliss put the past behind her to carve out a new future for herself with someone as nice as Philip Gregory.

Not that Fliss would ever forget or stop loving Charles Bellamy, she realised. But after all the lonely years without him, Fliss, above all people, deserved her place in the sun – Paris in the fall. Even September in the rain . . . the tune Ross was playing as she left the restaurant.

Twenty-One

Hal's duties included preparing breakfast and doing the washing-up afterwards. He had just finished making coffee and toast when his wife appeared wearing her night things, a white satin nightgown and a matching dressing gown, her face devoid of make-up, which was highly unusual in her case. Normally, she refused to be seen, even by him, without her full complement of foundation cream, rouge, powder and lipstick.

She said faintly, 'I don't want any breakfast. I'm going back to bed. I feel unwell.'

'In which case, I'll send for the doctor,' Hal replied, 'but not before you've rung up Fliss Bellamy to apologise for last night.'

'Ring up Fliss? *Apologise?* Why on earth should I?' Bess stared at her husband disbelievingly.

'Because you were in the wrong! You behaved badly, and the only honourable thing to do is admit it.'

'*I* behaved badly? What about *her*? She accused me of being mindless and insensitive, in case you've forgotten.'

Drawing in a deep breath, going in at the deep end, knowing the time had come to tell his wife a few home truths for her own sake as well as his, Hal said, 'Hasn't it occurred to you to wonder why? You began by spreading silly rumours about Philip Gregory's so-called hole-and-corner affair with, in your own words, "some brazen young floozy". You later referred to Fliss as a "monument", accused her of being stuck in a time warp. Then you had the damned cheek to rake up her ex-husband, saying in that mindless, insensitive way of yours, no wonder he had left her for another woman. To add to the list, you also referred to that "po-faced" daughter of hers.

'To add insult to injury, you refused to dine in the company of Philip Gregory, making an exhibition of yourself into the bargain. Later, in the car, on our way home, you blamed me for not telling you that bloody awful puce lace dress you wore last night made you look fat. Well, quite frankly, my dear, it did! Why? Because it was too small for you. You said, "Why I bought it in the first place, I can't imagine." Well, if you can't, *I* can! Because you haven't learned how to grow old gracefully, as Fliss has done, to accept that you are no longer the slender young girl you used to be.

'And why the dyed blonde, over-permed hair and inch-thick make-up? Why must you forever regard yourself as the life and soul of the party? What are you so afraid of? Learning how to put a curb rein on that silly wagging tongue of yours? Admitting that you are now in need of a size eighteen, not a size fourteen wardrobe?'

'So what is it you want me to do?' Bess uttered bleakly, dismayed by her hitherto lenient husband's suddenly harsh attitude towards her. 'Apart from ringing up Fliss Bellamy, I mean?'

Hal said quietly, 'First things first. The rest will come later.'

'The rest of what?' she asked anxiously.

'The rest of our lives together,' he said, pleased that his plain speaking had not escalated into a full-scale row as he had suspected it might.

Bess, apparently, had been shocked into the realisation of her shortcomings to the extent of dialling the Mirimar and asking to speak to Mrs Bellamy. Closing the kitchen door on the conversation, Hal knew that Fliss would accept Bess's apology wholeheartedly, without reservation.

When Bess returned, he said, 'Thank you, my dear. Now hadn't you best be getting back to bed while I ring up the doctor?'

'Doctor?' Bess frowned. 'I don't need a doctor. I feel fine. Hadn't you better made some fresh coffee? If there's anything I can't stand, it's lukewarm coffee!'

Grant Edwards had driven Stella home to the Villa Marina late that night. It was well past the witching hour of midnight when, after a final, lingering goodnight kiss, he said quietly, 'No regrets?'

'Not one,' she assured him. She smiled happily. 'How about you?'

'Need you ask?'

Getting out of the car and standing on the pavement, she waved and blew him a kiss as his tail lights disappeared into the effulgent semi-darkness of a starlit August night.

Returning from her midnight assignation with Ross, Thea asked, 'Stella, is that you?' She was surprised and delighted to see her again, thinking how well and radiant she looked, a far cry from the troubled girl she had last seen two weeks ago. Obviously her country holiday had done her the world of good.

Stella said breathlessly, 'May I come to your room? Oh, Thea, I really need to talk to you, to tell you what's happened. I'll probably burst if I don't.' She laughed. 'Not to worry, the baby is still intact. I decided to keep it, after all.'

Upstairs in her room, Thea made coffee and listened intently to Stella's account of her week in the country, told in fits and starts as it occurred to her, a bit like a bird hopping from twig to twig, and not making sense at times.

'You see, I'd been there before with Brian Felpersham, so I really shouldn't have gone back there at all. I decided to leave early the next day, by taxi. I'd have left straight away, only the telephone lines were down, so I had to stay overnight.

'Grant was very kind and understanding. He offered to have dinner sent up to my room, but I went downstairs to the restaurant. He knew I was pregnant because he'd guessed as much, but he begged me not to go ahead with the abortion. His ex-wife had had an abortion without telling him, you see.

'He hadn't a full-time receptionist, so when he offered me the job, I accepted. I couldn't face continuing at the beauty salon, so I said yes.

'Then, when Grant told me he loved me and wanted me to marry him, to bring up my child as his own, how could I possibly have said no? I'd loved him all along, you see – from the first moment I met him – though I wasn't prepared to admit it.

'Now I'm here to work my week's notice at the salon. Then I'm going back to The Inn Thing to begin a whole new way of life with the man I love. No fuss, no bother, just a quiet register office wedding. Oh Thea, I'm so happy. Completely, blissfully happy for the first time in my life.' She added shyly, 'And I do really want my baby. Just to think, if it hadn't been for you, none of this would have happened.'

Thea still wasn't sure exactly what *had* happened.

Fliss said at lunch next day, 'Bess rang me this morning to apologise for calling me a "monument", and all those other things besides. Raking up your father's desertion, for instance.' She paused momentarily, then, 'Tell me, Thea, did I overstep the bounds of propriety in offering to share Phil's weekend in Paris? The truth, now.'

Thea smiled. 'If you mean do I object to the idea of you and Philip sharing a room overlooking the Champs-Elysées, no, I don't. I happen to think that the pair of you were made for one another, and I wish you both all the luck and happiness in the world.'

Fliss said quietly, 'How about yourself and Ross? I may be wrong, but I have the feeling that all is not quite as it should be between you. He'll be going away soon, back to Paris, and you'll be returning to London to pursue your own career. How will you bear the separation, I wonder?'

'With difficulty, I imagine,' Thea confessed. 'But I've really no choice in the matter, have I? I've agreed to marry him one day, if and when he is free to remarry. It could take years, but I'll wait for him however long it takes. Now, let's change the subject, shall we?' Scarcely able to bear the thought of Ross's departure, she didn't want to talk about it.

She said, 'I'll miss South Bay, my friends, the boutique, the theatre, the art gallery. I've been happy here. I wish this summer would last forever.'

'Nothing lasts forever,' Fliss said. 'Sometimes things change for the better. I dare say Bunty, Stella, June and your two old ladies would agree with me.' She knew all about their various ups and downs from Thea's letters and phone calls, and her daughter had just been bringing her up to date with some of the latest developments. 'I'm so pleased that Stella has decided to keep her baby, that she has found a decent man to care for her after that ghastly Brian what's-his-name. Thank God she had the sense to end the affair when she did.'

Thea laughed. 'You ain't heard nothing yet. Wait till I tell you about last night, that shemozzle at the Villa Marina I mentioned. June's mother turned up out of the blue to take June back to Batley, and I've never been so scared of anyone before! I thought she'd throttle me with her bare hands when I marched in to June's room to confront her.'

'You did *what*?' Fliss whistled softly under her breath. 'No wonder Bess Hardacre referred to you as "po-faced"! Stonewall Bellamy would have been nearer the mark! What if you'd been killed?'

Thea said, tongue in cheek, 'Then I wouldn't be here having lunch with you, would I?'

Meanwhile, workmen had moved into the Laurels to begin the alterations. Lorries were parked in the roadway, to the annoyance of the hoteliers who complained, in a body, to Bill Cumberland regarding the ill-timed commencement of the reconstruction.

Their spokesman put the matter in a nutshell. Visitors in search of peace and quiet had objected strongly to the noise from the Laurels, even more so to the contractors' vehicles cluttering the esplanade from morning till night.

Bill had apologised for the annoyance, and pointed out that he'd been obliged to accept the contractors' starting date; had done so rather than delay the work till the middle of winter. In any case, the summer season was virtually over, or would be in a fortnight or so, when the Sun Court closed, the beach donkeys were taken to their winter quarters, and when they, the hoteliers, had swanned off to Spain, the Bahamas or wherever, in search of sangria and sunshine.

Now, Abigail and Violet, safely ensconced in the west wing of the Villa Marina, were enjoying a life of comparative luxury in a self-contained flat with a modern bathroom and kitchen, sharing a bedroom, not that they minded occupying twin beds close enough together to allow them to hold hands before bidding each other goodnight and God bless.

At times, Violet deeply regretted the loss of her son from her life. But she did not regret the break with her daughter-in-law, Hester, and never ever did she regret that she and Abby were destined to remain together for the foreseeable future. No longer were they paupers eking out a poverty-stricken existence together in a decaying, ghost-ridden house, but reasonably well-off old women well able to afford trips to town now and then, to enjoy home-made soup, roast beef and Yorkshire pudding, plus apple pie and custard, in a pensioners' café near the town square. And, following this, they would walk together, arm in arm, purchasing little treats for their supper – a quarter of roast ham, for instance, a quiche, sausage rolls or, blissfully, chocolate eclairs.

As time drew on inevitably and the close of the summer season approached, Ross and Thea spent as much time together as possible before their September leave-taking.

Curiously, despite their passionate awareness of one another, they found little of importance to discuss, almost as if they were strangers, unwilling to overstep the demarcation line between them, afraid of embarking on forbidden territory.

Ruth could scarcely credit the treatment she'd received at the hands of John Barratt who, having appointed himself spokesman on behalf of Joan, Eva and Daniel, had told her in no uncertain terms, that her interference in their lives would not be welcome.

'*Interference*?' She'd stared at her son-in-law disbelievingly. 'In what way have I ever interfered in your lives? I've done everything in my power to help you, in case you've forgotten, to the extent of planning your weddings to the last details. No easy matter, I can assure you, in the event of a double marriage.

'I've made you welcome in my home, bent over backwards to accommodate you, despite your reprehensible behaviour on your last visit. Now you dare to stand in judgement of me when you, John Barratt, were entirely responsible for my present predicament! After you had been carted off to bed to sleep off your disgusting hangover, on the occasion of our fortieth wedding anniversary, my husband and I quarrelled violently, and he left me. You were the main cause of that quarrel. And to think I stood up for you and my daughters. Now *this*!

'Well, I'll not stay where I'm not welcome! As for you Joan, and you, Eva, are you going to sit there like dummies, saying nothing in my defence? Apparently you are! My God, and to think I've wasted the best years of my life on a couple of weaklings like you! Frankly, you disgust me, the pair of you!'

'Oh, come off it, Mother,' Joan advised her laconically, 'there's no earthly reason why you and Father shouldn't make up your quarrel. This divorce talk is a nonsense, and you know it! We – John, Eva and Daniel and I – have talked it over at length, and were in full agreement that you and Father should patch up your quarrel and stop behaving like a couple of characters in a soap opera.'

Perhaps they were right, Ruth thought. Swallowing her pride would not be easy, but if safeguarding her future meant going cap in hand to Philip, then it must be done. No way could she contemplate living alone.

Following the family conclave in Birmingham, made sick at heart by her daughters' rejection of her – their own mother – she had flatly refused to stay a moment longer under Eva's roof, despite her younger offspring's tearful reminder that she was welcome to spend the weekend in the spare room, as arranged. Daniel had agreed to that, so what was the point or purpose of spending the night in a hotel room before rushing back to South Bay early next morning?

'Because I choose to do so,' Ruth said coldly. 'And spare me your crocodile tears! What I do from now on is none of your business!'

'Believe me, Mother, I never meant this to happen. It was all John's doing. Well, you know what he's like!'

Ruth said bitterly, 'Oh yes, I know *exactly* what he's like. An arrogant bully at heart, capable of bending other people to his will, including yourself and Daniel. Power has gone to his head like the strong drink he's so fond of. He's riding high at the moment. Riding for a fall, if you ask me! When that happens, don't say I didn't warn you!'

* * *

She rehearsed beforehand what she would say to Philip when she visited his flat on her return home.

Of necessity, she would need to say she was sorry for any distress she had caused him by way of the threatened divorce proceedings against him. That he would agree wholeheartedly with her suggestion of making a new start together, especially when she mooted the idea of selling the red brick house and buying a cottage, she entertained no doubt whatsoever. She had always possessed the ability to wind him round her little finger when the need to do so came uppermost. And that need certainly came uppermost now, she realised, as she knocked on the door.

A voice called out, 'Miss Mould, is that you? Come in, it's not locked. Sit down, make yourself comfortable; I'll be out directly.'

Bemusedly, Ruth entered the apartment, amazed by the changes wrought by Philip during his tenancy. Every vestige of rubbish had been removed; the walls had been painted primrose yellow; the divan was covered with dark green, box-pleated material. There were new armchairs, a deep apricot in colour, shaded lamps scattered about the room, and fresh flowers on the mantelpiece and on the glass-topped coffee table between the chairs. Obviously he had created his own space since their separation, a realisation that Ruth found oddly disturbing.

Suddenly he entered the room, looking fitter than he had done for years. Seemingly neither surprised nor overjoyed to see her, he said pleasantly, 'My dear, how kind of you to pay me a visit. I've been hoping that you would.'

'You have? May I ask why?'

'Well, far better to discuss things face to face, don't you think? Details of the divorce settlement and so on. Far better to part amicably, as friends, rather than enemies.'

He smiled. 'Please sit down. May I offer you a glass of wine, tea or coffee? By the way, if you're wondering what's happened to the kitchen, I've had it moved through yonder. It's small but adequate for one person, and I couldn't stand the sight of a sink and draining board in my living quarters.'

Sitting down, refusing his offer of refreshment, Ruth said tautly, 'The reason I came here . . .' She swallowed hard. This was proving harder than she'd imagined.

'No need to explain,' Philip said briskly. 'Naturally, you need to put your own house in order, to stabilise your plans for the future. I shan't stand in your way. It's only right and fair that your future is financially provided for. I've put the shop and the boutique up for sale.'

Ruth uttered sharply, 'But where will you go? What will you do? This shop and the boutique have been your life, your reason for living for the past thirty-odd years! You can't turn your back on them as easily as all that!' She added bitterly, 'As easily as you turned your back on me.'

'Don't, Ruth. There's no point in raking up the past. It's the future we have to think of now.'

'That's why I came. I've acted hastily and I'm sorry. I want us to make a fresh start, to sell the house and buy that cottage you wanted, or one like it. We don't need a big house any longer. The children have their own lives to live, and I know they are anxious about the divorce. They want us to get together again, and frankly, so do I.'

'So you've discussed it with them?' Philip frowned.

'Not in detail.' Ruth bit her lip, wishing she had held her tongue, not wanting Philip to know about her abortive trip to Birmingham and its conclusion. 'They were naturally concerned about us. Well, why don't you *say* something?'

The old familiar note of harshness had entered her voice, that querulous tone he knew so well. He said quietly, 'I know what you *want* me to say, but that's not possible. I have plans of my own to consider. I shall be leaving South Bay quite soon now, next month as a matter of fact, when the boutique has been dismantled and the summer season is over.'

'But that's damned ridiculous and you know it! What do you intend to do? Travel the world with a knapsack on your back like some silly teenager? A man your age? Huh, a fine spectacle you'll make of yourself, I shouldn't wonder!'

Throwing caution to the wind, her voice rose shrilly. 'All well and good for *you*, but what about *me*? What about *my* future?' She got swiftly to her feet, angry beyond belief. 'I might have known better than to come here in the first place, cap in hand to a selfish beast like you! Well, why not admit it? You don't give a damn about me!

'Oh, I get it! There's someone else, isn't there? There has been all along! And I can guess who! That – shop-girl of yours! I'm right, aren't I?'

'If it pleases you to think so,' Philip said gently, compassionately, 'but you are entirely wrong, as it happens. Now, shall I escort you downstairs, or can you find your own way out?'

Twenty-Two

Dismantling the boutique, Thea denuded the hangers of their summer bounty of sun-tops, put them back in their boxes, disrobed the dummies and emptied the draw-out shelves of silk scarves, tights and stockings. She remembered, with mixed feelings of sadness and joy, how much this little shop had meant to her throughout the summer months.

Stella had gone off, in high spirits, to her quiet wedding. By dint of patient questioning, Thea had finally made sense of her initial garbled version of events: the name of her bridegroom, for instance, and what he did for a living. Having imagined him to be a waiter at the curiously named The Inn Thing, relief swept through her when she knew that he owned the hotel. Not that she had anything against waiters, but it had worried her to think of the glamorous Stella and her husband working as a waiter and receptionist in some kind of sleazy, off-the-beaten-track roadhouse.

The fact that Stella had been there before, with Brian Felpersham, had added to her sense of unease.

'Oh, I know what you're thinking,' Stella said wistfully, 'that Brian deserved his come-uppance when his business went bust and his wife left him.'

'Really? I had no idea,' Thea murmured sympathetically. 'What happened exactly?'

Stella shrugged her shoulders dismissively. 'Apparently the law caught up with him at last. Her Majesty's Inspector of Taxes, to be precise. His wife decided to leave him when she realised the amount of money he had squandered on other women. I can only thank God that Grant persuaded me to tear up the thousand-pound cheque Brian had given me to go ahead with the abortion.'

At this point Thea had stopped worrying about Stella's choice of a husband. Obviously she had chosen wisely and well, finding a decent man who would care for herself and the child.

There had been a farewell party in Bill Cumberland's apartment on the eve of Stella's departure, to which he'd invited Thea, Philip Gregory, June, Luke Carter, Grant Edwards and, of course, Bunty – to act as his hostess on what had proved to be a memorably happy occasion.

Thea had liked Grant Edwards, a charming, quiet, handsome man, at first sight, and had known instinctively that he and Stella would be happy together.

Bill had gone to town on the food and drink. There was smoked salmon, cold roast pheasant, chicken and mushroom vol-au-vents, fresh watercress, canapés, quiche lorraine, pasta, bowls of fruit salad, Jersey cream, Black Forest gateaux, and enough champagne to float a frigate.

Not that Grant had drunk much, Thea noticed, and she guessed why not. When the party was over, he'd be driving Stella to her new home, and he wanted to keep a clear head for so important a journey.

At some point during the evening, Bunty had whispered in her ear that she and Bill were hitting it off just fine together. 'And would you believe it,' she confided, 'he invited the two old girls from next door to join in the celebration.

'When they declined the invitation, he asked me to make certain to save them some smoked salmon, roast pheasant and a couple of slices of Black Forest gateau to take up to them tomorrow. Wasn't that kind of him?' She added, sotto voce, 'How do I look, by the way? Do I look fat in this dress? Is my nose shining?'

Thea smiled. She said, 'Your nose isn't shining, but your

eyes are. And in case you hadn't noticed, so are Bill's whenever he looks your way, which is most of the time. To my way of thinking, the man is head over heels in love with you, just as you are with him, and he probably wouldn't even have noticed if you'd turned up this evening wearing a bin liner!'

'Well, ta very much,' Bunty quipped merrily in her lilting Scottish accent. 'I'll take that as a vote of confidence then, shall I?' She added wistfully, 'I just wish I looked as lovely as Stella does tonight. June too, come to think of it. Have you noticed that her boyfriend has had his hair cut, by the way? And he's wearing a decent suit of clothes, for a change?'

'There's a reason for that,' Thea explained quietly. 'This is their wedding day. They were married, first thing this morning, in the South Bay Register Office. I was sworn to secrecy, but they intend to announce it later, when the party's over. They just felt it would be unkind of them to spoil Stella's special occasion.'

'*Gosh!*' Fairly gobsmacked, Bunty enquired, 'So where are they spending their honeymoon? Surely not upstairs in June's room? The mind boggles!'

'No, of course not. They've booked the honeymoon suite at the Mirimar for the weekend, then they're spending a week or so with Luke's parents. They'll be having their marriage blessed in church during that time.'

Philip had been delighted to accept Bill's invitation to renew his acquaintance with an old friend, and Thea had been glad of his company. In Ross's absence, even with friends around her, she felt like a soloist lacking an accompanist. How strange, she thought, that she and Ross had seldom spent uninterrupted time together, never been to the theatre or a cinema together, never dined or danced or been to a summer show or a concert, all the simple pleasures of life that most couples took for granted.

Smiling, sipping champagne, joining in the celebration, she envied Stella, June and Bunty's new-found happiness, so richly deserved. Stella with a wedding and a baby to look forward to; June a honeymoon and a church blessing; Bunty anticipating a proposal of marriage in the near future.

Philip said concernedly, 'Thea, are you all right?'

'Sorry? Oh yes, of course. Why do you ask?'

'You seemed miles away.'

'I suppose I was.' She smiled up at him. 'Just thinking.'

Philip decided to take a chance. 'About – Ross?' he said quietly. 'Fliss told me. I hope you don't mind?'

'I'm glad she did. I'd have told you myself, only there isn't much to tell. He's going away soon, back to Paris. I just wish – oh, I don't know – that I could envisage a future together, but I can't. The future seems a blank to me at the moment.'

'And this celebration party isn't helping much, I imagine,' Philip said understandingly. 'Standing on the fringe of other people's happiness? I know the feeling. But then, the future is always an unknown quantity, a bit like taking a step forward in the dark, never knowing what tomorrow may bring. The only thing to do, in my experience, is to take that step in the dark, with the hope of better times ahead.'

Thea said wistfully, 'You're thinking of Fliss, aren't you? Wondering if I mind your having fallen in love with her – if I shall ever resent your taking over my father's place in her life. The answer is no! I shall dance at your wedding, one of these fine days!' She added, tongue in cheek, 'Just as long as I shall not be called upon to wear a Victorian poke bonnet and carry a fur muff!'

Philip laughed. 'As if! You know, Thea, one of the nicest aspects of marrying your mother will be having you as my stepdaughter. The kind of daughter I've always longed for and never had, until now.'

When the celebration party was over, well past midnight, when Stella and Grant had driven away to their new life together, and after June and Luke had shyly announced that they were man and wife, to the pouring of more champagne and more toasts to the happy couples involved in the night's proceedings, Thea went slowly upstairs to her room to look out of the window at a starlit sky above the dark waters of South Bay washing in on the shore.

Ross would be home now, she thought, tired after his long stint at the Mirimar, probably thinking of her, wondering, as she was, what the future held in store for them.

She imagined his suitcases, already half packed with his belongings in readiness for his return to Paris a week from now. She could scarcely bear the thought of his departure from her life. What would they find to say to each other at the last moment, on a railway station platform? she fretted inwardly. All the foolish, inconsequential things that people usually said to each other from train windows. 'Take care of yourself'; 'Safe journey'; 'Promise you'll write to me?'; 'I'll miss you so much'; 'Remember that I love you'; 'Goodbye, my love, goodbye . . .'

Returning to London aboard a Golden Arrow Express from York Station to King's Cross, Thea remembered, with tear-filled eyes, that prior to his leave-taking Ross had simply held her tightly in his arms until the last minute, saying nothing at all except, 'I love you, Thea, and I shall go on loving you till the day I die, whether or not you love me in return. I shall always recall, with joy, the first time we met. You, my darling, and *Liverpool from Wapping*. Remember?'

Remember? Of course she remembered. Never, ever was she likely to forget anything about him: his looks, his charisma, his hands on a piano keyboard, the feel of his arms about her, the touch of his lips on hers. Most of all, the sparkling engagement ring he had given her that evening in the shelter overlooking South Bay: a testament of faith in some far-off future together which, even now, she regarded as an impossibility, considering their present circumstances, the lengthening of the distance between them. He in Paris, she on her way home to London to begin her career as a stage designer.

Fliss said, 'I expect the house seems cramped after the Villa Marina?'

She was right. Thea looked out of her bedroom window at the street beyond. This was a typical London suburb, pleasant enough, with leafy trees showing the first hint of autumn. Soon the pavements would be thick with falling leaves.

Not that the house was in the least cramped. Built in the Victorian era, the downstairs rooms were spacious, with handsome marble fireplaces, deep skirting-boards and high ceilings. The stairs were broad with polished banisters. All was dear and familiar to Thea, and yet she felt strangely disorientated – a natural reaction, she supposed, after four months' absence.

Fliss was in the kitchen when she came down, making preparations for their evening meal. A wise woman, she kept quiet, not making idle conversation, asking no questions about the train journey, her daughter's feelings at leaving South Bay. There was no need. She knew exactly how Thea was feeling, but confidences could not be forced, and so she got on quietly with what she was doing: peeling potatoes at the kitchen sink, brushing lamb chops with olive oil and adding a sprinkling of herbs in readiness for the oven.

This was a pleasant kitchen, overlooking the back garden, with an Aga cooker, practical modern fittings, plenty of cupboard space and laminated work surfaces, a tall refrigerator, and pink and red geraniums and busy Lizzies on the window sills.

Suddenly, Thea sat down at the kitchen table. Burying her face in her hands, she sobbed, 'Oh, Fliss, I'm sorry! I'm so unhappy! Please help me!'

'Why, darling? What's wrong?' Fliss dried her hands and sat down opposite.

'It's Ross. I've let him down so badly. I should have gone with him to Paris; stood by him through thick and thin and to hell with convention. Oh, Fliss, I've been so selfish, so prudish. I sensed a barrier between us. Now I know it was of my own making.

'If I'd thought about it more clearly, I'd have realised that Ross could never turn his back on Colette. The poor woman has suffered enough. I should have told him I loved him enough to help and support him in every way possible, during and after those soul-destroying prison hospital visits of his, but I didn't.'

'And now?' Fliss asked compassionately.

'Now, all I want is to belong to him body and soul. To be with him, to take care of him, to ease his burden, not add to it. After all, I could study design in Paris, just as well, perhaps even better than here.'

Fliss asked mildly, 'So what's stopping you?'

'You, for one thing,' Thea admitted. 'Leaving you alone in a house far too big for just one person.'

'Ah.' Fliss smiled mysteriously. 'But I may not be on my own for very much longer. You see, darling, Philip will be joining me once his business affairs in South Bay have been settled, and prior to our weekend in Paris.

'No strings attached. He may well decide to travel further afield to come to terms with his past before committing himself to an unknown future. I shall not stand in his way. Meanwhile, I'll have my own work to occupy my mind. Commissions for children's book illustrations are rolling in quite merrily at the moment, so I'll remain financially independent, whether or not Philip and I end up as man and wife one of these days.

'So you see, Thea, we are pretty much in the same boat, you and I. Both of us attached to human beings who have been hurt or mistreated by life in some way or another. I know, for instance, that it will take Philip some time to come to terms with the loss of his home, his wife and family, and

I'm prepared to wait, in the wings, until he is entirely certain of our future together.

'You, on the other hand, have a man, head over heels in love with you, every bit as unhappy as you are, and for no good reason, when all you have to do is ring for a taxi to Heathrow, book a seat on the first available flight to Paris, and *voilà*! Well, don't just sit there, do it!'

'I will, but not tonight,' Thea said mistily. 'I'm staying here with you tonight – just like the old days, remember, when we came home together from a theatre or cinema matinée, a visit to Regent's Park Zoo, Madame Tussauds or wherever.'

Fliss smiled. 'Of course I remember. How could I ever forget?'

Thea said, 'I love Ross, but I shall never love anyone in the way that I love you.'

'Oh well, if you're about to talk nonsense, I might as well get back to peeling potatoes,' Fliss protested, returning to the sink. 'Of course you love me, I know that. I'm your mother, for God's sake. You're *supposed* to love me, so cut out the sweet talk and start setting the table.'

Opening drawers, finding a tablecloth, napkins and cutlery, Thea said, 'About Philip – I thought things were cut and dried between you? At least I hoped so. What I mean is, you wouldn't send him away from a misplaced sense of loyalty to my father, would you?'

'That thought had never entered my mind,' Fliss said crisply. Turning to face her daughter, frowning slightly, she realised, for the first time, Thea's reluctance to play the role of the 'other woman' in Ross Drummond's life.

She said firmly but kindly, 'Thea, my love, you mustn't allow what happened to your father and me to cloud your own life. It's all in the past now. Quite simply, he fell out of love with me, in love with someone else. I can't blame him for that. We had so little in common, you see.'

'Not even me?' Thea asked wistfully.

'No, not even you, my darling.'

'But you never uttered a harsh word against him,' Thea said bleakly. 'Why didn't you? Why did you let me go on believing that he loved me, that you loved him, too, and would welcome him back with open arms if he came home again, one day?'

'Because he did love you, Thea. You must believe that. It was myself, not you, he had fallen out of love with, but you were far too young, at the time, to understand what had happened, and why.'

'Thank you for telling me,' Thea said. 'But what about Philip? Would you really want him to go off somewhere on his own to get over losing that awful wife of his?'

'Of course not, but I won't try to stop him, if that's what he needs to come to terms with the past. I'm a strong believer in individual freedom, allowing even the people one loves – them most of all – the time and space to make their own choices, reach their own conclusions.'

'The way you did with my father? The way you have done with me?' Thea asked gently.

'Well, yes, I suppose so.' Popping the potatoes into a pan of water, Fliss said thoughtfully, 'I lived in the hope that Charles would come back to me one day, not from a sense of duty or guilt, but because he loved me enough to want to come home. He chose not to. That was *his* decision, which I learned, in time, to accept and to live with.

'The same applies to Philip. If we end up together one day, the choice must be his, not mine. I know how I feel about him, but I must be certain, in my own mind, that he feels the same way about me.'

A kind of role reversal, Thea thought, remembering Ross, who had given her both the time and space to reach her own decision regarding their future, knowing that if she came to him, it must be of her own free will, because she loved him enough to want to be with him, despite the obstacles ahead of them.

Tomorrow, she thought, with an uplifting of her heart, she would prove to him how much she loved him. Tonight belonged to her mother, as she had intended it should.

After supper, mother and daughter sat together near the log fire Fliss had lit in the front room, talking over old times and making tentative plans for the future.

Fliss said, 'If Philip asks me to marry him, I'll buy a new skirt, wear my Bellino blouse, and carry a bunch of whatever flowers are in season at the time, hopefully primroses.' She added anxiously, 'You and Ross will fly over from Paris to attend the wedding, won't you?'

Thea laughed. 'Well, that all depends.'

'On *what*?' Fliss demanded, tongue in cheek. 'No, don't tell me, let me guess.' She added, more seriously, 'Oh, my darling, so you really intend to give me a grandchild? How wonderful!'

When the fire had sunk to ashes, Thea went upstairs to bed, filled with thoughts of tomorrow, her reunion with the man she loved, whom she would ring up from Heathrow when she knew the time of her arrival in Paris.

Tears filled her eyes when, later, entering her room, Fliss smoothed her bedcover and bent down to kiss her goodnight, as she had always done throughout the years of her childhood, and beyond; a beloved, fragrant, everlasting presence in her life, to whom she had always turned, and would continue to do so, for total and complete love and understanding.

'Goodnight and God bless, my love,' Fliss whispered. 'I'll leave the landing light on, shall I? Just to remind you, as I used to, when you were little, that you were not alone in the dark.'

Twenty-Three

'The leaves of brown came tumbling down, remember, that September, in the rain.'

Standing forlornly among the crowds thronging Charles de Gaulle airport that wet September afternoon, Thea recalled the faintly dismissive note in Ross's voice when she'd rung him to say she was coming to Paris, and to give him the time of her arrival.

She had gained the impression that he had other, more important matters on his mind at that moment. He said, 'If you're sure it's what you really want.'

'Of course it is! Why? Don't you want me to come?'

'You know I do. But why the sudden decision?'

'I can't explain now. I'll tell you when I see you. In any case, it wasn't a sudden decision. I've given it a great deal of thought. I really need to see you!'

'And I you. We have so much to talk about, to discuss. Look, darling, I'll be there to meet you around five o'clock.'

The time was now twenty to six, and there was still no sign of him. Cold, lonely and a little frightened, Thea waited near the main exit, staring out at the pouring rain, glancing around the concourse, desperate to catch sight of his tall figure hurrying towards her, hands outstretched to greet her, the feel of his arms about her, the thrill of his lips on hers.

Had he mistaken the time of her arrival? Had he left a message for her which she had not received? Enquiring at the reception desk, she discovered they had no message for her. So what had gone wrong? Had he been held up by the heavy evening traffic of home-going commuters from the city centre?

Car lights had been switched on now, creating a fairyland of twinkling head and tail bulbs, for all the world like rubies and diamonds against the amber glow of the street lamps and the background of steadily falling rain.

At six thirty, checking his phone number against the address book in her shoulder bag, Thea rang his apartment. There was no reply. Seriously worried, fearing that he had met with an accident, she took decisive action and phoned for a taxi to the apartment. There was bound to be a concierge on duty, she imagined, someone who might know what had become of him. She had to find out.

Or could it be that he had decided not to meet her after all? But no, Ross would never have done such a thing. Perhaps he had lost track of the time, had not heard the telephone ring when she'd called. Likelier, she suspected, he had gone to the prison to visit Colette, a tender subject which he had thought best not to mention when he'd received her joyous morning call with news of her flight. He did not know – how could he? – that her jealousy was a thing of the past.

Without this essential forgiveness and understanding, there could be no settled future for herself and Ross. She had carried the burden of insecurity and misunderstanding of Ross's marital problems to the detriment of his and her own peace of mind; had accepted his engagement ring as a kind of hostage to fortune – some pie-in-the-sky notion of happiness and security when the time was right.

Selfishly, she had acted in her own best interests, not his, not stopping to think how the distance she had insisted on maintaining from his own life and desires would affect their relationship in the long run.

Paying the taxi fare and entering the apartment block where he lived, a tall, narrow house with bleached shutters to the downstairs windows, in what appeared to be a student quarter of the city, Thea thought it would be little wonder if he had changed his mind about the future, if he no longer loved and wanted her. Had she kept him waiting too long?

Sick at heart, she approached the concierge's cubbyhole in the stone-flagged lobby, finding a plump, dark-haired woman seated at an old-fashioned bureau littered with bill-spikes and ledgers. 'Pardon, madame,' Thea murmured, 'I am looking for a Monsieur Drummond. Is he at home?'

'Who wants to know?' the woman demanded hoarsely, pushing back a pair of heavy-framed spectacles to her forehead. 'I do not spy on my lodgers. They are free to come and go as they please.'

'I beg your pardon, madame. I didn't mean to imply otherwise. It's just that M Drummond arranged to meet me at the airport some time ago, and he hasn't shown up. My name is Thea Bellamy. I'm a friend of his from England. I hoped that you might have news of him.'

The concierge glanced at Thea curiously. 'Are you ill, mademoiselle?' she asked bluntly.

'No, not ill, just tired and anxious. It's been a long day.'

'A friend of his, you say? I regret, mademoiselle, but I know nothing of M Drummond's movements or his whereabouts. He went out this morning and he hasn't been back since, that is all I can tell you.'

'Then may I please wait here for him?'

The woman shrugged her shoulders. 'Do as you think best. He has been delayed by the traffic, most likely. That is not my concern. I have work to do, a living to earn.'

Sinking down on a horsehair sofa in the hall, close to tears, Thea stared at the doorway leading to the street beyond until, with a deep sigh, throwing aside her pen, Madame Robillard took pity on the girl. She said brusquely, 'You are cold and damp, mademoiselle. God forbid you should catch a chill sitting there. I will give you a spare key to M Drummond's apartment. It is on the top floor, the best apartment in the house. Go there and wait for him, and do not blame me if he is angry, upon his return, to find his privacy invaded!'

'Thank you, madame,' Thea murmured gratefully. 'You are very kind.' She smiled. 'And you speak very good English.'

Madame Robillard chuckled. 'But of course. Why not? My father was English, my mother French. The mistake I made, early on in life, lay in marrying a Frenchman and coming here to live with him in this so-called city of romance, growing older and fatter by the minute, assuming the characteristics of an archetypal French patrone, bust, black bombazine bodice and all. Being stern and implacable at all times to put the fear of God into my lodgers. Impecunious students, most of them. But Ross Drummond is different from the rest, a charming individual who has been with me for a long time now. A quiet man, a musician to his fingertips. A very private man with his own secrets to keep. But you know all about that, I dare say?'

'Yes, I do,' Thea admitted. 'You see, madame, I'm in love with him, and I came here to tell him so, to tell him just how much I love him.'

Madame Robillard smiled wistfully. 'High time someone did,' she said softly.

A twisting stone staircase with rickety wooden banisters led up to Ross's apartment. Feeling half afraid, Thea opened the door and stood on the threshold of a spacious studio beneath a skylight window. Hearing the swift beating of rain hammering against the panes of glass, aware of a subtle infiltration of light from the massed effulgence of the city highlighting the ceiling above the dais on which stood Ross's Bluthner grand piano, Thea felt like an intruder, a voyeuse.

Unable to see clearly, perhaps not wanting to see clearly, she moved forward into the room like a blind woman, not switching on the lights – not that she knew where they were. She was glad of the enfolding darkness surrounding her, and thought how different was this apartment from Ross's milieu in South Bay. There everything had been neat and tidy, cut and dried. Simply a dwelling place, not a home.

Here, she noticed through the gloom, sheafs of music were scattered on the floor near the piano; stacks of books, in disarray, on top of a bookcase. A sprawling chintz-covered sofa sat near the French windows, which led to a rooftop balcony. There was a wood-burning stove in a corner of the room, a basket of logs on the tiled hearth. A white, wrought-iron garden table bore the remains of the meal Ross had eaten before he had left the apartment: bread and cheese, fruit, a pot of honey, a cafetière of coffee near a crumpled table napkin, as if he had quit the room in a hurry.

Two doors led from the main room, one of which gave access to a bedroom containing a double, unmade bed with rumpled sheets and pillowcases, a massive, typically French wardrobe and a chest of drawers. The other door connected the main room with a narrow passage leading to the bathroom and kitchen, neither of which was clearly discernible from the eerie half-light of the living room.

Feeling her way, Thea made use of the bathroom, recognising the fragrance of Ross's citrus soap and aftershave as she washed her hands and face and smoothed back her hair from her forehead, aware, as she did so, that she was trembling despite the tweed suit and the cashmere sweater she had worn on her journey from Heathrow, seemingly a lifetime ago.

Returning to the studio, she opened the stove, hoping against hope that a spark still remained among the ashes with which to rekindle a fresh log from the basket. Kneeling near the hearth, she recalled the words of an old song from Ross's bar-piano repertoire. 'In love's smouldering embers, one spark may remain . . . I'll be content with yesterday's memory, knowing you think of me once in a while.'

Such romantic, foolish lyrics. But what if all she would have, from now on, was the memory of a burnt-out love affair? What if Ross told her that he no longer wished to share his life with her?

Glancing about the room, it occurred to her how little she really knew about the man she had met in South Bay, apart from what he had chosen to reveal to her in that clinically neat and tidy flat of his in Lissom Grove.

This, his real home, portrayed a different picture entirely. It was the home of a man uncaring of neatness. That of a man at odds with himself and the world: witness the scattered music near the grand piano, the piles of books on the bookcase, the uncleared table, the unmade bed, as if the need for self-expression, recognition of his worth as a pianist, had reached fever pitch, leaving little or no room in his life for anything else . . . not even herself.

In that case, the sooner she left Paris, the better. He need never know that she had been here to pry into this secret world of his, this untidy, lived-in apartment of his beneath the rainwashed skylight, reflecting the glow of lights from the most romantic city on earth. Paris in the rain. September in the rain.

Getting up from the hearth, collecting the few items of luggage she had brought with her, she decided to ask her strange new friend, Madame la Patrone, to ring for a taxi to the airport. With luck, she would avail herself of a cancelled seat on the next flight to Heathrow.

Coming here had been a mistake, she knew that now. She had no part to play in Ross's life from now on. But never would she forget the charm of this place, this oasis beneath the steadily falling rain of a wet evening in Paris, in which, had things been different, had she known for certain that Ross still loved and wanted her as much as she wanted him, they might have been happy together.

If only she knew of his true feelings towards her. If only some small part of herself had invaded his living space: a snapshot, a sea shell garnered from the sands of South Bay.

Then, turning at the door for a last glance about the room, suddenly she saw it! How could she possibly have not noticed it before? There it was, glowing softly on the wall above the fireplace: a small original oil painting of moonlight on the sea, by John Atkinson Grimshaw.

Thea hurried forward for a closer look at the picture. Tears of delight filled her eyes when she saw that it really was by Grimshaw, and realised its significance. Ross must have scoured Paris to find such a treasure, a reminder of their bittersweet love affair in South Bay. What it must have cost him, she couldn't begin to imagine, but money must have been Ross's last consideration in search of something so beautiful, so precious, so intrinsic a part of their love story.

The log she had placed on the fire spurted suddenly, rekindled by a spark from seemingly dead ashes, rekindling a sense of joy in her heart, a feeling of renewed energy and vitality, knowing that she occupied a corner of his life, after all.

It was then that she heard footsteps on the stairs, urgent footsteps hurrying towards her. The door burst open. Ross was on the threshold. They faced each other momentarily, not speaking, uncertain of what to say to one another. Then, as he came slowly towards her, words were not important. There was no need of words as they silently entered each other's arms and clung together. The pianist and his lady.

Slowly, during the hours that followed, together on the sprawling sofa in front of the glowing log fire, Ross spoke haltingly of Colette, whom he had visited earlier that afternoon.

'Something rather wonderful had happened,' he explained. 'Wonderful and totally unexpected. A kind of miracle. The man she loved, the father of her child, was at the hospital when I arrived; the reason I'd been sent for. The doctors needed my permission to let him see her; they feared his presence might worsen her condition, make her more confused, add to her distress.

'I thought differently. You see, darling, the man in question was the only one in the world for Colette. She attempted suicide when he left her. I knew that despite all her wild behaviour, the crime she committed, the murder of her child in a moment of madness, she had never stopped loving the man responsible for her misfortune.'

'Please go on. Tell me what happened,' Thea prompted him gently, aware of his struggle to put his feelings into words. 'No need to face this alone. No need to face anything alone ever again. I'll be here by your side whenever you need my help and support. Above all, my love.'

Picking up her hands, he kissed her fingers one by one. 'I needed you from the moment we met,' he said, 'and I shall go on loving you all the days of my life.'

Eventually, he continued, 'I spoke of a miracle. I can't be certain that Colette recognised, in the weary, middle-aged man beside her bed, her eager young lover of long ago. Of one thing I am entirely certain, however: she *knew* him with an instinct older than time. Holding his hand, she fell into a deep natural sleep. I'll never forget her face, as she slept, as if the pain and misery of the past had been washed away.'

'I'm glad. Poor Colette.'

Ross said, 'She deserved better. She was just a child when I met her, unable to cope with the harsh realities of life. I'll never believe that she meant to harm her son. She loved Louis.'

He smiled suddenly. 'I think it's stopped raining. Come and look at the view from the balcony.'

The air smelled sweet and fresh. 'This is my Paris, the Paris I love,' Ross said, his arm about Thea's waist, her head against his shoulder. 'Tomorrow, first thing, we'll buy bread and croissants for breakfast, fruit and fresh fish from the street market. Which reminds me, you must be starving.

Here I am talking of breakfast and you haven't even had supper. We could go out, if you like.'

'What time is it?'

'A little after midnight, but the bistro on the corner never closes. We could have Pierre's *spécialité de la maison*, tournedos Parisienne, a bottle of wine.'

Thea laughed. 'Better still, I could cook us an omelette. Make myself useful in the kitchen. Not that I'm the least bit hungry. I'm far too excited. Or, as Fliss would say, I've got past it.' She smiled up at him. 'A sensation of weightlessness comes next. But I'm already floating on air with happiness, being here with you.'

'A beautiful bride on her wedding night?' he suggested softly, taking nothing for granted. 'Or I'll sleep on the sofa, if you like.'

'Could you bear that?' she asked shyly. '*I* couldn't.'

Drawing her back into the room, Ross closed and fastened the windows behind them, shutting out the sounds of Paris: laughter from the street below, music from an apartment across the way. 'These Foolish Things'. 'The smile of Garbo and the scent of roses, the waiters whistling as the last bar closes.'

Alone in the bedroom, making ready for bed, suddenly Thea heard the sound of the piano. Ross was softly playing Beethoven's Moonlight Sonata.

When, a little later, he entered the room, she was fast asleep, smiling, hair spread about her on the pillows. Undressing, he lay down beside her. Taking care not to disturb her, all night long he held her in his arms, until morning came.